THE
PATCHWORK
HOUSE

RICHARD SALTER

First Edition

ISBN: 1-938644-22-0
ISBN-13: 978-1-938644-22-1

Nightscape Press
http://www.nightscapepress.com

for Jene, for ever

The Half-Truth

The police called at my apartment about two weeks after I returned from the UK. Two of Chicago PD's finest stood at my doorway at seven in the evening.

"Mr James Randal?" the taller of the two asked.

I nodded.

"I'm Officer Warrington and this is Officer Hunt. Can we come in please? We'd like to ask you some questions."

I acted surprised to see them and blustered something about this being out of the blue. Then I let them in. We sat down at my dining room table.

"We're here to ask you about Miss Bethany Harris," said the taller cop. Warrington.

"Is she all right?"

"We were hoping you could tell us that, sir. Her parents have reported her missing. Have they been in touch with you at all?"

I injected some alarm into my tone. "Yes, they called me about a week after I came back from England. I told them Beth and I weren't together anymore, and I came back to the US alone. When did she go missing?"

Warrington didn't answer my question. Instead he asked, "Has Miss Harris been in touch with you since you returned?"

"No. I made it pretty clear I didn't want to see her again. I assumed she'd return to the States of her own accord."

"No, Mr Randal, she never came back."

I carefully allowed myself to sound frustrated with them that they didn't know what had happened to her. "Have you talked to the British police?"

"Of course, but they don't know where she is either."

"What about Derek Jackson?"

"What about him?"

"Have you spoken to him? Does he know where she is?"

"No, sir. He's missing too."

I sat in silence for a moment, pretending to let this sink in. I fidgeted with my hands and then rubbed my chin, trying to look as agitated and concerned as possible.

"So look, we're not together anymore but I want to help if I can."

"We appreciate that, Mr Randal," said the other cop, Officer Hunt. "Can you maybe tell us what business you had in the UK?"

"Er, sure. Well my dad buys properties at auctions all over the world. He buys them, does them up and resells them. He's usually too busy to see the houses in person so he sends me to do it. I took Beth—she was my girlfriend then—because she'd never been to England. She was so excited. She loves Jane Austen. I think she assumes every house in England comes straight from Sense *and Sensibility*."

"Was this Binsham Park?"

"Yeah that's the place."

"How long were you there?"

"Just the weekend. Arrived Saturday morning and returned Sunday evening."

"And you didn't return together."

"No… We had an argument. We broke up and I left on Sunday morning. I went to London to see some relatives and then I took the flight home on Monday evening as planned. I expected to see her at the terminal, thought we might talk about what had happened, but she was a no show. I assumed she'd decided to stay in England longer. I've not heard from her since. I kind of expected her to call me, at least to get her stuff back."

"Was she living here full time?"

"She was planning to. She'd listed her apartment. Most nights she was here with me."

Warrington asked, "And the other couple who stayed at the house with you?"

"Oh, right. Derek and Chloe. Well Derek is an old friend. I'd not seen him in years. Right before Beth and I flew out, I read Chloe's status online. She was mad at him because they were meant to go to Vegas for the weekend, their first trip away without the kids in years. At the last minute Derek realized his passport had expired so they couldn't go. I invited them to stay with us instead, at the house. Not quite the same as Vegas but at least it meant they could get away for the weekend like they planned."

"Have you had any contact with Mrs Jackson?"

"Chloe? No."

"The British police talked to her and she said she left her husband at the house and returned home alone as well. Am I to infer anything by that?"

There were tears in my eyes now. They weren't fake tears, though I wasn't crying for the reason the police thought I was.

"I caught... I saw Derek and Beth..." I trailed off. It wasn't the truth, not by a long shot. But it was painful even to lie to them about it.

Warrington backed off on that line of questioning. There was no need for me to spell it out, thankfully.

"Did anything else, unusual happen at the house while you were there?"

I chose my next words *very* carefully.

"I was only there the one night. There were strange noises and some furniture moved around when we weren't looking. It's a creepy place, that's for sure."

"And what about the car?"

"What car?"

"The SUV your father rented."

"Oh, yeah. Derek totaled it."

"You sure?"

I nodded. "Yeah my Dad called me, all mad that the car got wrecked and he had to pay the deductible. Derek and Beth went off in it. I didn't see it again before I left. Dad said nobody was hurt so I didn't worry about it."

"That's true, there's no evidence that anyone was hurt." Warrington paused. He seemed about to show me something, but decided not to. I knew what it was — a picture of the car. I knew exactly what had happened to it. I wondered why he didn't show it to me. Instead he stood up. Hunt and I followed suit.

"All right then, Mr Randal," said Warrington. "We won't take any more of your time. If you hear anything, please let us know."

He handed me a card. As I took it I noticed my hand was shaking. Was it from grief? Or perhaps it was guilt because of the lies I told. I hoped they would believe the former.

"Thank you, officers, and if I can help in any way just call me. Oh and also…"

"Yes, Mr Randal?" said Hunt.

"If you find her, please let me know. Despite what happened, I'd hate for anything bad to happen to her."

"Of course. We'll call you as soon as we hear anything."

I showed the officers out. When they were gone I collapsed against the back of the door and sighed. The sigh quickly turned into sobs. I must have sat there crying for at least half an hour. Just that past week I had finally managed to get some sleep at night, and now it seemed I was in for more insomnia.

The Truth

CHAPTER 1

I hated the flight but Beth was too excited to care. By the time we landed at Heathrow, my legs were stiff and my bum cheeks were asleep. Beth just called me an old man and spent the entire time in the airport giggling like a schoolgirl whenever there was an announcement.

Had I been away that long? The accent sounded so odd. Not just the announcements. Overhearing folks walking by, they sounded exaggerated.

"Do I sound like that?" I asked.

"Yes you do."

Amazing what you get used to.

Traffic was mercifully light and it wasn't long before we were leaving London and heading out west. Since neither of us had slept much on the plane, we dozed off.

I woke up with a stiff neck and quickly roused Beth. I knew she wouldn't want to miss this.

Hedgerows bordered narrow roads with occasional breaks to allow access to fields. Beth was groggy for a moment and then wide awake, staring out the window. We passed through a village with its black and white Tudor houses, stone bridges over tiny rivers and a medieval stone church. Save for the smattering of cars, some road signs and a couple of shops selling modern conveniences, the village looked as though it had not changed in centuries.

Beth gasped at every sight, from the market square with its thatched roof to the kids playing Pooh-sticks on the bridge. She squeezed my hand whenever she saw something quaint or olde-worlde and pointed things out to ensure I saw them too.

The house was a fair drive from the village, along twisty-turny single-track roads. The driver slowed down often, struggling to see around every blind corner as the high banks obscured what lay ahead. Every time we rounded a bend, I expected to see a local hurtling towards us in a beat-up old Land Rover, moving too fast to avoid a collision. Beth loved all of it.

We passed the occasional farmhouse but after a while there was nothing but the odd tumbledown barn or rusted-out tractor. We must have gone a good few miles before we reached Binsham Park. The car pulled up outside a large white gate about ten feet high. We got out and the driver unloaded our bags. I tipped generously and sent him back to London.

The gate and railings were a little taller than us, painted immaculate white. Once beyond the gate, a gravel driveway led a few hundred metres before disappearing around a wide corner, flanked on either side by freshly mown lawn. Giant evergreens flanked the driveway beyond the grass.

"Do you think your dad will sell it to us?"

"Sure, if you have a few million pounds lying around."

"The house is a bit small though." Beth nodded towards a small cottage to the right of the path, standing behind the railings to the right of the gate.

"That's the lodge, dummy," I said. "I think the groundskeeper once lived there." Beyond the lodge was a tiny garden, not too big but beautifully kept. A high stone wall marked the edge of the property, mostly obscured by the giant firs.

"We have to walk," I said, nodding in the direction of the path. "I know that will be hard on your poor American feet."

She flashed me a sardonic smile and set off up the lane at a run, her shoes crunching on the gravel.

"Last one there has to go see a British dentist!" Beth said.

I took my time following her, partly because I'm a lazy bastard but mostly because she left me with both bags to carry.

It took a good ten minutes to reach the top of the driveway. As I rounded the last bend, the trees cleared, the path opened up into a wide gravel space, and Binsham House came into view. Even from here I could see that mishmash of architecture in its disparate parts.

Ahead was our vehicle, a four-by-four, rented by my dad and sitting waiting for us. It gleamed white in the afternoon sunlight. Beside that was a pickup truck, carrying a ride-on mower and various other pieces of gardening equipment on its trailer. *For Peat's Sake* was written on the side of the truck. Arthur the groundskeeper was around somewhere then. That was good news because he had the keys to the house and our car.

On the right of the driveway was a meticulously maintained herb garden bordered by low hedgerows. The garden was as large as it was fragrant, an astonishing mix of heady odors from an array of plants, dancing with insect life. Beyond that was a stone wall, which wrapped around the house before disappearing behind trees.

The house itself was like someone had thrown together every significant period of British architecture into one gestalt. Part Gothic, part Tudor, part Victorian, part several other styles, it was obvious the house had been built in stages, decades apart. I read that one part had burned down and been rebuilt many years ago, but the place was already such a mish-mash of styles it was hard to tell what was new and what was original. The front door was unassuming, as if it belonged on an urban townhouse. The windows ranged dramatically in size and shape, as if the architect's young kid had ripped up a bunch of plans and stuck random bits together on one page.

I watched the expressions on Beth's face. Even though Mr Darcy might never have lived in a house like this, I could tell its age and size impressed her. I'd seen my fill of English country houses in my time, but I too found this was something unique. The few photos on the web hadn't done it justice.

At the far end of the house stood a separate building with two sets of wide doors. This was obviously a garage. Later I'd check to see if Dad had unknowingly purchased a couple of classic sports cars.

Beth was drinking it in. "It's so odd. Beautiful, but… odd!"

"The grounds are supposed to be amazing."

She was already off around the near side of the house. I dropped the bags and made to follow her, but something caught my eye in the near ground floor window. I approached it slowly, watching my reflection approach at the same rate. Jeez I looked awful! Had the flight really taken such a toll on me? I looked so beaten up! I blinked and the reflection was gone. I was up against the window now, staring inside at a small room with a fireplace and several pieces of furniture covered in dust sheets.

I took a step back, but now could only see the vaguest of reflections in the glass.

Weird. I needed a shower clearly.

I hurried after Beth and joined her in a paved courtyard behind the house, enclosed by low walls, spanning the length of the building all the way up to the garage. The courtyard had benches and flower beds at regular intervals, and an ornate stone fountain in the centre, not running.

Behind the low courtyard walls lay a huge lawn, maybe a couple of acres in size. The right side of the lawn was bordered by trees, and on the left was a wooden fence beyond which were rolling hills and meadows, and not a single building as far as the eye could see. Ahead of us, at the end of the lawn, was the lake, broad and stunning.

"I feel the urgent need to wear an empire waist," Beth said. She ran out onto the lawn and started spinning like a little kid, taking it all in. I smiled but I was still feeling a bit off after the weird reflection I'd seen. A cough from behind me made me jump. I turned to find a grey-haired man with angular features and a slight stoop. He shook my hand.

"Sorry, I didn't mean to startle you. Arthur Baker, the groundskeeper. You must be James?"

"That's right. Great to meet you."

"Welcome to Binsham Park. I hope you had a good flight."

"Not bad," I lied. "This place is truly amazing."

"Thank you, most kind. Worked here all my life, I have, since I was a little lad helping out my dad. We've been groundskeepers for the Logan family for as long as they've owned the house."

"What happened to them?"

Arthur scratched his nose. "Oh, old Percy passed away a month or so ago, left no heirs. Very sad. He's buried in the little cemetery down by the lakeside. The last five generations of the Logan family are there. It's consecrated ground, you know? Wouldn't mind being buried there myself someday. Lovely spot."

Arthur stared wistfully towards the lake for a moment and then seemed to return to the present. He looked me in the eye. "So now your father owns the place?"

"Yes, he's asked me to check the state of the building and the grounds. No complaints on the latter."

"Well that's good to hear. I take it he plans to resell?"

"Probably, though he's been known to keep houses he falls in love with."

"Hello," said Beth. She had approached quietly and now stood with her hand outstretched.

Arthur shook it. "Hello, my dear," he said kindly.

"Arthur is the groundskeeper," I said.

"Oh, well, what can I say? This place takes my breath away."

Arthur seemed pleased. "Well that's lovely to hear. Your accent is quite charming. Whereabouts in the States are you from?"

"Chicago."

"Oh really? I've always wanted to visit. Before I forget, here are your car keys. The man who delivered your car left them with me. Also, the keys to the house—don't lose them, they're my only complete set. The lodge key is on that ring too. It's the one with the blue cover at the top."

"You don't live in the lodge then?" Beth asked as I took the keys from Arthur.

"Oh goodness me no! My father lived there for a time but it's not really big enough for a family. I have two daughters, you see, although they're pretty much grown up now. My youngest, Amelia, she works for me. We live in Colmsford village a few miles down the road. I think my wife would have left me long ago if we'd been cooped up in that little lodge all this time!"

"Well thanks for everything," I said. "There's no electricity, right?"

"That's right. Cut off two weeks ago along with the gas and the phones. Luckily it's not too cold at night or the pipes would freeze! I'm hoping someone will move in before winter so the bills will be paid again."

"Oh right, sorry for the delay. There was a snafu at the bank and the utilities haven't set up the new accounts yet. But don't worry, my dad will be paying all the bills including your wages, Arthur."

He shifted uncomfortably. "Well I appreciate that. I was a little concerned, I'll be honest."

"I don't blame you. Thanks for carrying on looking after the place. We'll make sure you keep getting paid while my dad owns the house, and we'll let interested buyers know your services are part of the deal."

Arthur brightened considerably at this news. "Oh thank you, I appreciate that. I've put many years into this garden and I'd hate to see it neglected."

"It does look wonderful."

"Thank you, kind of you to say."

"Dad understands it's best not to try to fix what isn't broken."

"A fine philosophy. I'll be off now then. Oh, speaking of broken things. Couple of nights ago we had some vandals. They broke a window but didn't do any damage inside the house except to move some stuff around. I didn't see anything taken. The police weren't much interested. Anyway, window's fixed now so I'm just warning you in case you hear anything."

"Thanks."

"Just one more thing before you go, Arthur," Beth said.

"Of course, my dear."

"Tell me about the ghosts."

I scoffed at that, I must be honest. I wasn't expecting her to be so blunt.

"Which one?" Arthur replied. His smile was pleasant, not mocking.

"All of them," she said. I groaned inwardly. Beth didn't often embarrass me, likely not half as much as I embarrassed her, but now was one of those times.

Arthur didn't seem to mind at all. "Well, very quickly," he said, "because I'm sure you'll meet them yourself at some point. They're all very friendly, so there's really nothing to worry about. There's the ghost of Percy's grandfather. He got the clap, so they say, and died in the master bedroom. He's been known to make quite a racket at night but he's harmless. Then there's the lavender lady. Nobody knows who she is, but she's seen walking down the staircase now and again, and flitting about the kitchen. You can smell the lavender wherever she's been. Of course it could just be fragrances from the herb garden carried by the breeze, but I think she's real. Lastly there's the little drummer boy. My, he can only be about seven or eight, but he walks around the grounds banging his little tin drum. You can hear him from inside the house on some nights. He moves fast though, you likely won't see him if you look outside. At least, I've never seen him."

"You've seen the others?"

"I've heard Percy's grandfather, and I've seen the lady several times."

Beth clapped her hands together. "Thank you so much for your time, Arthur."

"No problem at all, my dear. A delight to meet you both. If you need anything, you can call me on this number." He handed Beth his business card. "If you can get a signal out here. I rarely can. I'll be back on Wednesday so I won't see you before you leave, but maybe next time, yes?"

We thanked him and he walked away. A little while later we heard his truck start up and the wheels crunch on the gravel path and then fade away.

Beth and I looked at each other and then ran for the house. I slowed down and let her go ahead. She wasn't getting inside without me; I had the key!

I caught up with her and unlocked the door, then followed her in, heaving both our bags on my shoulder. It smelled a bit musty inside, but it wasn't unpleasant. The hallway was probably a dozen metres deep, but it stretched off for some way to the right. The red wallpaper was faded but in good condition, and furniture covered in white cloths lined the walls. At the back of the hall, an unassuming staircase allowed access to the upper floor. Ahead and to the left were heavy wooden doors, and in the distance on the right a double door stood open, with the kitchen beyond. That's where Beth headed first while I looked through the door to the left.

This was the room I'd seen from the outside, probably a drawing room. It was small compared with the hall, but still afforded plenty of space for several chairs and a centre coffee table, all covered with dust sheets. There was an iron fireplace set into the wall to the right of the door. The ancient smell of pipe smoke permeated everything. The room needed a good airing, but it was comfy.

Returning to the hallway, I noticed an old-style rotary telephone on a small table near the foot of the stairs. It was green and squat, with the receiver cradled on top. I used to play with one of these when I was a kid, my parents having long since replaced it with a cordless. I picked up the receiver but it was completely dead, even though the phone was plugged into the wall. It was unlikely anyone was going to reconnect the phones on the weekend. I checked my mobile but there was no signal. This might be one of the few places in the country, other than the Scottish Highlands or the London Underground, where mobile phone coverage was still hard to come by.

The room opposite the front door by the foot of the stairs was much more opulent than the drawing room. It was a beautiful living room with ornate decorations covering every inch of the ceiling, cherubs, angels and the like. Again the furniture was covered, and the unmistakable form of a grand piano stood in the far corner. The thick glass windows were interspersed with stone dividers. Gazing through them revealed the grounds and in the distance, the lake. It was so peaceful.

Until Beth poked her head around the door.

"Oh my God, is that what I think it is?"

She hurried over to the piano and pulled off the dustcover. She gasped when she saw the black wood of the instrument. Reverently, she opened the keyboard and pressed a few keys. The quiet tones were so pleasant in this space, which added resonance and natural reverb.

Beth sat down and started to play. She never could resist, and certainly not when the piano was this fine. As the beautiful notes of the second movement of Beethoven's *Pathétique Sonata*— Beth's favourite piece—filled the room, I joined her. I had sold a few musical instruments on my various jaunts around the world. I would often recommend to my dad particular items of value that might be worth selling individually, rather than as part of the house itself, so I had a fair idea of what to look for and what was worth some cash. Sometimes I could really help capitalize on his investments that way. This was a rare Bechstein in perfect condition. There wasn't so much as a scratch on it. I took out my phone and snapped a few pictures of the piano for evaluation. Then I took one of Beth playing. That one was for me.

"Can we buy this?" she asked, stopping abruptly.

"I'll ask Dad if we can have it shipped to Chicago."

She knew I wasn't serious, but the way she gazed at the instrument made me want to make it happen.

I reached over and one-fingered the only tune I knew how to play: Ode to Joy. As I played, I sang along using words I made up as I went along.

"This old house is really scary,
We might see a ghost with luck,
Let's make sure to turn in early,
So we have some time to" –"

"Enough of that," Beth said. She closed the piano lid abruptly, nearly pinching my fingers.

"What?" I asked as I followed her into the hall. "I was going to say 'tuck', as in 'tuck you in'! What did you think I meant?"

"Shut up and come see the kitchen."

She led me past the stairs to the double doors at the far end of the hallway. Stepping through, it was clear we were moving into a different age. This was likely the part of the house that had burned to the ground and been rebuilt. The windows were larger here, with wider panes and wooden framing. The décor was a huge change from the other rooms we'd seen in the Gothic section of the house. The flooring went from creaking hardwood to unforgiving stone. As a kitchen it was dramatic; a huge space with two great iron stoves, a huge slate-topped workspace in the centre and an enormous fireplace you could stand in, filled with pots, pans and a roasting spit. Of course, we stood in the fireplace and stared upwards into the dark chimney.

"I wonder if this goes all the way out," I said.

"I don't see daylight."

"Well no, it doesn't go straight up to the roof."

"Is it a kinky fireplace, Jim?"

"I believe it's very kinky, my dear. Much like the lady standing in it."

"Ho ho."

"Hark! I hear Santa."

She laughed at that and gazed upwards again. "I think he'd get stuck."

We stepped out of the fireplace and opened a door beside it. Stairs led up so we followed them around a bend until we came to a modest-sized, self-contained apartment. The windows were small but they didn't have bars like I'd expected.

Beth almost seemed disappointed. "I thought this would be where the lord of the manor imprisoned his ex-wife or something."

"More likely just the housekeeper's apartment. Shame though. You could lock up your ex, tell everyone she's dead and find yourself a new young hottie to marry."

"And when you're bored with her you can lock her up here too."

"Perfect," I agreed. "I'll get right on it."

Downstairs again, we passed from the kitchen into a conservatory filled with all manner of exotic plant life, and then onwards to a giant ballroom with a stage at the far end and doors on either side.

I found the key to the door on the right and we stepped into a narrow corridor. The only light came from a window in the external door at the far end. Two more doors stood at either side of us. Opening the one on the left revealed a darkened dressing room filled with mirrors and little else. The other door opened to steps leading down into the blackness.

We stopped there, just listening. The unmistakable sound of ticking rose from the dark.

"Is that a clock?" Beth asked.

"Could be a time bomb."

Beth mock-punched my arm. "I didn't realize there was a basement."

"I guess there's no windows down there so you wouldn't know from the outside."

Beth shivered. "I don't like it."

"The basement or the dark?"

She linked her arm around mine and gripped my hand. "The ticking."

I listened. It *was* strange. It didn't tick-tock like a normal clock. It seemed to skip beats ever so slightly, sometimes sounding rushed and sometimes falling behind. The slightly arrhythmic beats weren't loud or particularly ominous, but they were unpredictable. Like listening to a short piece of music in an imperfect loop, where the beat would restart slightly too early each time around. I'm not particularly musical, but it bothered me. For Beth, it must have been torturous.

"Let's go back," Beth said. I agreed and together we went back through the ballroom to the conservatory. There were several different paths through this mini-maze of foliage, and we headed towards the back of the house this time. We passed by the back door we'd seen from the outside, at the end of a short corridor, and walked through an oak paneled dining room and then back into the living room again.

Beth went straight for the piano, perhaps intending to reset the off-kilter beat of the ticking basement with her own musical tempo. The distant sound of car tyres on gravel halted her.

Derek and Chloe had arrived.

CHAPTER 2

The driver was already moving off by the time we stepped outside to greet the newcomers. They stood in the driveway with their modest-sized luggage at their feet. Derek looked awkward while Chloe beamed with enthusiasm.

I'd never met Chloe before, just seen her picture online. She was blonde, plain-faced and a little plump. She was so happy to see us it was like we were long lost relatives. She hugged us both tightly and thanked us over and over again for thinking of them and for inviting them to stay with us.

Derek was more subdued. He was just as skinny as I remembered him, and didn't seem to have changed much. True there was some grey showing through his brown hair and he carried heavy bags beneath his narrow eyes, but he hadn't changed as much as I had expected. He seemed in a bit of a daze but he shook my hand and gave Beth a polite kiss on the cheek when I introduced her.

As we took their bags inside, Chloe could not stop talking. Her positivity was infectious rather than annoying, and for Beth she seemed to rekindle that initial bubbly delight in our surroundings all over again.

"Oh my God, it is amazing!" Chloe said as we stepped over the threshold.

"Isn't it?" Beth said. "It's like something out of a fairy tale."

"This is so much better than Vegas."

"I don't know about that," I said. I happened to quite like Vegas.

"Hey look," said Derek to me as the girls left us trailing behind in the hall. "Thanks for getting me out of the dog house."

"No problem, mate, any time." Already I was starting to sound English again.

"I thought she was going to murder me when I showed her my passport."

"It happens to us all. At least you checked before you got to the airport."

"Yeah, could have been worse."

"Later I'll tell you about the time I went to Nepal and left my passport on the plane. That wasn't a fun day."

Derek didn't seem particularly enthused to hear my story. We tagged along after the girls in silence. I struggled to find something else to say to him.

I remembered that Derek had always seemed timid and soft spoken. He took time to warm up to people, but we'd known each other for so long it was odd that he seemed so awkward. Still, it was years since we'd seen each other, so maybe he just needed a chance to remember where we left off.

I found the silence uncomfortable, so I filled it.

"Hey, what do you think? My dad bought a haunted house."

"Pretty sweet. Always dreamed we'd see a real ghost someday. Maybe this is our chance."

I'd managed to get a positive response from him, so I pressed on. "We were talking with the groundskeeper earlier. He said there are three ghosts and we'll likely see at least one of them."

"Can't wait." He spoke the words, but there was little enthusiasm in them. He gave a polite smile and then the awkwardness returned.

Beth and Chloe seemed to be getting on far better than Derek and I. They were all smiles and Oh my Gods and isn't this place just awesome. They returned to the hallway in a gaggle of glee.

"So Chloe, on a scale from one to ten, how great is it to be away from the kids for a weekend?" I asked, grateful for someone keen to talk to me.

"You have *no* idea," she said. "Oh sweet Jesus it feels good to be free, even for a little while. Although..." She pulled out her mobile phone. "I should really call my mum and see how they're doing."

"Relax, Chloe, they'll be fine," said Derek.

"Shit, there's no signal here."

"That's okay," Beth said. "I'm going into the village for food later. You should get a signal there if you want to come with me."

"Did you try the telephone?" Chloe asked.

I said, "Yeah, it doesn't work, sorry."

"Okay. I'm a bit worried that if something happens during the night, mum won't be able to get hold of me."

"I'm sure nothing will happen," Derek insisted, with a slight edge of frustration to his voice.

Clearly there was some friction between them. Beth picked up on it too. She grabbed Chloe's hand and started tugging her towards the front door.

"You haven't seen the grounds," she said, making Chloe laugh as she dragged her outside.

Derek watched them go for a moment, glanced at me and then seemed to come to a decision.

"Wait up," he called after Beth. "I'd like to see too."

He forced a smile at me and headed off after the girls. I tried not to take this too personally, but it was a challenge.

"I'm going to take a look upstairs," I shouted from the doorway, though they had already turned the corner and were out of sight.

I sighed and went back inside, closing the door behind me. I made sure it wasn't locked so they could get back in, and then headed to the stairs.

As I climbed them, the temperature dropped noticeably. I could feel the warmth of the hallway dissipate with every step. I'd expected it to be musty and airless up here, but there was an edge to the atmosphere, like stepping outside on a late-autumn morning.

At the top, the stairs turned ninety degrees to meet the landing, which was a long corridor that stretched in both directions, spanning the whole length of the house. To my right the corridor was shorter, since there was only the length of the hall and drawing room before the corridor ran out of house. To the left it stretched much further, covering the length of the kitchen, the conservatory and the huge ballroom on the lower floor. In places the corridor widened and narrowed, with differences in décor and door styles. At the far end one more door stood open. Small corridors branched from the main at occasional intervals between rooms. Windows at these points provided illumination, casting pools of light in patches.

I checked each room in turn. Most were bedrooms but I did find a bathroom and I made use of the spotless facilities. There was a library too, with a table in the centre and several large chairs, all hidden by more white dust covers. Light flooded the room via the wide window on the far wall, through which I could see the driveway and the herb garden, and the car directly below... Seeing it reminded me I still had to unload the equipment from the trunk, courtesy of Dad.

One wall of the library was entirely covered in books, and opposite this was a large, free-standing bookcase made of solid oak, uncovered, and laden down with thick tomes that must have been as old as parts of the house. This piece must have weighed a ton and I wondered how the hell anyone managed to haul it upstairs. I pulled a book from the shelf and checked the cover. *Basic Botany Volume VII*. Clearly old Percy loved his plants. I put the book back on the shelf.

I moved over to the wall shelf and my eyes were immediately drawn to a number of volumes with crosses on the spines. I pulled a couple of unique Bibles out, beautifully bound and possibly worth a decent amount in their own right. There were some Catholic texts as well that might be worth something.

At the end of the landing, furthest away from the stairs, was a large games room, complete with pool tables, darts and a bar. There wasn't a single bottle of alcohol behind the bar, and I wondered if Arthur had loaded it all in his truck one day and taken it back to his place. Or maybe Percy was a recovering alcoholic and had disposed of it himself. Too bad. I would have to ask Beth to stock up when she took her trip into town.

The last bedroom, next to the games room, was also the smallest. Inside was a simple bed, a bedside table and a small dresser. There were no dust sheets in here though, and a photograph stood in a frame next to the bed. It was the most lived-in of all the rooms in the house, simply by virtue of that photo. It was a black and white picture of a small boy with his mother. They seemed happy. So, had this been Percy's room? It was hard to believe he wouldn't make use of one of the bigger bedrooms.

I turned to the door, convinced someone was standing there. I expected to see Beth or Derek, but there was nobody there. I went out into the hallway but it too was empty. I tried to shake off the feeling that I wasn't alone and returned to the tiny bedroom.

I checked the drawer in the bedside table and found only a small Bible and a couple of pencils. There was an extra slot beneath the drawer though, inaccessible, and I became obsessed for a good ten minutes trying to open it. If there was a hidden drawer, I couldn't spring it open. Oh well, maybe Beth could take a look at it later. She was good at puzzles.

I left the room and headed back up the corridor towards the stairs. There was a section of wall with no doors. Behind it, I assumed, must be the servant's apartment. It was self-contained and had no access to the rest of the upper floor. I would probably suggest to Dad that he leave it as is instead of knocking through a door to make it into yet another bedroom. He'd be wise to spruce up the separate apartment and perhaps even expand it by subsuming one of the bedrooms. It would make for a great rental space or guest apartment, and there were half a dozen other bedrooms for the main house. One less wouldn't make any difference.

I spun around to face the door to the games room again. I would have sworn under oath that someone was standing there, though how I could have known that while looking the other way, I couldn't explain.

A door slammed downstairs and I heard a voice call out. No doubt Derek and the girls returning.

"Come on up here!" I called. "Bring the bags!"

I had a sudden idea, something that would be really funny. I moved quietly into the library, just as I heard footsteps on the bottom of the stairs. I quickly ducked under the white sheet covering the table in the middle of the room and pulled myself in close to the central pillar, trying hard not to let my elbows or knees poke the fabric and give myself away.

I heard someone outside the door and then the door creaked open.

If it was Beth, she was already onto me. Otherwise she would have called out my name by now, wondering where I was. So it was either Derek or Chloe perhaps. Even then, it was odd that they hadn't said anything. It was even odder when I heard the door close again.

The footsteps moved closer to me, creaking on floorboards. I held my breath, waiting to spring out and terrify whoever it was half to death.

But I couldn't move.

I wasn't frozen stiff. I could shift my position. Something was preventing me from leaping out like I'd planned to. To my surprise, all the hair on the back of my neck stood on end. Instead of holding my breath voluntarily, I couldn't breathe at all. The footsteps moved over to the window, and a shadow fell over the dust cover.

I knew it couldn't be Beth or Chloe. The figure didn't move like a female and the footsteps were too heavy. But Derek was a skinny guy, so maybe he was deliberately walking slowly and making more noise with each step than necessary.

This was ridiculous. It was clearly Derek trying to get his own back on me. I forced myself to move, pushing forward against the dustcover and emerging from under the table. I threw aside the white sheet and burst out into the room.

The empty room.

CHAPTER 3

There was nobody in the library.
Did Derek leave? How had he done it so quietly? The
door was closed and I hadn't heard it open again. What the hell?
Who had come in here?

Unnerved, I hurried back into the deserted corridor. Derek
could have ducked into another room. One way to be sure. I
entered a bedroom on the opposite side to the library, a little
further away from the stairs, and went over to the window at the
back of the house.

Beth, Chloe and Derek were walking back across the lawn
towards me. The two girls were arm in arm, Derek a few steps
behind. They were about to reach the courtyard, but it was
obvious they hadn't yet been back in the house since I'd seen
them last.

I spun around, listening for any sound. Nothing. Who was in
the room with me? Did I imagine it or did I just have an
encounter with Percy's grandfather? My skin tingled in fear and
excitement. I tried to recall every detail of what had just
happened before the memory faded. I didn't know whether to be
terrified or exhilarated. I had hoped to encounter something
while staying here, but in all honesty I had fully expected the
night to pass with no incident whatsoever. The prospect of there
being a real ghost to hunt, not just rumour or a groundskeeper's
stories, but a real entity in this building…

I had to tell Derek. Even if he was pissed at me or being shy or whatever the hell was wrong with him, he would love to hear about this.

I hurried down the stairs and across the hallway, opening the front door just in time to see Beth, Chloe and Derek standing there.

"You look very pale," Beth said as she stepped in. She gave me a brief kiss. "Are you okay?"

"Oh my God, you have to listen to what happened to me," I said eagerly as they all assembled in the hall. I recounted my experience in as much detail as I could. Beth and Derek seemed unconvinced despite my excitement. Only Chloe seemed to hang on my every word.

"First of all, lame prank, mister," Beth scolded me. "Second of all, I think you just heard creaky floorboards."

"What if it wasn't just creaking?" Chloe said, intrigued.

"What do you think, Derek?" I asked.

"I don't know. I'd have to hear it for myself."

What was up with him? I brushed it aside for now.

"So listen, it's kind of cold upstairs. Not drafty, there's just a chill up there. Anyway, I suggest we make camp down here. The warmest room seems to be the one just next to the front door. We could even start a fire if we can find some wood."

"And if the chimney's not blocked," Beth said.

"Why don't you take Chloe into the village to get food and she can call home."

Beth took the car keys from me. "While you boys can get reacquainted."

"Don't get lost!" I called as the girls headed out the front door. "Oh and remember we drive on the left here. Wait, I need to get the stuff out the car first. Give me a hand please, Derek."

We followed them outside. While Beth was adjusting her seat and the mirrors, I opened the trunk and pulled out one of two large canvas bags. Derek grabbed the other and while the girls drove off, we hefted the weighty bags into the house.

We took them into the drawing room and placed them carefully in the corner.

"Right," I said, "let's see what we've got."

I unzipped the first bag and pulled out a digital SLR with tripod and a case full of lenses. Next was a video camera with night vision lens, a laptop, cables and a huge battery pack. It was fully charged so I plugged my smartphone in right away. The other bag contained two double ultra-thin sleeping bags, neatly rolled up, and two gas lanterns and a mini camping stove.

"Do you mind taking these to the kitchen?"

Derek nodded and left the room. I booted up the laptop and wondered again what was wrong with my old friend. He was so quiet. As a teenager, when we used to hang out all the time, he would have been fascinated and utterly convinced by my possible encounter with a ghost. I wondered if perhaps Chloe had been haranguing him the whole ride and he was simply feeling cowed. Still, with her gone, he should have lightened up a little. Perhaps parenthood had just drained him so much he could only function on the most basic of levels.

I started up the video camera and took a panning shot of the room.

"Hey, Dad," I narrated, "it's me, Jim. This is the drawing room and it smells of pipe smoke and the wallpaper is peeling. The rest of the house is in great shape, but this one room will need some work. I have some other suggestions too, but first let me show you the hallway."

I picked up the camera just as Derek was emerging from the kitchen.

"Dad, you remember my old friend, Derek? Derek, say hi to Dad."

Derek waved awkwardly and ducked out of the shot.

I spent the next hour going from room to room, taping each one and providing commentary and suggestions. By the time I got upstairs, the natural light was fading so I switched on the camera's low-light filter. I was in the library upstairs when I heard the car return. I looked out of the window and saw Derek going out to meet the girls. He seemed talkative with them, not shy at all. As I watched, he even laughed at something Chloe said. If he'd been in the doghouse with his wife, he was out of it now. Their voices were muffled and I couldn't make out words, but there was definitely more good humour. Was it just me he was pissed at? What the hell did I do?

The car itself was right below the window. I had to peer downwards at quite an angle to see the back end of it. Now I couldn't see the trio either, so I assumed they had returned to the house. The blip of the car's alarm activation and the sound of the front door closing confirmed that. I finished filming in the library and told Dad I would be photographing many of the rarer books and getting them appraised, just in case there were any collectible first editions on the shelves that could make some bonus cash.

I headed downstairs and into the kitchen, still filming.

"Smile, everyone," I said as I entered the kitchen.

Beth turned around to welcome me and immediately ducked away, hiding her face.

"Argh! Put that thing away."

"Don't tell me you hate being filmed," Chloe said.

"Yep, Beth hates being on camera," I said. "You'll make an exception this weekend, right?"

"Hell no."

Chloe shook her head. "If I was as pretty as you are, I'd go looking for cameras to take my picture," she said.

Beth smiled and let her guard down for a moment. "Aw, you're sweet."

"How are the kids doing, Chloe?" I asked.

"Oh just fine thanks. Mum's got everything in hand so we can *finally* relax!"

"Excellent."

"Dinner is served," Beth said. She opened two bags filled with Chinese takeaway. Another three bags of snacks and junk stood on the counter by the sink. Clearly we weren't going to be hungry this weekend. Chloe opened cupboards until she found crockery and utensils, and pulled out enough for all of us.

"Can we get some light in here please?" Beth asked as she opened containers and put spoons in them.

Derek headed for the door. "I'll get the lamps," he said. It really was getting quite hard to see in here.

I taped him leaving the room and then shut off the camera.

"So, Chloe," I asked, "just how much trouble is Derek in over the passports?"

Chloe laughed. "None. Well, none anymore, not since we saw how amazing this place is."

"Better than Vegas?" I asked her.

"Well we're spending a lot less money, that's for sure."

"I'm so glad you invited these guys," Beth said, still hiding her face in case I started the camera up again.

"Oh what? You can't stand the thought of being alone in this house with me?"

"Ugh, God no. You're *so* dull."

Just for that I turned the camera back on, and then moved in closer to try to get a shot of her face. She held up a bag of nachos to block me. Derek came back with the lamps. He'd brought the chill with him it seemed. Beth hugged herself and Chloe zipped up her jacket.

"That's a heck of a draft you've let in," Chloe commented as Derek turned on the first lamp. There was a momentary hiss of gas and the lamp fired into life.

"One should be enough for now," I said. "Let's save the others for later."

Derek put down the lamp and we all grabbed stools. Beth spread the various dishes over the counter and I put away the camera, grabbed a plate and helped myself. The others dived in too.

"Thank God for that," Beth said. "I thought you were going to film us eating."

"Screw that, I'm too hungry."

"Pass the sweet and sour please," said Beth.

Even Derek seemed to come out of his funk for a little while. At first there wasn't much conversation; we were too hungry to talk. But after a while our stomachs realized that we weren't going to be starving them all day and we slowed down enough to take a breath.

I was the first to take a pause. "This is good. I'm surprised you found a Chinese takeaway in the village."

"So were we," Chloe said.

"I thought we were going to have to buy a bunch of cans and cook over a little camping stove," Beth said. "And then we nearly drove right past this tiny little take out joint."

"It was pretty busy," said Chloe. "Always a good sign."

"Didn't realize how hungry I was," Derek said.

I stared at him for a moment as he ate. His appetite seemed to have lifted the air of grumpiness he'd carried since he arrived. Of course it wasn't going to last.

"Chloe, I hope you paid Beth for half this stuff," he said between mouthfuls.

"No, Beth insisted on paying. You should say thank you to our gracious hosts."

The temperature seemed to take a dip again.

"It's okay, hon, we can pay our way. It's the least we can do after Jim and Beth were nice enough to invite us."

"This trip isn't costing us anything," I said, "so it's fine, we can pay. I know things have been a bit tight for you guys—"

"We're not poor," Derek snapped. I wasn't the only one to detect the accusation behind Derek's words. Beth looked at me awkwardly too. We all fell silent for a moment while Derek's words hung in the chilly air.

Beth broke the silence. "How about if we go back tomorrow then it's on you?" she suggested.

"Yes all right then," Chloe agreed, but this didn't seem to placate Derek.

"That's okay," Derek said in a forced tone. "Jim has all the money, so let him pay."

"I have my own money, thanks very much," Beth said. Now she sounded pissed.

"Oh, so both of you are doing well. That must be nice."

"Derek," Chloe said.

"No, it's okay. It stands to reason that if you don't have to work two jobs with stupid hours just to put food on the table for your three kids, it's much easier to swan around the world staying in nice houses and spending most of the year playing computer games."

The atmosphere was so frosty I could almost see my breath turning to mist in the lamp light.

"Derek, you need to calm down," I told him.

"Calm down? Sure I'll calm down. It's your fucking fault I'm stuck with my shitty life while you never have to lift a bloody finger."

"Excuse me?" It was Chloe's turn to be angry now. She rose from the table. Derek knew he'd gone too far; all his bluster faded immediately.

Chloe advanced on him. "It may be hard and we've had to make a lot of sacrifices, but I love you and I love my children. I don't regret anything and I certainly don't consider my life to be shitty."

"Hon, I didn't mean... I meant financially..."

"I know exactly what you meant, Derek, and—" Chloe stopped suddenly. She stared upwards. "What was that?"

We all looked at her and then followed her gaze to the ceiling. I'd felt so awkward while they argued that I was ignoring everything else around me. Now we all sat in silence, staring at the light fixtures.

I broke the silence. "What did you hear?"

"Shh."

We stayed dead still, all looking up. I couldn't hear anything. Nobody spoke, wondering if whatever Chloe had heard might happen again. I opened my mouth to speak.

There was a bang from above, a *huge* bang, so loud it was like a bomb had gone off upstairs. All of us jumped to our feet. There was absolutely no mistaking it. The house was far too solid for the bang to cause anything to move, but we'd all *felt* it too, like a very short, very violent earthquake.

We froze, gaping in shock at each other.

After a moment I asked, "What the hell?"

We stood in stunned silence for about a minute, our food forgotten, staring at each other, then at the ceiling, then back to each other again. Nobody made a move.

"Should we pretend that didn't happen or go take a look?" Derek asked.

"I vote we check it out," I said, putting down my fork and reaching for the lamp.

"I'm not going anywhere," Chloe said, a slight tremour in her voice. "And you're not leaving us in the dark."

"It's not dark yet," I assured her. "You'll be fine."

"I don't think we should go up there," Beth said.

"I want to know what that was. Are you volunteering to take a look?"

"Hell no. Why are you taking the lamp?"

I stopped. I was halfway across the kitchen on my way to the hall. I felt a bit guilty for walking off with the only light and leaving them all in the gloom.

"We'll take the other lamp," Derek said, firing up the spare. "You girls stay here while we go take a look."

"Men go find big bang," I grunted. Nobody laughed.

Derek carried the spare lamp and headed out into the hallway. I passed my lamp back to Chloe and followed him. My heart beat loudly and my balls receded into my abdomen. As I left the kitchen, I flashed the girls a brave smile to try to mask how I felt.

Derek was nearly at the bottom of the stairs. I hurried to catch up. It really was very dark inside the house now and I cursed Dad for screwing up the utilities. When he told me there would be no electricity, I'd seen it as a fun challenge, to survive the night in a haunted house in the dark. That was before the bang. Christ that was loud! It was far more than a bump in the night. It wasn't even the sound of something falling over. We'd all felt it reverberate through the entire house.

What I wouldn't give to just be able to turn the lights on.

Slowly, we ascended the stairs.

CHAPTER 4

The only sounds were the creaking steps beneath our feet and the hiss of the camping lamp. I should have gone to get my phone from the charger so I could use the flashlight app. Or I should have picked up one of the torches from the supply bag. Instead I had no light source of my own and I could only see by the light of Derek's lamp, which cast eerie shadows along the walls and safety rail as we neared the top of the staircase.

"Tell me about the ghosts in this house?" he whispered as he stepped onto the landing.

"There are three of them, the groundskeeper says. The noisy one is the grandfather of the last occupant, apparently. He died in one of the bedrooms and likes to throw stuff around."

"Which room is above the kitchen?"

"There's an apartment at the back of the house. That door at the back of the kitchen leads up to it. But the bang came from the library. I'll show you."

"Is that where the old man died?"

"Nope. Maybe he's just an avid reader."

These were the friendliest words Derek and I had shared since he'd arrived. It felt like we were teenagers again, sneaking off to go ghost hunting in Gibbet Lane late in the evening, in the village Derek grew up in. I came to that village as a twelve-year-old after moving from place to place all my life. Hafferty was the first place that felt like home, and Derek was the first friend I kept for longer than a few months.

Now here we were, chasing a ghost in an old, creaky house.

I was scared, my stomach was threatening to eject my dinner all over the carpet, and I had to fight the urge to run back downstairs. But I *loved* it.

I could tell Derek was finally enjoying himself too. We advanced down the long corridor like a pair of spies on a mission. The lamp was making our immediate surroundings very bright, but it abandoned the rest of the upper floor to total darkness.

"Why not turn the lamp off?" I suggested.

Derek did so. We waited while our eyes adjusted, and sure enough there was still enough ambient light to see a little further than the lamp had allowed, once our eyes adjusted. In a way it was less scary up here without the lamp, although there were plenty of darkened areas along the corridor in which shadows could thrive.

I moved past Derek to the library door.

"In here," I said, somewhat unnecessarily, and stepped inside.

Derek was right behind me.

The room was empty. No movement, no ghosts, nothing weird at all.

"Whatever it was didn't come from in here," Derek said.

Indeed, everything was how it used to be.

Except it wasn't. Not even slightly. Something really fundamental had changed. Disbelief gripped my senses. My hair stood on end and my hands started to shake.

I raised a trembling finger to point to the bookcase.

"What is it?" he asked, firing up the lamp again. The light chased the shadows into the corners and lit up the most astonishing sight that defied explanation. To Derek, who had not been in here before, everything looked totally normal. But not to me.

"When I was up here, before dinner, the bookcase…" I couldn't finish what I was saying.

"What? Tell me!"

"The bookcase was over there."

I pointed to the right side of the room. The space where the bookcase used to be was empty. Now, impossibly, it stood on the other side of the room, directly in front of the book shelves on the wall.

"Are you sure it moved?" Derek's incredulity was obvious.

"Of course I'm sure."

I moved closer. I didn't want to go anywhere near the bookcase, so instead I went to the place it had been standing earlier in the day. Sure enough, the carpet showed four deep indentations where the heavy piece of furniture once rested.

"That doesn't prove anything. Maybe it was moved before we arrived."

I couldn't believe what I was hearing. "You think I'm lying?"

"I think you might be playing one of your oh-so-hilarious pranks, Jim."

I stared at him for a good long minute. "Try and lift it," I said eventually.

"What?"

"Try and lift the bookcase."

"Okay." Derek placed the lamp on the reading table in the middle of the room and crossed to the bookcase. He tested it by using both hands to try to lift one end, and of course it didn't move. Then he wrapped his arms around it and placed his hands under the top shelves. He heaved. It didn't shift so much as a millimeter.

"So it's bloody heavy," Derek said. "Maybe it was moved before we arrived."

"Moved by whom?" I stammered. "And why?"

"I don't know. You tell me."

I was really starting to get pissed off with him now. I'd invited him here, given him a chance to salvage his weekend away from the kids for the first time in forever, I'd got him out of the doghouse with his wife and I'd done it entirely of my own volition. I had done a good thing for my old friend and he was essentially calling me a liar.

Suddenly I realized something. "I can prove it."

"How?"

"Back downstairs."

I ran from the room, back to the stairs and hurried down. I heard Derek following me at a slower pace, his swinging lamp making my shadow lurch across the wall as I descended. I burst into the kitchen so suddenly it made the girls jump.

"So, what was it?" Chloe asked.

I didn't answer. Instead I went straight for my camera, opening it up and hitting rewind.

Derek entered behind me, his lamp increasing the ambient brightness in the kitchen.

"Jim thinks a piece of furniture moved," he said.

"And that caused the bang?" Beth asked.

"Jim thinks so."

I shook my head, my eyes locked on the camera's LCD screen, watching the images flick by in reverse. "Not just a piece of furniture," I said, glancing up at Beth. "A fucking heavy bookcase that would take a team of people to lift—ah ha!"

I stabbed the play button and thrust the camera at Derek triumphantly. He peered at it. The girls gathered around, unsure of what they were looking for.

"Well I'll be…" Derek said, the colour draining from his face.

"See, the bookcase was on the other side of the room!"

"Holy shit."

"What? I can't see," Chloe complained.

"Then come upstairs."

"I don't want to." Chloe looked visibly upset now.

"Please, I want to be sure we're not crazy."

Beth agreed to come with us. I think Chloe came too because she didn't want to be left downstairs alone. All four of us went out into the hall. I grabbed a lamp and ducked into the drawing room before we went upstairs. I took my now fully charged smartphone from its cradle and picked up two torches. Rejoining the others, I gave Chloe my lamp and switched on my torch, passing the other to Beth. Now we all had a way to see in the dark, and we needed it because the natural light was all gone.

The sun had set on Binsham House and I was now convinced that something was in here with us.

We shuffled upstairs to the library. It reminded me of an old Berenstein Bears book I read as a kid. It was about three bears investigating a spooky old tree. It was one of the first books I ever remember reading to myself. I loved that book. The three bears, one with a light, one with a stick, and one with the shivers.

But we were four, we were adults, and by God half the reason we'd come here was to see a ghost.

I showed the girls the bookcase, the indentations in the carpet, and the footage on the camera again.

We stood in the library in stunned silence.

"I can't explain it," Beth said.

"Do you have a bunch of people hiding here?" Derek accused me. "Will they all pop out and say boo any minute? Did you invite some other old friends to meet us here? Are Ben and Nick going to show up at the front door and say hi as if they've just arrived?"

"I swear we're the only people in the house. And if I did set something up, surely I wouldn't wait this long to spring the surprise. I'd have scared you all hours ago. Besides, it would take at least six people with lifting gear to move this bookcase. I mean look." I went over to the place the bookcase used to be and shone my torch on the floor. "The fucking floorboards are bowed where it used to stand. The wood is less faded. That bookcase hasn't moved for *years.*"

Derek *still* didn't look convinced. What the hell was his problem? I wasn't making this shit up. This wasn't some elaborate ruse designed to freak everybody out.

We went back downstairs to the kitchen and tried to finish our food. Nobody was hungry anymore. We were all a bit shell-shocked. Nobody spoke. I could tell their brains were busy doing the same thing mine was: trying to work out what could have picked up something that heavy and moved it clear across the room.

The next bang was nearly too much for Chloe. She shrieked and dropped the glass she was holding. It didn't fall far and it didn't shatter, but the sound it made as it hit the table made us jump again. The bang had come from the library again. I wondered if the bookcase had moved back to its original position, or somewhere else entirely.

"I don't like this," Chloe said. "I think we've pissed something off."

I could see my weekend plans disintegrating before my eyes.

"Chloe, it's fine," I assured her. I wasn't ready to leave and I knew that would be her next suggestion. "It's *weird* but it's fine. I mean how cool is this? A real ghost."

"I guess." She gave a brave smile. "But it sounds angry to me. Derek, what do you think?"

"I think we should try and get it on camera."

I grinned. "Now you're talking."

"Really?"

"Really. We've got a video camera, a still camera, we've got night vision lenses, we've got a tripod...

"We have a laptop with a huge hard drive," I added.

"So, let's set up a camera at the top of the stairs, and another in the library."

But Chloe was still not convinced. She was clearly looking to her husband to agree with her unspoken intentions.

"You want to stay?" she said, in a tone of voice that made it clear this was the wrong decision.

"I want to see what this thing is."

"Is anyone going to ask my opinion?" Beth said.

I slid off my chair and put my arm around her. "You're not scared, right Beth?"

"I'm scared, I don't mind admitting it. But I'm curious too. I want to see if it will do anything else."

"Sorry, hon," Derek said, aware that his wife was outvoted and likely to take it out on him. "But how often do we get an opportunity like this?"

Chloe sighed. "All right then, we'll stay."

"But promise me this, Jim," Beth said.

"Sure, name it."

"If this thing, whatever it is, if it gets violent with us, if it threatens us or puts us in danger, we leave. Okay?"

I looked at Derek and he nodded. "Okay," I said. "First sign it's hostile towards us, we jump in the car and I will drive you wherever you want to go."

"Not many options," Chloe grumbled.

It was settled. I suddenly felt really excited. This was our chance to capture real paranormal activity on camera!

"Okay," I said. "Here's the rules. Nobody goes anywhere alone. We even go in pairs to the toilet. We've all seen enough scary movies to know what happens when folks are separated. Everyone carries a spare torch even if they have a lamp. Derek and I will set up the cameras upstairs. Why don't you two clear up in here and then setup the drawing room for us to sleep tonight?"

"Sure, leave us to do the women's work," Beth said.

Derek ignored her. "How much free space you have on the camera?"

"Oh I'll plug it into the laptop and download the recording directly to the hard drive. I have extra-sized battery packs for the camera and the laptop—Dad went to town on batteries because he knew we'd have no power. I can setup the digital camera in the hallway to take a picture every ten seconds, and have the video camera rolling constantly in the library. I'll have to turn the quality down a bit to save space, but it should be able to last all night."

"If only everything would last all night," Beth said.

"Ha ha."

CHAPTER 5

Ten minutes later, Derek and I were working to set up our equipment at the top of the stairs. I attached the night vision lens to the DSLR camera and then configured it to go off every ten seconds with no flash. Then I handed it to Derek, who held it while I descended a few steps and then reached through the wooden bars to take it from him. I tried placing it in various positions until I was satisfied the camera had the best view of the landing, pointing towards the library. Derek took masking tape and wrapped it around the camera and the railing several times, being careful not to obscure the lens or the controls.

I checked to make sure it was taking pictures and then we moved to the library.

"Turn off the lamp a moment."

Derek did as I asked and the hissing ceased. Then I turned off my torch.

It was quite astonishing how dark it was. It wasn't just a case of our eyes having to get used to the gloom. We literally couldn't see a thing. I held a hand in front of my face and wiggled my fingers. I saw nothing.

I broke the silence. "Now that's dark."

Both of us lived in the city. It was virtually impossible to shut out the light. At night, streetlamps illuminated our apartments through curtains or shutters. Electronics cast an eerie glow with their standby lights. But here, in this room, with our lamps off and the video camera powered down, even though there was nothing covering the window, we stood in pitch darkness.

"Wow," I said. "You still there?"

"Yep," said Derek. "I don't remember being anywhere so dark before."

I looked towards the window. It must have been an overcast night because we couldn't see stars or the moon.

"You could shut yourself in a meat locker with the light off, I suppose," I said.

"Not my idea of fun. If you turn off all the lights in my flat and go in the bathroom with the door closed, it might get this dark."

I chuckled. "Is that something you do a lot?"

"I think we should turn the lights on now."

"Scared?"

"Not yet. Getting there."

The gas lamp hissed into life again. We blinked and shielded our eyes from the sudden intrusion. Once my eyes had adjusted, I glanced around the room. Nothing had moved this time. Derek placed the lamp on the centre table.

He worked on the tripod while I powered up the video camera and laptop and connected them together. Both had extra-capacity battery packs with a full charge, so in theory they should last throughout the night. I checked my iPhone. The time was 9pm. It felt like the middle of the night already.

The camera was rolling and I checked the images were going straight to the laptop hard drive. Then I paused it and mounted it on the tripod.

"We should try to cover as much of the room as we can," Derek said.

"Over here should do it." I picked up the tripod and moved to the corner next to the window, away from the wall shelves. Derek followed carrying the laptop, keeping the connecting cables slack. I stood the tripod up and checked the test image on the laptop Derek was holding. I shifted the camera to take in the impossible bookcase, the area where the bookcase *used to be*, and the covered table and chairs in the centre of the room. Derek was still holding the laptop, so I went over and grabbed him a small side table, removing the plant on it first.

As I adjusted the camera position, Derek picked up the lamp from the centre table.

"So I guess you weren't that keen on coming," I said. I had to bring it up at some point. If he was pissed at me, I wanted to know why and I didn't want Chloe answering for him.

"No, mate, it's fine, really. It's good to see you." That was obviously a lie. "Pass me the tape would you? I want to make sure nothing knocks this tripod over." I handed him the tape but I wouldn't let him change the subject.

"If it was up to you and not Chloe, would you have come?"

"Well I had to make it up to her so I couldn't say no."

"That's not what I asked."

He let out a deep breath. "What do you want me to say, Jim? You want me to say no? Okay no, I probably wouldn't have."

"Why? Is it me?"

"Jesus… You don't give up, do you? We've hardly spoken in years. We have different lives now. It was like a stranger calling me up out of the blue to ask if I'd like to spend the weekend in his big scary house. Things are so different now. We're not the same people. Plus there's the whole charity thing of you helping us out, and while I appreciate the sentiment I fucking loathe being treated like we're in need of handouts."

"I can understand that."

Still he wasn't telling me the full story. He was holding something back.

We were pretty much done so I dropped it for now. At least he was talking to me and we had a common goal to pursue. That took some of the awkwardness away. Satisfied that the equipment wasn't going to shut down automatically, run out of batteries or just fall over, we went back downstairs.

In the drawing room, with the door and window shutters closed, it almost seemed cozy. The dust covers were gone revealing comfortable leather furniture. The carpet was old and a bit worn, but it was clean. This was by far the warmest room in the house so we didn't need to roll out our sleeping bags just yet. We would all be sleeping in here tonight. Our original plan was to give Derek and Chloe their privacy (and Beth and I, ours) but after what had happened we all agreed to stick together. We were all tired, but nobody wanted to turn in so early in the evening. None of us was sure we could even sleep.

Chloe announced that she needed to pee, so we suggested she use one of the downstairs toilets, a small room under the stairs accessible from the hallway. Derek and Chloe went together. While they were gone, I had my first chance to talk alone with Beth since they'd arrived.

"See, you asked for ghosts, I deliver ghosts. Am I good or what?"

"Pretty wild, for sure," Beth said. I held her for a while and enjoyed the feel of her body pressed against mine.

"It's a shame we can't spend the night alone," she said. I got quite aroused at that, just the idea that she wanted to be alone with me tonight. Sometimes that's all it took.

"Well, we're here tomorrow night too. So if nothing bad happens tonight then perhaps tomorrow we can find our own place to sleep."

"That would be nice."

"Or if we're dragged into hell tonight, perhaps we can find a nice hotel for tomorrow night instead."

"That sounds good too. The hotel bit, not the hell bit."

I didn't want to let her go.

"Hey, maybe tomorrow you and I could slip away to the woods behind the lake, or the Victorian garden, maybe have some open air fun?"

"Oh that does sound naughty," she said. God how I wanted to take her somewhere private right now. Damn ghost! "But what if Arthur comes back?"

"He's not back until Wednesday."

"You never know, he might have forgotten something."

"Well we can ask Derek and Chloe to act as lookouts for us. We can do the same for them."

"I don't want to ask them that! It's embarrassing."

"Then I'll talk to Derek about it. I'm guessing he would love to take advantage of some rare alone time with Chloe."

"If he talks to you at all."

"You noticed that then?"

"Hard not to. Did you talk to him upstairs?"

"A bit. He says he's just unsure of where we stand after so much time barely talking. But to me it's like we've never been apart, you know? Some people you just know you're always going to be friends with, even if twenty years has gone by and you've never seen them."

Beth held me a little tighter. She could probably feel how horny she was making me, but she didn't move away. If anything she pressed harder against me. "I know what you mean," she said.

I kissed her, trying not to let myself get carried away.

"I hope you packed condoms," she said.

"If I didn't I wouldn't worry. Dad will have thrown a pack in the supply bag." She laughed at that and we moved apart a little. My body ached for closeness again but there was something I wanted to ask before the others returned. "Did Chloe say anything to you about Derek?" I asked.

"Oh we got on really well, we talked about everything. She's so nice and friendly. So English! I really like her."

"I'm glad to hear it. So what did she say?"

"Just that she's as confused by his attitude as we are. He was reluctant to come and she thinks he only said yes because he screwed up so badly with the trip. She thinks he's pissed at you about something, but she doesn't know what it is and he won't talk to her about it."

"Yeah I don't know what it is either."

"You've pissed off a lot of people in your time, Jim. There could be so many reasons."

I grabbed her close again with a mock growl and kissed her.

Just as the door opened and Chloe walked in.

"Oh I'm sorry," she said. "We can come back."

Beth and I parted awkwardly.

"It's okay," I said, grateful for the semi-darkness.

Derek followed Chloe into the room. She seemed more comfortable now, being in a smaller room with the rest of us. It had been an hour or so since the banging from upstairs, and the house was quiet now.

"I can't believe how dark it is," Chloe said.

Beth sat up, leaning on her hands stretched out behind her. "Yeah I hope the lamps don't burn out."

I opened the supply bag and pulled out three more cans of gas.

"I think we'll be okay."

Chloe settled into one of the winged-back arm chairs. "So what do we do now?"

"I have cards," Beth said.

I walked over to the corner of the room where a wooden cabinet was mounted into the wall. Something about it just screamed *board games inside!* to me. The cabinet wasn't locked. I swung the door open and sure enough saw six or seven battered boxes stacked on top of one another.

"Who's up for Monopoly?" I asked, pulling out the first box. "Cluedo? Scrabble? Wow, all the classics. No Trivial Pursuit, which is a fucking relief and no mistake. No Pictionary either, and for that we can all be grateful."

"Are you suggesting we spend the night in a haunted house playing board games?" Chloe scoffed.

"If you'd like to go poking around upstairs, please be my guest."

"What's Cluedo?" Beth asked. "Is that like Clue?"

"Yes, its Clue," I told her.

"I hate Clue. Something else?"

Chloe piped up. "Well I like Monopoly."

Since nobody objected, I lifted the box and brought it to the table.

"Monopoly it is."

Derek sneezed suddenly, making us all jump. Obviously we were all still a little on edge.

"Did your dad put some wine bottles in that bag?" he asked.

"No but Chloe and I bought some from the village," said Beth.

"They're in the kitchen, right?"

"Of course."

Derek stood up. "I'll go get them then. I'll get some glasses and see if I can find a corkscrew."

"No need," Beth said. "They're the bottles with the twist off caps."

"Classy," said Derek. "Be right back."

"Whoah, where are you going?" I scolded him.

Derek made a show of repeating himself. "To get the wine from the kitchen?"

"Not on your own, remember?"

He sighed and grabbed the spare lamp and a torch. "Fine. Come on, Chloe. Help me grab the wine while they setup the game."

Beth and I were alone again. We opened the Monopoly box and took out the pieces. The game board was tattered but still serviceable, and while the money and the cards were dog-eared and in many places torn and stuck together with Sellotape, there weren't too many pieces missing. We also had enough playing pieces, though the iron was gone.

"It's a woman, isn't it?" Beth asked, out of the blue.

"I'm pretty sure it's supposed to be a boot," I replied, holding up one of the Monopoly pieces.

"Not the game. Derek's beef with you. It's a woman. I don't know which woman, but something Chloe said really stuck with me. She was telling me how she got pregnant the first time she slept with Derek. She always wonders if he's only with her because of the children. If she hadn't got pregnant, would he have stayed?"

"They seem to be getting on okay."

"Yeah I suppose so. But I wonder if that's why he's pissed at you."

"What did I do? Sneak into Derek's flat and stick pins through all his condoms?"

Beth screwed her face up at me. "She seems to think that Derek was only with her on a rebound though he's never confirmed it."

"And you think he was rebounding from the true love of his life?"

"How eloquent, Mr Harlequin Romance."

"So what does this have to do with me?"

"I have no idea. I'm just guessing. But the reason he's pissed at you could be something to do with how he ended up with Chloe."

"You're reaching," I said. "The timelines don't match up. I haven't seen Derek in eight years. He's been with Chloe for, what, seven?"

"I think so. Maybe it was a delayed rebound. Did he ever date any women you dated?"

"No I don't think so. I was pretty self-absorbed in my late teens and early twenties, so it's possible."

Chloe and Derek returned with the wine.

"All quiet?" I asked them.

"Not a sound, thank God," Chloe said.

Derek sniffed loudly, as if to challenge the silence. "Kind of disappointing," he said.

Chloe placed two bottles of wine on the table and opened a third as she sat down. Derek handed out a glass to each of us.

"Just three bottles then?" I asked with a smile.

"That's just for me," Chloe said.

"Don't drink too much," Beth warned her, "or you'll have to keep going to the bathroom during the night."

"Oh good point. Can we get a chamber pot in here or something?"

We all turned up our noses and laughed at that. We chose our playing pieces and started the game. The wine was a cheap red but it was quite pleasant and helped sand the rough edges from our little group. Even Derek was mellowing. Between the ghost hunting and the alcohol, something resembling my former friend began to surface. We even told Chloe and Beth about our experience on Gibbet Lane.

"We used to go down there quite a lot when it was dark," I said. "Our parents thought we were each at the other's house, but instead we snuck off to Gibbet Lane."

"It was quite a long walk too."

"Yeah but it was so spooky, and there were so many weird stories about it. How could we resist?"

"We never took a video camera, did we?"

I shook my head. "No, missed opportunity there. Neither of us owned one. I had an old cine camera somewhere though."

"So," said Beth, "did you ever see anything?"

I glanced at Derek and said, "We didn't *see* anything, no."

"So what did you hear?" Chloe asked, catching on.

"We were walking down the lane towards the crossroads in the middle," I said. "There was a grassy area in the center with an old tree, and that's apparently where they used to hang highwaymen caught robbing people on the London Road."

"So why did they call it Gibbet Lane?" Beth asked, interrupting. "If they hanged people from a tree, you don't need a gibbet."

"I don't know! Hello! Trying to tell a story here. So this is a narrow lane, barely wide enough to get one car down. On both sides are these tall grass-covered banks and beyond that is just fields, so there isn't much light other than from the moon.

"Derek was walking along the top of one of those banks, and I walked in the lane. You felt it more than me, right?"

"Yeah," Derek said. "It was so weird. All of a sudden, no warning, no buildup, suddenly there's this booming noise and the whole bank shakes. Literally it shakes. But not like an earthquake where it's constant movement. No it was like BOOM, BOOM, BOOM, three times in a row."

I picked up the story. "The second boom actually knocked Derek off the bank. The third boom we heard behind us, because we were running the hell away."

"I've never been so scared," said Derek. "I remember the first boom making me stumble and the second one was violent enough to knock me off."

"He crashed into me and then we just took off."

"So what was it?" Beth asked.

"We don't know," I said. "To this day we have no idea."

"People we talked to suggested it was a rabbit underground kicking the inside of its burrow."

"Bloody strong rabbit!" I said.

"Someone else said it could have been a water pipe that got blocked."

"Seems really unlikely given the lane is bordered by fields. I don't know why anyone would run a water pipe along it, and underneath one of the banks. Makes no sense."

Derek nodded. "A mystery," he said.

"Bullshit!" said Beth

I stared at her with my mouth open. So did Derek.

"It's not bullshit!" I insisted.

"I know. I just wanted to see the look on your face."

"Just for that I'm going to buy out your entire hotel chain and demolish the lot."

Chloe turned to Derek. "Didn't you tell me you failed A-Level maths because you went ghost hunting?"

Derek shifted. He looked uncomfortable. "Yeah we went out the night before the exam."

"Did we?" I didn't remember that at all.

"Yeah we did. I wanted to stay home and revise, but you insisted."

"Oh so it's *my* fault you failed maths? I managed to pass it."

"Not really a surprise there, Jim. You did fuck all work all year and just strolled through the bloody exams. What did you get, straight As?"

"I got a B in History…"

"Meanwhile us lowly humans had to put in some actual fucking work to get good grades. It didn't matter if we had a big exam coming up, you still wanted to go bloody ghost hunting."

"You could have said no."

"I *should* have said no. Do you know what happened when my dad saw my maths mark?"

He didn't have to tell me. I remembered all too well the bruises Derek sported when his father's temper got the better of him.

We all fell silent after that. The game went on for another ten minutes but Derek had descended into a funk and I wasn't really in the mood either. Only Chloe and Beth kept the game going through sheer determination. But in the end we gave up before it was done, declaring Beth the winner because she had the most money and property.

Chloe yawned dramatically. "Maybe it's time to get some sleep."

Thankfully it was still warm in the drawing room, and I think we were all glad we'd decided to bunk down in here together rather than venture upstairs to separate rooms.

We all had to use the bathroom again. Derek and Chloe went together and returned without incident. Then Beth and I took our turn.

When we got back to the room, Derek and Chloe were already wrapped up in their sleeping bag, fast asleep.

"Parents," I whispered.

"Shhh, this is probably their first sleep in years!"

"You know what I'm scared of, more than anything?" I asked as we climbed into our double sleeping bag.

"Things that go bump in the night?"

"No, I'm scared of taking a freezing cold shower in the morning."

"Oh shit!" Beth said, too loudly.

"Shhh!"

But it didn't matter. Derek and Chloe would have slept through anything.

Beth whispered anyway. "I hadn't thought of that."

"It's not too bad. I've stayed in one of Dad's houses before where there was no hot water. You get used to standing *beside* the shower and sticking bits of yourself in. It's almost bearable that way. The worst part is washing your hair."

"Maybe we should just go jump in the lake."

I laughed gently. Beth yawned and I took that as my cue to turn off the gas lamp, plunging the room into total darkness.

"Can't you leave it on?" Beth asked.

"The gas will run out. Don't worry, I have the flashlight right here. I'll put it on the floor right by our heads. And remember, if you have to go to the loo before dawn, you can wake me up and I'll go with you, okay?"

But she didn't answer me. I could tell by her breathing she was already asleep. It had been a very long day, even though 10:30pm was only 3:30pm for us. Still, we had slept so badly on the plane. I was glad she'd fallen asleep before me. It meant she wouldn't be the only one left awake.

I couldn't get to sleep right away. I was wondering if the cameras upstairs had captured anything interesting, assuming they were still running. I should have gone to check them but I wasn't feeling brave enough to go on my own. Plus it would be really hard to get out of the sleeping bag now, not just because I didn't want to wake Beth but also because it was so warm and comfortable in here and I felt like…

***

I woke suddenly. I had no idea what had startled me, and it was so dark it was hard to tell whether or not my eyes were open.

I listened for a moment, but I couldn't hear anything aside from loud snoring coming from either Derek or Chloe. I reached outside the sleeping bag and grabbed my smartphone. Switching it on, the light hurt my eyes and I had to blink rapidly. The luminous display danced in front of me, an illusion caused by the contrast of light and dark, but still unnerving. It was 11.30pm. I'd been asleep just an hour.

Strangely I didn't feel tired. Instead I experienced again the same feeling I had while hiding beneath the table in the library. My heart was beating fast and my hair was standing on end.

Why? I turned off the phone and listened, trying to make out if there was any sound in the room beyond my three sleeping companions' breathing. There wasn't anything else. I waited to see if my eyes would adjust to the dark, but there just wasn't any light, however faint, for my vision to get used to. I tried closing my eyes and going back to sleep, but I was hyper-aware now. I couldn't relax. What had spooked me? Had I heard something just before I woke? I turned the phone back on and switched on the flashlight app. The camera flash lit up with surprising brightness, aimed at the door in a focused beam of light. I sat up and swept the light slowly around the room. The light moved over the wall by the door, passing over a side table, the alcove in the corner with the empty vase, the fireplace ahead of me, with its metal grate and wooden mantle. Another recessed area to the left of the fireplace, with empty shelves. I kept going, my hearing still trying to filter out the others' snoring, trying to detect any hint of something that didn't belong.

Something rustled to my left. I jumped, jerking my light towards the source. It was just Derek, turning over. His movement caused Chloe to turn onto her side too. Their breathing quieted down after that. There were no other sounds in the room.

So I kept going with the light, sweeping it over Derek and Chloe's sleeping bag and beyond them to the shutters over the window. I twisted my body as the light moved past the corner of the room to my rear left and then right behind me. I swung around so I was now looking over my right shoulder and followed the circle made by the phone's light. Then I moved it across the corner to the right of the door, and back to my starting point.

Nothing unusual.

I switched off the phone and lay back down next to Beth, trying to listen to her gentle breathing, letting it wash over me, trying to relax. I stared up at the ceiling, though of course now I could see nothing at all.

And that's when I realized.

I'd checked the room at eye level, but not above my head.

I snatched my phone up and stabbed at the on button. The light glared in my face again, casting the room in a dull, blue pallour. I didn't turn on the phone's flashlight again, I just used its regular illumination to see by.

And then I looked up.

In the centre of the ceiling was a chandelier that wasn't terribly opulent, but was in good condition. I knew this because I'd seen it in daylight. Right now I couldn't see it at all.

The centre of the ceiling, right above my head, was black.

Quickly I turned on the phone's flashlight and aimed it upwards.

The blackness swallowed the beam. It was like anti-light. The lit circle shone on the ceiling around the edges of something black where the chandelier should be. Something that shouldn't be there. Something that would not reveal itself no matter what angle I shone the light.

And then it moved. Very very slowly, almost imperceptibly at first. I found myself reaching over to Beth, trying to shake her awake.

And then it *turned*.

I'm sure it *looked at me*.

It had no eyes, no shape, no form, but it was looking at me. I knew it. I felt it in the core of my soul. It was watching me. It knew me.

It hated me.

And then it fell from the ceiling, like it had let go. It fell right towards me. For a brief second, I saw something form in the centre of the black mass as it dropped.

I screamed and dropped my phone. My arms flew up to protect my head.

But there was nothing. Nothing touched me.

I picked up the phone again, shaking. I aimed it upwards, hardly daring to look.

There was the chandelier. No blackness, no inexplicable shadow.

But it was in here, with me, with us.

I used the light from the phone to find the lamp. I turned the valve and it hissed into life, filling the room with warm, comforting light.

The others didn't stir.

I got out of the sleeping bag and searched the whole room. I looked beneath the table and under the chairs, even in the fireplace. My eyes kept returning to the ceiling, wondering just what the hell I'd seen.

Finally, satisfied that the four of us were alone in here, I got back into the sleeping bag.

This time I left the lamp on.

But I didn't sleep. I couldn't sleep. My mind just kept on replaying what I'd seen on the ceiling, over and over.

I don't know how long I lay there. I was damn glad I'd left the lamp on though. I didn't have to stare into the darkness imagining what was sitting there ready to pounce at me.

It was then I heard footsteps.

It was background noise that wasn't there before; quiet enough so that I couldn't be sure what I was hearing but loud enough to be sure it wasn't just something natural. It was a creaking, like floorboards bowing under someone's body weight. I'd heard that rhythmic creaking before. I'd heard it whenever anyone had descended the stairs earlier that evening.

Someone was coming down the stairs right now.

I glanced at my sleeping companions. All present and accounted for. I hoped I'd fallen asleep without realizing it and one of them had left the room. But no. Neither was I dreaming. My flesh crawled. The more I listened, the more certain I was that somebody was almost gingerly descending.

The footsteps went quiet. I froze in place, sitting up in my sleeping bag. I strained to hear. Why had the sound ceased?

Oh God, more footsteps, but not descending the stairs now. They were crossing the hall.

They were coming closer.

I climbed out and stood up, looking around for some kind of weapon. The fireplace didn't have a poker or I would have snatched it up. Not that it would do me any good, but an iron bar in my hands might have lent me some courage.

"Guys, wake up!" I hissed. They didn't even stir. I didn't dare speak louder. I didn't want to let anything outside know we were in here.

But it knew.

The footsteps grew louder now, unmistakable. And then they stopped, right outside the door.

Silence.

Just the regular breathing of my companions, and the hiss of the lamp.

Half of my brain wanted to throw open the door and confront whatever was out there. The other half, the half that won, wanted that door to stay shut until dawn, when I would jump in the car and leave this place and never come back. I had to wake the others but I couldn't move. I just stared at the door, standing like I was ready to run—though there was nowhere to run to.

Now I was aware of another noise. It was coming from the door. It was a scratching noise, like someone was running their nails down the outside of the door. I'd had enough.

"Wake the fuck up," I shouted.

Beth sat bolt upright. Derek and Chloe stirred.

"Wake up," I screamed. I didn't care what might hear me; I just didn't want to be facing this alone.

"What is it? What's wrong?" Beth asked, climbing out of the sleeping bag. She rubbed at her eyes and blinked at me. "Are you okay?"

"There's something outside the door. It's trying to get in."

"What time is it?" That was Derek. He was fumbling for his phone so he could answer his own question.

"Derek? What's going on?" Chloe asked.

Beth got up and linked her arm through mine.

"What's the matter? What did you hear?"

"I heard footsteps coming down the stairs," I replied, aware that I sounded like a raving madman. "And then they crossed the hallway and stopped. I wanted to open the door and see who was there, but there was this scratching noise, like nails on the wood."

Was I losing my mind? We all listened intently but there was no sound coming from the other side.

Derek went over to the door.

"Do you want me to open it?" he asked, his hand grasping the handle.

"No," I cried. "Yes! God, no."

I think he was laughing at me inside, though he kept a straight face. Instead of opening the door, he put his head against the wood and listened.

"What can you hear?" asked Beth.

He held up a hand for silence. Impatiently we waited for his verdict.

"There's nothing out there," Derek said at last. "I'm going to open the door."

I took a step backwards. Beth gazed at me in concern.

"Perhaps best not to," she said to Derek.

"Bullshit," he said. "If it's a ghost I want to see it. That's why you invited us here, right Jim? For a spot of jolly ghost hunting? Well let's go hunt the damn thing. It can't harm us, so let's go harm it."

"Derek, it moved a bookcase," Beth reminded him.

"It's trying to scare us. It wants us to leave. If it's the grandfather of the last owner then it's pissed that the house isn't in the family anymore. So let's make it angry, let's get it fired up some more and then we can take its picture. We'll post it on every website and tweet it and put it on Facebook until it goes viral, and every wannabe ghost hunter in the world is going to descend on this place and your dad can charge a fortune to let them stay in a genuine haunted house."

Beth was shaking her head. "I don't think we should make it mad."

"It's not trying to get us to leave," I said. I don't know how I knew that, but I got the strong impression it was just flexing its muscles, and if it wanted us out it would have picked us up and hurled us through the window by now.

"Of course it wants us to leave! This isn't our house. The family has lived here for decades and now you think this ghost is just going to sit there and let the place fall into the hands of investors or some dumb footballer?"

"Keep your voice down, please," Chloe said, taking his arm.

But Derek's rant was over. The wind had gone out of his sails somewhat. Perhaps the ghost—there was no doubt in my mind any more—was just trying to drive a wedge between us. It wouldn't be hard, given the inexplicable frostiness Derek had shown towards me from the moment he arrived.

"I'm going to take a look."

Derek crossed to his sleeping bag and picked up his phone and his torch. He switched the torch on and selected something on his phone, likely the camera. Then he crossed back to the door.

"Derek, love, I think we should probably keep the door closed," Chloe said.

"No, I'm going to take a look. And if there's nothing there then I'm going to get the camera from the landing. If it came down the stairs like Jim says it did, then it must have passed the camera and there must be a shot of it."

"I'll come with you then," said Chloe. She didn't sound very brave, but she obviously didn't want to let him out of her sight.

"Let's all go," I said.

"I'm not going," said Beth.

"You want to stay here alone?"

"No, you're going to stay here with me!"

"Chloe and I will go," Derek said. He handed his torch to Chloe and had her stand a few feet from the door, shining the light towards him. Then he put his hand on the door handle again, and held his camera ready. Before he opened it, he put his ear against the door one last time to see if he could hear anything.

We waited in silence.

Bang.

The door shook with the force of the blow. Derek staggered backwards and fell to the floor. Chloe screamed. I think I screamed too.

"What the fuck was that?" Beth breathed.

Derek stared at the door in shock, his bravado evaporated. Chloe went to him and helped him up, holding him tight. Beth's hand found mine and squeezed it.

We stayed like that for some time, just staring at the wood-panelled door in shock.

Eventually, Beth spoke up.

"This is ridiculous. We can't stand here all night."

And to everyone else's surprise, she grabbed the lamp, moved over to the door, turned the knob and opened it.

It was so dark beyond it was difficult to see if there was anything out there or not. As Beth stepped out into the hallway, I wanted desperately to go with her, to keep her safe. But I couldn't move. I felt like the worst boyfriend in the world. What if something took her? She was brave enough to go out there; I should be by her side!

"There's nothing out here," she said.

Derek grabbed the spare lamp and turned it on so that we'd still have light in the room. Then he took the torch back from Chloe and joined Beth outside the door. Chloe seemed as terrified as me, but she managed to move to the doorway even if she refused to pass through it.

"Look, over there at the bottom of the stairs," Beth said, and moved out of my line of sight.

Derek followed. "What the hell?"

Finally my curiosity won out over my cowardice. I gently pushed past Chloe and stepped into the hall. As I did so, I clicked on my torch. There was enough light coming from the lamp and Derek's light, but I felt more secure with my own torch in my hand somehow. If nothing else, I could use it as a weapon.

Beth and Derek were at the bottom of the stairs, down on their knees, sorting through a pile of... books.

"How did they get there?" I asked redundantly.

There were about a dozen of them. Beth had organized most of them into a neat pile.

"Did it throw them down?" Chloe asked. She had joined us now, unwilling to be left in the drawing room alone.

Beth nodded. "Yeah, they were scattered over the bottom few steps."

"Maybe it's trying to tell us something," Chloe suggested. None of us wanted to acknowledge that we were now calling whatever this phenomenon was an 'it'.

I bent down and took the first book off the pile. "These are just botany books. Check the rest of them."

Derek sorted through a couple while Beth worked through her pile.

"This one's about bird watching," Beth said, handing it back to me. "This one is Moby Dick."

"Here's a cookbook," said Derek, "and Dracula of all things."

"I don't get what this is supposed to mean," said Beth.

I handed the book back to her. "I don't think it's supposed to mean anything. I think whatever it is just grabbed some books and threw them down the stairs at us."

"I've seen more threatening spirits," Derek said.

I shook my head. "Don't forget the bang on the door, and the bookcase. Old Percy's granddad sure is a strong bugger."

"Jim, what's this?"

Beth was holding a book open in one hand and a photograph in the other. Clearly she'd just taken the picture from within the pages of the novel. I picked up the lamp and brought it closer. When I saw what it was, I gasped.

It was a picture of a pretty blonde woman, in her twenties, with large blue eyes and a radiant smile. I'd not seen her photo in so long; it was a shock to see it here.

"I know her," Beth said. "I've seen her photo in your old photo album. I've seen this photo!"

"Who is she?" Chloe asked, peering over my shoulder.

"Her name is Anna," I replied. "I used to date her, years ago."

"So what's her photo doing here?" Derek asked.

"Yeah that's what I'd like to know." Beth was staring daggers at me.

I gaped at her. "Okay, sure, that makes sense. I bring a picture of my ex-girlfriend on my weekend away with you, and I stash it in a book when I get here just for kicks. That sounds likely."

"How else did it get here?"

"I remember her," Derek said. "Where is she now?"

"As far as I know she's in Australia," I replied.

"And she's here tonight!" Derek announced, turning and waving his arms dramatically. Clearly he was enjoying my discomfort.

Nobody laughed at Derek's joke. I continued, "And no, I don't carry her photo around with me."

Beth wasn't convinced. "Maybe you brought it by mistake and tried to get rid of it by sticking it in a book before I saw it."

I had no idea how the photo had got there. A disturbing thought arrived in my head.

"Maybe the ghost, or whatever it is, maybe it brought it here."

"How convenient," said Beth icily.

"Well it's a bit of a coincidence isn't it? I hide this photo in the same book that gets thrown down the stairs."

Beth just stared at me. Then she tore the photo in half and returned to the drawing room. We all followed her, closing the door and switching off all but one of the lamps. Then we sat around the table again, quietly listening to see if anything weird was going to happen. Beth wouldn't even look at me.

"Tell us about these ghosts then," Derek asked, probably just to change the subject. "Three of them right?"

"Yeah," I said. "Arthur the groundskeeper was telling us about them. There's a boy with a drum, a woman who smells of lavender and the ghost of Percy's grandfather."

"Who's Percy?" Chloe asked.

"The guy who owned this place before he died and my dad bought it."

"So which one is throwing books at us and shifting furniture?"

"I think we can discount the little boy with the tin drum," I said. "Unless he's been working out." I laughed gently, trying to break the tension a little, but nobody so much as smiled. "So that leaves Percy's granddad and the lavender lady."

"Can we rule her out?" Derek asked.

"Sure," I said. "I didn't smell any lavender. Did you guys?"

They all shook their heads.

"So that leaves Percy's granddad," said Chloe.

"Arthur did say he tends to make a racket at night," I told them.

"He must be really pissed at us," Beth said while she looked at me, making it clear that the ghost wasn't the only one who was mad.

Derek nodded. "So it's the old man then. Any reports of him moving furniture?"

I shrugged. "No idea. Arthur only talked about him briefly, just said he's noisy."

"Does he have a name?"

"Percy's granddad? Well he must have, but I don't know what it is."

"We could ask him," Beth suggested.

"Or maybe the books give a clue to his name," Derek suggested.

"I think that's a stretch," I said.

"Feel free to come up with a better suggestion," Derek snapped.

All of us sat quietly for a moment.

"Are you going to tell me why you're so pissed off at me?" I asked him after a time. I knew why Beth was mad, however unfairly, but the cause of Derek's ire was a mystery.

"Drop it, Jim," he said, in a warning tone.

"Maybe I won't. Maybe you're going to tell me what's up with you."

"I don't owe you an explanation. I don't think I owe you anything. You don't need anything from me so just drop it, okay?"

I put up my hands and backed off. "No problem, Derek. I'll leave you be."

"Thank you," he said.

Well there was no doubt about it now: he really didn't like me and me alone. So now the only person here who could tolerate me was Chloe.

We sat in silence for a short while and then Chloe said something.

"What if it's not one of the three known ghosts," she suggested quietly. "What if it's a newcomer? What if it's Percy himself? How long ago did he die?"

"A month," Beth said.

"Well there you go then, maybe it's the ghost of Percy."

"He was an old man when he died," I said. "How's he going to lift a bookcase?"

"He's a fucking ghost, Jim," Derek said. "Who the hell knows what he's capable of?"

I ignored his abrasive attitude and went with the positive. By calling it a ghost, Derek was admitting that I wasn't crazy. I was sure he'd try to find some kind of explanation for the bang on the door and the books on the stairs. But no, he was seemingly as convinced as I was. And he hadn't seen the thing on the ceiling.

"It makes sense though, right?" Chloe pushed on, putting a hand on Derek's arm to try to get him to calm down. "Percy dies having lived in the house all his life. He leaves no heirs so the house has to be sold. And we're the first ones to stay here overnight. Stands to reason. He wants us gone."

"You may be onto something there," I told her. "But I still don't think it wants us to leave."

"Maybe it… he just wants us to know he's here, so that your dad won't be able to sell the house at all."

"Or it could be Arthur," Beth piped up. "He could have the house wired up with special effects. It could be a big ruse to get us to leave."

"How very *Scooby Doo*," I said with a forced smile. "I'll unmask him for a Scooby-snack."

Beth regarded me coldly and my smile vanished.

"It's actually the most logical explanation," Derek said.

"Well it might explain the thumps and the footsteps, but it doesn't explain moving the bookcase, or the thing up on the ceiling either." I pointed to the chandelier. Everyone else stared at it.

"What thing on the ceiling?" Beth asked.

"I saw it while you were all sleeping. It was a black mass, clinging to the chandelier. I pointed my phone's light right at it and it came at me."

"Came at you?" Beth said.

"Yeah, it just sort of... hurled itself at me. And I saw a face."

"It had a face?" Derek was leaning in now.

"Yeah I'm sure of it. But it was only a fraction of a second and then it was gone. I swear it had a face but I couldn't draw it for you or anything, or pick a guy out of a lineup. I couldn't even tell you if its nose was big or its mouth was wide. It was in motion, fluid."

"And what happened when it came at you?"

"Well I kind of... screamed and covered my head, and then it was gone."

Chloe swallowed. "I will never sleep again."

We sat in silence for a while. Beth yawned, but none of us felt willing to climb back into our sleeping bags.

"So is it time to leave?" Beth asked.

I checked my phone. It was 12.30am.

"It's the middle of the night, where are we going to go?"

"We can take turns to drive back to London," Chloe suggested. "You can stay at our flat. The kids are away so there's lots of room."

"Thanks but it might be easier to drive to the nearest city and rent a room."

"What is the nearest city?" Beth asked.

I shrugged. "Hereford, I suppose. Once we're back in civilization I can check some websites and see if I can get us in somewhere."

"We're not leaving!" Derek said.

"Hon, I think we're not wanted here," Chloe said, putting a hand on his arm.

"No way, I'm not leaving until we get this thing on film."

"Derek, I'm with the girls. I think it's time to go."

"You can go if you like."

I shook my head. "We're not leaving you here alone."

"Nothing's going to happen to me," he said. "You can come pick me up in the morning."

"You're not serious, are you, hon?" Chloe's tone was pleading. "I can't leave you here, I won't leave you."

"Stay with me then."

Chloe continued, "But this is crazy. Out of the four of us, you were the only one who didn't want to come. Now you don't want to leave."

"Now I know there's a ghost, I want to stay. I want to find out who it is and what its motives are. And I want it on camera."

"We won't leave you," I said again. Regardless of his attitude, he was still my friend. He was still the only person in the village I grew up in who took the time to reach out to me, the new kid. It was a lonely life moving around so much, and to have a friend like Derek had been a lifesaver—and I mean that probably in a literal sense.

"Then we're all staying."

And that was that. Beth didn't look happy about it. Or she might have been pissed at me still. Chloe was veering halfway between terror at the prospect of staying and anger that her husband didn't want to leave.

"I'm going to get the camera on the banister. Hopefully it got a good shot of whatever came down the stairs."

"Shouldn't we wait until morning?" I said.

"I want to check we got something now. If the camera's at the wrong angle we could end up getting no good shots the whole night."

"Oh Derek, stop it," Chloe said. "None of us wants to go upstairs now. Let's just stay in here."

"I didn't say you had to come with me."

"We made a rule, remember," I said.

"Bollocks to your rule. If anyone wants to come up with me then be my guest. If not, I'll go alone. I'm just going to grab the camera from the top of the stairs and come back again. I'm not going to hang out and drink piña coladas with Percy's granddad in the library."

Beth, Chloe and I glanced awkwardly at each other, each hoping someone else would volunteer first.

Derek laughed. "For God's sake, it's either a ghost or a hoax, and the sooner we find out the sooner we can get some sleep."

Somehow I didn't think Derek really cared that much about sleeping. He was on a mission now. Perhaps this was the most exciting thing to happen to him in years. Or perhaps he longed for fame, and believed this was his chance to grab it.

I had to admit, while part of my mind recoiled in terror at the thought of seeing that dark mass again, another part dearly wanted to get it on film. Not because I wanted to become famous and get on TV, necessarily, but because it would be pretty cool to have actual evidence of a real life haunting.

Derek clicked on his torch and went to the door.

"I'll come with you then," I said. I would never forgive myself if I let him go alone and something happened to him.

Beth didn't look too happy about that. "We'll be fine," I whispered to her. I picked up the spare lamp, turned on the gas and followed Derek into the hall.

He was already at the foot of the stairs, using his torch to illuminate as much of the upper floor as its beam would reveal. I stood back so as not to blind him with my lamp. After a moment he seemed satisfied that there was nothing up there and he started climbing. I followed him, keeping back a few steps. Our eyes never wavered from the landing. When Derek reached the base of the guard rail, his head at floor level, he shone the torch up and down the corridor and craned his neck to see. The camera was attached to one of the wooden beams about two feet above Derek's head. He reached up and switched off the automatic setting—the camera had likely already taken a few snaps of Derek's torchlight dancing over the walls. He placed the torch between his teeth, climbed another couple of steps and reached out to the camera again. This time he started taking off the drafting tape holding it in place. It was very loud, the noise echoing in the long corridor running the length of the whole house. I raised the lamp to help Derek see what he was doing. It seemed to take forever but eventually the camera came free.

Derek pulled it through the bars and then took the torch out of his mouth. "Should have brought a knife," Derek said drolly as we headed back down the stairs.

We made it to the drawing room without anything weird happening and closed the door behind us. Chloe and Beth looked relieved.

"Nothing happened," I told Beth. Derek ignored us and sat down with the camera. Quickly he began flicking through photographs.

"What time did you hear the footsteps?" he asked me.

"I don't know, maybe around quarter past twelve."

"Okay, well your camera is screwed up, because the photos have the wrong date on them. The timestamp says they were taken around three in the morning."

"That is weird. I double checked the date and time when I set it up."

"And something else that's weird. It took a picture of us going into the library, and coming back out again after we set up the video camera. But later on there are more pictures of just me."

Derek handed over the camera and I looked through some of the pictures. They were of Derek coming out of the library and going back in, but I wasn't in them.

"You didn't go in the library alone, so where am I?"

"Scroll back to just before those photos and you'll see both of us," Derek said. "I don't remember going back in after we were done in the library though."

"I think our friend is playing with the electronics," Beth said.

"And that's not the only thing," I said. Have you seen how much battery is left? With the extended battery this should have been good at least until dawn."

"How much is left?" Beth asked.

I shook the camera, like that would make the slightest difference, and checked it again. "A few minutes," I said. "I'll have to charge it again before we put it back upstairs."

"So lots of weirdness, but nothing concrete," said Derek.

"Is there anything else you've found?" I asked him, handing him back the camera.

Derek took it from me and said, "I'll let you know. I've not got to the photos taken when you heard the footsteps yet, and with the timestamps messed up it's really hard to tell where they are. I wish I could plug this into the laptop."

"No no no," Chloe said. "You're not going back upstairs!"

"I have to anyway. The video camera battery is likely nearly dead as well, so we need to recharge it.

"Uh oh," said Beth. She was holding out her smartphone. The battery level was critically low.

I checked mine too and saw the same. Yet we'd charged ours off the recharger station when we arrived.

While Chloe and Derek checked their own phones, I went over the recharger. Thankfully it was still showing a decent amount of battery left.

"Maybe power is only draining upstairs," I said as I plugged my phone and Beth's into two of the sockets. I had two bays left, and Derek reluctantly handed over his phone (nearly dead) and the camera and I plugged them both in.

"Now I really want that laptop," Derek said again. "Who's coming with me to get it?"

None of us moved.

"We need to conserve our light," I said.

"We need to leave," Chloe snapped. "Who's to say the car battery isn't dead too? Maybe we should get it running before it goes flat."

"That's a really good point, Jim," said Beth.

"The car hasn't been upstairs," Derek protested.

"The point is we don't know what's causing the drain or if it's limited to anywhere," I said.

Derek shrugged. "Okay, well why don't you go out and see if the car starts?"

"I'd rather be all ready to go in case it only has enough juice to start the once."

"Oh Jesus, fine. Let me get the laptop and then we can all go together. Deal?"

"Okay then," I agreed, picking up the spare lamp again. "Let's go."

"You don't need to come with me. Really, it's fine. Just start packing stuff we'll need. Bring food too, I'm getting hungry."

I thought Chloe would protest Derek going upstairs alone, but I think she was just relieved we were finally leaving. A weight seemed to have lifted from her. She gave Derek a kiss and a smile before he switched on his torch and left the room, the door staying open behind him. We listened as his footsteps ascended the stairs.

"Right," I said, making the others jump. "Chloe, pack as much food as you can. Beth, bring the charger with the phones still plugged in. I'll bring the two supply bags—they shouldn't be too heavy without the tripod and stuff."

The scream, when it came, made us all freeze in place. We stared at each other in shock.

"Derek," Chloe screeched.

The three of us barrelled out into the hallway. I barely remembered to grab the lamp as we went. Beth clicked on her torch but Chloe had nothing. She was already running for the stairs despite the darkness. Beth hurried after her, doing her best to keep the steps lit so that Chloe wouldn't trip.

The scream came again, but it wasn't from above. I paused with my foot on the first step.

"Guys," I called.

"Chloe wait up," I heard Beth call upstairs on the landing. "Jim's trying to tell us something. Chloe!"

Clearly she couldn't make Chloe stop. I tried calling up again.

"Hey Chloe," I yelled, loud as I could. "Derek's down here."

Another scream, definitely from the kitchen. It wasn't loud this time, but it was clearly in pain. It was also clearly coming from Derek.

I couldn't wait any longer.

"Beth, if you can hear me, I'm in the kitchen!"

But there was no response. I had to help Derek. I ran the length of the hall, my swinging lamp causing shadows to lurch at me as I passed by. I stepped down into the kitchen and looked about me. The room was empty but for the detritus we had left from our abandoned meal. There were no more screams, the room was utterly silent.

"Derek?" I called, not as loudly as I'd intended. "Derek, are you there?"

No response. Maybe he really was upstairs. Maybe there were pipes or ducts that relayed sound from other parts of the house. Perhaps all I'd heard was an echo of Derek calling from upstairs.

If I went upstairs now, I could be abandoning him. Maybe he was in the conservatory, or even in the ballroom. Perhaps he was in the upstairs apartment and the sound had carried into the kitchen via the narrow stairway. I shone the light in that direction. The door was closed but perhaps some sound filtered through. But how would Derek gain access to the apartment? There was no way in from upstairs.

I listened for another few seconds and then I couldn't stand it anymore. I had to check on Beth. I retreated from the kitchen, back into the hallway, and hurried to the foot of the stairs. As I came around the bottom bannister and started my ascent, I was aware of someone coming down from above.

I jumped, my heart in my mouth, and raised the lamp.

It was Derek, torch in hand.

"What the fuck, man?" he said, confused at the look on my face. "Something wrong?"

"Derek, where were you?"

"I was in the library. I've got the laptop, see?" He shined his torch at the computer tucked under his other arm.

My head was starting to spin. What the hell was going on?

"Where's Beth and Chloe?"

Derek just stared at me. "With you in the drawing room, no?"

"Oh God, oh God no."

I charged past Derek, taking the steps two at a time. When I reached the landing, the upstairs was quiet.

Derek came running up behind me. He was no longer carrying the laptop so he must have left it at the bottom of the stairs.

"Where are they, Jim? Where did Chloe go?"

"She came up here, looking for you. We heard you screaming, so she just ran up here. Beth followed her with a torch."

"I wasn't screaming. I was just disconnecting the laptop. I didn't see or hear anything. Wait a minute, if Beth followed Chloe with a torch, are you telling me that Chloe didn't have one?" Derek sounded mad as hell.

"Yeah she just ran out without thinking. We heard you scream and she was off. I tried to stop her…"

"I didn't hear a fucking thing!"

We'd reached the library now. It was so quiet up here, apart from us arguing.

"Beth?" I called. "Chloe? Where are you?"

Icy tendrils clutched at my chest. I couldn't have lost both of them, it just wasn't possible. It was a big house, but it wasn't *that* big.

"We need to check every room. Maybe they stumbled in the dark and hit their heads."

"Both of them?" Derek sounded incredulous. "Chloe!" he called. "Answer me, damn you."

Inside the library everything was as it had been. The camera still stood on the tripod in the corner, and opposite was the bookshelf that had moved earlier that evening. The dustcovers were still on the centre table and the chairs around it.

We left the library.

"Split up," Derek commanded. "I'll go search the bedrooms and the games room. You go back past the stairs and check those rooms.

"I don't want to lose you too."

"You won't, we'll keep calling out, okay?"

"Okay."

"One thing I want to know before we part, Jim."

"What?"

"Why did I meet you coming up the stairs? Why didn't you follow the girls immediately?"

"I heard you screaming too, but it was coming from the kitchen. I tried to call them back down but they couldn't hear me. I had to go see if you were all right."

"And was I in the kitchen, Jim?"

I hung my head, feeling like a chastised eight-year-old. "No."

"When we've found them, Jim, you and I are going to have words."

It was almost a relief when we parted ways.

I checked each room in turn in the section of the upstairs above the hall, the living room and the drawing room. I called the girls' names as I searched, and I could hear Derek doing the same thing. I was so mad at the fucker I could barely think straight. If he hadn't gone upstairs alone to get the laptop, we would all still be together. And if I hadn't wasted time trying to help him, I might have seen where they went. Now Beth was missing, presumably still somewhere in the house but unable to hear me. More to the point, it was likely that Derek was going to get lost too. And then what was I going to do? I couldn't just drive away and leave them here. I didn't think my nerves could take searching the house on my own, even though that's pretty much what I was doing.

"Derek?" I called out along the corridor.

"I'm here. Found anything?"

"No, nothing," I replied in the direction of his torchlight.

"Keep looking."

Well *obviously*.

By now I'd run out of rooms to check. The corridor this side of the stairs was much shorter than the other side. But if neither girl was answering then it was pretty clear to me then that we weren't about to find them.

And then Derek was calling me.

"Over here."

I had already returned to the corridor, intent on joining Derek in his search. Now I broke into a run, heading towards the dim glow from his torch, illuminating an open door frame in the distance.

"Did you find them?" I called as I ran, but Derek didn't reply.

I became paranoid, as I approached the lit doorway, that the light would go out or the door would slam as I reached it. Then Derek and whoever he'd found would be lost to me too. Instead I burst into the room to find Derek crouched over the prone-positioned body of Beth.

Relief and concern crashed over me. She was here but was she okay? I hurried over to Derek, my lamp sending shadows scurrying into the corners of the room. Beth was on the floor beside the bed. I knelt beside Derek and cradled her head in my lap.

"She's fine, I think," Derek said. "Just unconscious."

"We need to wake her."

"You can try, I didn't have any luck." Derek left me with her and moved to the doorway, shining his torch up and down the corridor. "I reckon she's in one of these rooms but in the same state as Beth. We need to search again, every room, and we need to check in cupboards and behind beds. She's probably knocked out too. She could be anywhere."

I nodded to him. "Get started. I have to stay with Beth, okay?"

"But what about Chloe?" he said urgently. He was obviously losing his mind with worry. I could hardly blame him.

"Let me try to wake her up. If I can't, I'll carry her from room to room looking for Chloe if I have to."

"Okay. I'll start in the games room."

"Yell if you find her."

And he was gone. I pulled the dust sheet from the bed and grabbed the blanket underneath. I wrapped it around Beth, concerned she might be cold. Then I lifted her onto the bed and held her close to me. I had no idea what had happened to her or why she wasn't stirring. Whatever it was I hoped it wasn't permanent.

"Come on, Beth, wake up. *Please.* Don't leave me here on my own."

The door slammed. I jumped up. The door to this small room was closed now. I'd not felt a draft.

"Derek," I called out. Had he locked me in here?

I went to the door and tried the handle. It opened with no resistance, which was almost more of a surprise than finding it locked.

I saw Derek's torch light coming from the doorway to the games room. Moments later, he emerged.

"What was that bang?"

"The door slammed. I didn't touch it."

"Are you okay?"

I was surprised to hear his concern given how he'd been treating me all this time. It stood to reason though. Without me he would be the only one looking for Chloe.

"Jim?"

Beth was awake. The door slamming must have woken her. I rushed over.

"Derek, she's awake," I called as loudly as I could.

"What's going on?" she asked, still groggy.

Derek appeared in the doorway.

"Beth?"

"Is that Derek?"

"Yeah, love. It's Derek and me. Take it easy for a moment, get your head together."

"Screw that," Derek snapped, coming over to the bed. "Beth, listen to me. Chloe is missing. Do you remember what happened?"

Beth scrunched up her face in concentration.

"I don't know," she said. "I think I was following her. Derek was calling out for help. She was running along the corridor with no flashlight. I was sure she would run into something or trip. I tried using my flashlight to light her way. Where *is* my flashlight?"

She tried to rise but I stopped her, easing her back down again.

"What happened after that?" Derek said. I wanted to thump him, but at the same time I understood his urgency.

"She ran in here, I think. I followed her and…"

She trailed off. Her eyes went wide and she started whimpering.

"What, Beth? What did you see?"

"Oh my God," she whispered. "Oh my God. Poor Chloe. Poor Chloe."

Derek was pacing up and down the small room now, going crazy with frustration.

"What the fuck did you see, Beth? Fucking hell, just tell me!"

I stood up and placed myself in between the two of us. "Calm down, Derek. If she could she'd be helping you."

"Fuck," Derek yelled. "Keep trying, okay? Keep asking her. Please, I'm begging you. How can I face the kids if she's not with me when I go home? What am I going to tell them?"

"We'll find her, I promise." I wished I felt so sure. If Beth followed Chloe into this room, then where was she now?

"Okay, okay, keep calm," Derek told himself, pacing again. "There's only one room left to check."

"Percy's room?"

"Right."

"Listen, Derek." He was already in the doorway, eager to be off and looking, but he paused and turned back to me. "If Chloe was in here and something happened, she might not be on this floor any more. Maybe this thing took her somewhere else. She might be downstairs."

Derek tugged at his hair in frustration. "All right, okay, why don't you two look downstairs then, and I'll go through the bedrooms again."

"We should stick together—"

"There isn't time! Please!"

"Okay, we'll go down."

And with that, Derek was gone. I turned back to Beth who was still clinging on to my shoulder.

"Honey, can you hear me?"

"Of course I can hear you."

"Good. Listen, do you have any idea what happened to Chloe? We're going to leave, all four of us, but if we can't find her then we can't leave, right?"

Beth nodded and detached herself from me. She swung her legs over the edge of the bed and put her head in her hands.

"I think I saw what you saw, on the ceiling."

"The black mass?"

"Yeah. And you're right, it does have a face but it *moves* and I can't tell who it is or really what they look like... It's like it's *trying* to have a face but it's not sure how. Oh God, it was horrible."

"What happened to Chloe?"

"It was all over her. I've never seen anything like it. I didn't know what to do or how to help. I think I must have fainted or something. I've never fainted before in my life! Really, I don't know what happened next."

I looked around the room uselessly. Aside from the bed and a small dresser, there was no space in here for anything else, and no wardrobes or cupboards. Even the bed was a single.

"Why was Derek screaming?" Beth asked suddenly.

"He wasn't. Or at least he says he wasn't. He says he was in the library when you came upstairs and he didn't hear you at all."

"And where were you? I thought you were right behind me!"

"I'm sorry, I heard Derek screaming from the kitchen. I called up to tell you but I got no response. Derek sounded in agony, I couldn't leave him."

"But he was in the library the whole time?"

"That's what he says. I know he's mad at me about something but I don't see a reason for him to lie, do you?"

"No. He wouldn't put Chloe through that deliberately."

"Maybe he had a plan and it went wrong."

Beth shook her head. She shuddered.

"Try not to think about it."

"I wish," she said, a tear appearing in the corner of one eye. "Oh God, Chloe! I should have helped her."

"Nobody blames you," I assured her.

"Derek does."

CHAPTER 6

We passed Derek on our way to the stairs, and I made sure he knew we were heading down.

"Beth didn't see what happened to Chloe," I assured him. It was a lie, but what good would the truth do him? He'd just get pissed at Beth and he'd be no closer to finding his wife.

He looked fraught, at his wits end. We left him throwing open cupboards in the biggest guest bedroom.

Beth and I descended the stairs, holding each other close. We had the one lamp between us.

"Before we start looking for Chloe, you need light in case we get separated."

"I'm not leaving your side," Beth said.

"Just in case. The thought of you waking up in that room with no light…"

Beth shuddered again. "Point taken."

So we entered the drawing room.

And we stood with our mouths open.

Everything was gone. I held the lamp high to be sure, casting light as far as we could see into every alcove and corner.

It was as if we had never been in the room. The dustcovers were back on the furniture, and all our stuff was missing. There were no sleeping bags, no charging stations, no phones, no spare torches and no spare lamps. Even the Monopoly had disappeared, presumably put back in its cupboard. We hurried over and opened the door. Sure enough, the game was back in its box with the other games as if we'd never unpacked it.

"What the fuck?" was all I could manage.

"Please tell me you still have the car keys."

I reached into my pocket and felt their reassuring weight.

"Yes, but without our phones… Shit. I should never have put them all in the charger together. We should have kept one."

"If you had then the battery would be dead by now," Beth said.

She was probably right. But I could have turned it off and conserved what little was left. Still, I'd never expected this. Our stuff wasn't just gone, it was like our presence in this room had been *erased*.

"We need to leave," I said.

"So let's find Chloe and go."

"Right."

We headed back out into the hall.

"I wish the phones were connected," I said. "Then I could call my cell and follow the ring."

"You're assuming it would get a signal."

"Didn't Derek leave the laptop at the bottom of the stairs?"

"I didn't see it on the way down."

We stepped back into the hallway. We could hear creaking floorboards from the upper floor, but most likely this was just Derek charging around up there, looking for his wife. The laptop was gone, assuming that was where Derek had left it. He wouldn't have had time to put it anywhere else.

Then we went to the kitchen. Someone had cleared away our abandoned meal too. No dirty plates, no bags or tubs of food, no half-finished drinks.

"This ghost is damn tidy," I said.

"I don't like this," Beth said.

"No argument there. So why are we stopping?"

I was on my way to the conservatory, but Beth was standing in the kitchen just in front of the door to the upstairs apartment. She was staring at the table with a quizzical look on her face. She clicked on her torch and lit up the tabletop.

"Come on," I urged her. "Let's find Chloe and leave."

"Hang on, Jim. This is just weird."

"Yeah, the ghost cleaned up. All of this is weird. Let's go."

Beth shook her head.

"This is not just cleaning up. Look."

She kept the angle of her torch low so as to illuminate anything sitting on the surface. There was nothing at all.

"What's your point?"

"Jim, the ghost has *cleaned the fucking table!*"

I laughed at that. The image in my head was almost worth the price of admission to this night from hell. And then I realized what she meant.

We had not been careful eaters. We'd spilled grains of rice, splashes of sauce, flakes of spring rolls, all over the kitchen table. Since we'd never finished our dinner it was certainly odd that the empty bags, the leftover containers and the dirty plates had all gone. But Beth was right, there was absolutely no trace of our meal. The table was completely clean. I took my lamp over and peered in close.

"Even if you accept that there's a ghost in the house that can move a bookcase, it doesn't explain this."

"You know what it's like?" Beth said.

"What?"

"It's like we were never here."

A chill gripped me when she said that. The gravity of her words settled on my shoulders and I realized she was completely right.

"Are we ghosts?" I asked. It seemed a logical conclusion.

"Well you don't look like Bruce Willis."

"And you don't look like Nicole Kidman."

Neither of us laughed.

"Maybe that's the answer," Beth said after a moment's pause.

"The answer to what?"

"The answer to what happened to Chloe."

I blinked. "I don't get you."

"Maybe she's gone, just like our stuff, and our food and the fricking crumbs on the table. Maybe she was never here."

"That's ridiculous."

"Then where the hell is she?"

"Well you mentioned the alternative back in the drawing room."

"Did I? Oh, the bottom of the lake?"

My grim expression told her she was now thinking what I was thinking. But we had to keep looking, and calling. We could hardly abandon her.

Footsteps came crashing down the stairs in a serious hurry. Beth and I flashed alarmed glances at each other and then we moved back to the hall door. Derek was running towards us, a determined expression on his face.

"She's in the apartment," he said as he pushed past us.

"Are you sure?" I asked.

"I heard her, through the wall." He didn't wait for us. He burst through the door to the upstairs apartment and bounded up the steps two at a time, torchlight swinging wildly in his wake.

"Chloe?" he called, even as he disappeared around the turn half way up the stairs. "Chloe, are you there?"

Beth and I hurried to follow. What a relief to know where she was. Maybe now the four of us could jump in the car and leave.

But it wasn't to be.

As Beth and I reached the top of the stairs, we saw Derek run back from the small living space to the bedroom.

"Chloe," he called. "Where are you?"

"Chloe?" I said. Beth and I joined the search.

We must have checked both rooms a dozen times. We threw open cupboards and closets, checked the tiny bathroom and even looked under the bed. Chloe wasn't here.

"Maybe you heard an echo of her voice coming through pipes or something," I said. "Like what happened earlier when I thought you were screaming in the kitchen but you were in the library upstairs."

Derek shook his head. His torch was still sweeping over every single item in the room.

"She told me, I heard her through the wall. She said she was trapped in the apartment."

"Shit," I said.

"So either she was lying," Derek said, smacking his hand against one solid wall in frustration, "or she was lost, or she was moved after I spoke to her."

"Well the only entrance is via the kitchen, and we were in there for a while. The apartment door never opened.

"Maybe there's another way in?" Beth said.

I shook my head. "What does it matter if there is? She's not here. We need to keep looking and we need to hurry."

Beth caught my expression. "You're worried about the light aren't you?"

"I'll search this place in pitch darkness if I have to," Derek spat, although he did click off his torch. Now the only light came from my lamp. It had been using the same canister since the sun went down. I had no idea how long one canister would last but I was guessing it was nearly exhausted. And when the lamp went out we would have to rely on our torches. We each had one, but given the drain on the other batteries earlier that evening, it was likely they wouldn't last too long either. I didn't want to be in this house when we ran out of light.

Beth was clearly of the same mind. Derek looked angry with us for even considering abandoning the search, but then his face turned grim and he moved away. I guessed he too had taken a moment to realize how fruitless—and terrifying—it would be to search for Chloe without light.

"We should search the kitchen cabinets for matches, torches, candles, anything we can use," Beth said.

I nodded. "I'll come with you. Are you staying here?"

Derek shook his head. "I heard her calling from somewhere. I have to keep looking."

"Voices carry in this house," I told him. "Keep looking and we'll join you when we've found more light."

Reluctantly, Derek followed us down the stairs and back to the kitchen.

"Did you clean up in here?" he asked when I set the lamp down on the centre counter.

"Wasn't us. Even the crumbs have been swept away."

Derek didn't respond to this. Clearly it was information he just didn't know what to do with right now. He clicked on his torch. "I'm going to the ballroom."

"We'll go via the living room and meet you there, okay?"

But Derek had already pushed through the door to the conservatory and didn't acknowledge me.

Beth and I turned our attention to the various draws and cupboards. We opened each in turn, searching for anything useful.

"Next time I invite an old friend on holiday with us, remind me not to, okay?"

"Our next vacation will be in Hawaii," Beth said.

We found some string and a half-used book of matches, but no candles or torches. I considered taking one of the large kitchen knives with us, but in the dark it was likely more of a hazard to us than to any entity we could or couldn't see.

Holding hands for moral support, Beth and I ventured back into the hall. We both gazed at the front door as we passed by, dully lit from a distance by the gas lamp. How much we wanted to just open the door, get in the car and drive away.

But then I thought of Chloe, all alone, in the dark, somewhere in this house. One glance at Beth told me she was thinking the same thing. We couldn't leave with Chloe still missing. Despite how he'd treated me, it wouldn't be fair to Derek to abandon him without the car also.

And so, wordlessly, we turned from the front door. I glanced into the drawing room in case our equipment had mysteriously returned. It hadn't. So we moved on to the front room. Upon entering, we stood still by the door. I lifted my lantern so that it cast an eerie glow into the room without dazzling our eyes.

It was no surprise to see the dust cover had returned to the piano. The stool Beth had sat on to play was back to its original position against the wall, and the shutters I had opened were now all closed.

At least this house was being consistently weird.

"I guess Percy's grandfather was a neat freak," I said.

"It's more than that though. It's like everything is back how it was before we arrived. Like we'd never even been here at all."

I shivered. Maybe that was our fate now, to wander the corridors of this house like ghosts ourselves, never able to leave. If we tried to change anything it would reset like a video game, back to the start of the level. I wondered if the grounds still lay out there beyond the black windows, or if instead there was now just infinite nothingness.

Beth moved over to the piano and uncovered it again. She lifted the lid and gently plink-plinked the highest key.

"Come on, we need to find Chloe," I urged her. Why was she wasting time?

"I'm just seeing if the room resets again. Okay, let's go."

We pushed through the door into the dining room. We had barely spent any time in this room so it was hard to tell if it had also changed. We were looking around for any possible hidden doors when a distant banging stopped us dead. It was coming from beyond the conservatory, probably in the ballroom. Beth and I stared at each other for a good twenty seconds, listening. Whatever was causing it, Derek was likely involved.

We rushed from the dining room, past the back door corridor and on through the conservatory. We didn't stop, hurrying onwards to the ballroom at the end of the house.

"Where have you two been?" Derek asked. I could see his torch was perched on a table, its beam aimed at one of the two locked doors on either side of the stage. In his hands was a fire extinguisher.

"We've been looking for Chloe," I said, making my way over to him. "What are you doing with that?"

"Trying to break the door down."

"That's a really bad idea. That thing could explode."

"I couldn't find anything heavier."

"Did you hear her behind the door?" Beth asked.

"No, but it's the only place we haven't looked. You checked the living and dining rooms, right?"

I nodded.

"And I checked every inch upstairs. So this is the last place she could be." He raised the extinguisher over his head.

"Wait," I called. Derek paused. "Let me try."

Derek backed away and I took his place. Holding up the lamp I could see the lock was dented but not wrecked. I paused, pretending to be thinking. In my mind I could hear the ticking again. I glanced at Beth and she was recalling it too. I didn't want to open the door but if Chloe was behind it, I didn't have a choice.

I made a show of pulling out the ring of keys Arthur had handed to me earlier that day.

Derek let out an anguished sound. "Fuck me! You had them all this time?"

"Just remembered," I said weakly. I put the lamp down next to the torch and tried to remember which key opened this door. On my fourth attempt the lock sprung and I opened it.

Beyond was total darkness. I grabbed the lamp and Beth and Derek shone their torches into the short corridor. The door to the right was still open and already we could hear the ticking. Drawing near, we paused at the top of the stairs that led down towards the noise that made my brain itch.

"I didn't know this house had a basement," Derek said.

"Dad didn't mention it. I suppose this must be fairly new too."

"I don't want to go down there," Beth said, clutching my arm nervously. I agreed with her. But I knew we were out of options. There was nowhere else to search.

Derek pushed past us but he too paused before descending. "What is that ticking? It's doing my head in."

"A clock, I guess…"

But he was already descending, crouching low and shining his torch underneath the floorboards of the ballroom.

"We should go with him," I said. I grasped Beth's hand and down we went.

What we found was something of a disappointment. It was obviously a wine cellar. One entire wall of the space covered by a built-in wine rack. Clearly Percy hadn't got very far with his hobby because there were only around twenty bottles in one bunch in the middle of the racks. If we survived until dawn I might just grab a bottle or three and get completely hammered by lunchtime.

There were a few other items in the room: a chair on the far side, a pile of dust sheets in either corner opposite the rack-wall, and a small pile of bricks behind the stairs. But our eyes were drawn to one object in the middle of the room, covered in a dust sheet. For a moment I thought there might be someone underneath the cover, standing motionless, waiting for our arrival. I was startled for a moment by its incongruity. What was it doing here? What was under the cover? It was the right height and the right width to be a person. But whatever was under the sheet was far too broad and round to be human.

Unmistakably, it was the source of the ticking.

Derek was ready to leave. "She's not here," he said. "Let's go."

"Wait," I told him. "Don't you want to see what's under there?"

"I'm guessing it's not my fucking wife, Jim."

Yet he stayed, hovering at the bottom of the stairs. Beth wanted to know what was making that incessant noise too. I held up the lamp as she approached, obviously fascinated by the strange item in the middle of the cellar.

Gingerly she took hold of the sheet and pulled it off. It fell to the floor like a lover's discarded robe, ignored and forgotten. All eyes were on the naked object underneath.

It was indeed a clock, but unlike any I had ever seen. It stood on a narrow column and had a bulbous globe on top with a flat face. At its base the column split into five protruding feet that sank beneath the poured concrete floor. It was beautiful, like something you might see in a palace or a museum. It must have been well over a hundred years old but the wood had been cared for meticulously, as had the brass plating and the iron hands. What was truly unusual about it, aside from its shape, was that it had five faces. They were arranged in a line of four, with the fifth clock face positioned above the others. From the looks of it, the timepiece was capable of keeping track of five international time zones at once. It reminded me of the kind of clock you'd see at airport terminals, where multiple faces would tell you the time in major cities around the world. Except this one pre-dated commercial air travel and possibly pre-dated international time zones too.

Beth and I gazed at it. Even Derek moved closer to get a better look.

In my years of assessing houses for my dad I had come across some unusual antiques—and I'd sold many of them on eBay and at auctions. This clock was unique.

"I've never seen anything like it," Beth said at last. I let my silence convey my agreement.

"Is it for showing the time around the world?" Derek asked.

I managed to refrain from telling him that this was obviously the case. On the one hand, it would have needlessly antagonized a man who was at least still speaking to me. On the other, I didn't want to end up proven wrong.

Three of the faces were working. They were keeping time and they were all in synch, almost impossibly so. The second hands click-click-clicked in unison. It was almost eerie to watch. The time they were showing was not the right time though.

The other two clocks were stopped, the one on the far right and the one on top.

"It's not ten-thirty, so why do three of the clocks say it is?" Beth asked. Nobody had an answer to that. The answer didn't seem to be that they were running fast or slow, because the three working faces were all equally wrong. The two stopped clocks had frozen at different times, one 10:40 and the other at 12:30. It was impossible to tell whether the time shown was morning or afternoon.

"Why is it here, in the cellar?" I asked. I didn't expect anyone to have the answer, I just felt it needed to be said.

"And why is its ticking so damn annoying?" said Derek.

We stared at it for some time. Two and a half minutes to be exact. And still none of us could answer the question why three running clocks all showed exactly the same wrong time, or what the clock was doing down here, or why its ticking was so jarring.

When the clock above the others started moving, we all jumped. Then we stared in fascination and mounting horror. Now the top face was ticking away the seconds at the same rate as the other three. We had no idea what it meant and we didn't know why it was doing it. But there was one fundamental difference between this clock face and the others below it, one thing that made my heart stop and my mouth go dry and every cell in my body resonate with primal, crawling, fear.

The clock was running backwards.

It didn't make any sense, and as we stood there watching it I had no idea why it stirred such dread within me. I couldn't take my eyes off it, and I was sure that Derek and Beth were as transfixed as I was.

What did it mean?

There was just something about it, the randomness of it starting up while we were watching, the impossibility of clockwork running in reverse without some reason behind it. Clocks didn't just run backwards on their own, did they?

A whole two minutes went by, and for a while it felt like we would never be able to tear our eyes away. It was moving faster now, the backwards clock. The seconds were turning back faster than the other three clocks could gain on them. The sound from the clock was almost random now, the rhythm lost in a storm of tick-tocks.

The trio of in-synch clocks now read 10:35. The backwards clock read 10:37 and it was counting down at a rapid rate. Very soon, all four clocks would say the same time.

And then they did. At 10:36, the fourth clock stopped for just a moment, and then started moving forward, in perfect synch with the other three.

"I don't get it," said Derek. Nothing had happened. The world hadn't ended. We were still standing here in a wine cellar in a haunted house, lit by a gas lamp that might die any second, staring at the most bizarre antique clock we'd ever seen.

"It's just broken, I guess," said Beth. I could tell she didn't believe her own words. "Or maybe it's measuring something other than time."

"We need to leave," I suggested. It was a little voice at the back of my mind, tiny but very insistent.

Get out now.

"I agree," Derek said. "Something's not right."

We all saw movement in the corner of the room.

"What was that?" Beth asked. She clicked on her torch. I moved the lamp aside so it wouldn't obscure our vision of what the torch was revealing. It was pointing at one of the piles of dust covers. It wasn't moving now.

"Are you going to take a look?" I asked. I didn't direct the question at anyone specifically. I was hoping either of my companions would volunteer.

"I'll look," said Derek. He walked between me and Beth and around the clock, keeping his distance from the creepy antique. He clicked on his own torch as he approached the pile. "It's probably just an animal," he said. "It'll leap out at me when I take away the cover." He'd reached the pile now. He put a hand out to grab the sheet when I realized something that sped me to the edge of insanity.

"Wait," I said.

Derek hesitated and looked back. "What is it?"

I was staring at the other corner, opposite to Derek's position. I pointed. I couldn't formulate words. Beth swung her torch into the far corner to illuminate what had me spooked.

The pile of dust covers in the other corner wasn't there anymore.

"Shit," said Derek.

Then the gas lamp sputtered and died.

I don't recall exactly what happened next. I remember the flicker of torchlight as Derek and Beth tried to locate the exit.

Derek yelled, "Get out!"

I don't remember making it to the stairs but I must have done because I don't think I've ever ascended a staircase as fast as I did right then.

It was the black shape. As I ran, not even caring if the others were following but dimly aware of torch beams moving around me, all I could see was that shape. It had been in the cellar with us, standing right next to Beth for who knew how long? Since we stopped looking at the pile of sheets in the corner perhaps?

The next thing I knew I was at the top of the stairs, fumbling in the pitch darkness. I wanted to get out, I *had* to get out of this house, but I was still aware enough to realize that if I turned back towards the ballroom I would have to go through that room, the conservatory, the kitchen and the hall to get to the front door. And that was too much. So I turned right. I went to the door at the end of the short corridor.

Beth was behind me. Derek too. I fumbled with my keys, relief flooding over me that I wasn't alone and that I wasn't the only one desperate to get out of that house.

"Find the fucking key," Derek said, his torchlight illuminating the entrance to the cellar. I glanced backwards too but it was impossible to tell if anything was coming after us.

Beth was whimpering, Derek was cursing. I was fumbling with the ring of keys.

"I need light!" I yelled, and this snapped Beth back to reality. She shone her torch at the lock and I selected one I'd not used yet. It didn't fit.

"Come on!"

I tried to calm myself, think carefully and choose wisely. If I did this out of panic, I'd never get the right key.

"Oh please, Jim, let us out!" That was Beth. The light was shaking.

"It's coming up the stairs, oh Jesus." Derek was losing it too.

And we could hear it now. Slow, steady footsteps ascending the stairs from the basement. It was in no hurry.

I forced my breathing to calm. I grabbed the torch from Beth who now couldn't hold the light steady. I chose the final unused key and thrust it into the lock. It fit.

I turned it, opened the door and the three of us spilled outside into the chilly night air.

I slammed the door behind us and re-locked it.

We stood there for a moment, wondering what to do. I directed the light around to see where we were. Definitely outside, but without the torches it would be so dark we might as well have stayed in the cellar. I lit up a door opposite us that allowed access to the garage. But there was no need to look in there. We had an escape vehicle already.

"We need to keep moving," Derek said.

The bang against the door made us jump.

"Oh God," Beth said.

I nearly lost it at that moment. Escape into the open air had seemed the logical way to evade what was after us. But I realized if we were safe, it was only temporary. I doubted a wooden door could stop this thing.

"This way," said Derek. He aimed his torch at the path leading to the front of the house and hurried off. I grabbed Beth's hand and followed him without looking back.

Our shoes crunched on the gravel driveway as we ran past the ballroom windows. Derek's light was pointed resolutely at the car, waiting beside the front door. My light was all over the place, fading into nothing as it got lost in the deep, crushing darkness.

I was convinced we wouldn't reach the car. I was certain that it was a mirage, or that something would step out of the shadows to intercept us. But it didn't.

As we approached, I took out the key and pressed the unlock button. The lights flashed and the car blipped. The internal light came on, a guiding beacon of safety.

We reached it and threw open the doors. Derek climbed in the back, Beth in the passenger seat and me behind the wheel. We slammed our doors and I shoved the key in the ignition. Now I was paranoid that the lights had sapped the last of the battery and it wouldn't start.

To my relief, the four-by-four roared into life, automatic headlights piercing the darkness ahead and illuminating the path to freedom. I put my foot on the clutch, shifted into first gear and reached for the handbrake.

"Wait!" Derek said.

"What? Fucking what?"

"We can't leave!"

"Chloe," said Beth. "We can't leave her."

I glanced nervously in the rearview mirror. I could see Derek's concerned face staring at the house. I couldn't see anything that might be approaching from behind the car. I was itching to be off. I turned on the high beams and instead of two laser-like columns slicing through the dark, the road ahead was now flooded with light. I still couldn't see anything behind us.

"I can't leave her in there," Derek said.

"We'll come back," I promised him. "We'll go get help and come back. We'll get a search party."

"They'll never believe us."

"We'll tell them she sleepwalked into the grounds and we've lost her, and we're terrified she might wander into the lake."

"Then why are all of us leaving?"

He had a good point. If we wanted to convince anyone to come help us find Chloe in the middle of the night, we would need to explain why at least one of us had not stayed behind to keep looking for her.

"Derek, we'll think of something. Let's go!"

"You go get help. I have to stay."

And with that, Derek got out of the car.

"No Derek!" Beth pleaded. "Please come back!"

And she got out of the car too.

What the hell? Was I the only one left with a shred of sanity?

I slammed my hands against the wheel in frustration. So close to escape. So close to driving away from this place and not having to spend another second in the dark. So close.

For a brief moment, I admit I considered leaving them there. If Beth had stayed in the car after Derek got out, I might well have done it. But I couldn't do that to Beth. I just couldn't, no matter how much my stomach churned, I couldn't leave her.

She would never, ever forgive me.

So I got out too.

From outside the car, the area was now well lit. The driveway was illuminated with enough distance between us and the shadows that if anything emerged, we'd have time to get back in. Behind the vehicle, the rear lights cast everything in a red glow. It wasn't as bright as at the front, but at least we could see some of the house and it didn't feel like something was about to leap out at us. The engine ticked over smoothly, a constant reminder that we had an exit and we should take it right now.

"Beth," I implored her. "Get in the car. We can go get help. If Derek wants to stay and keep looking, that's his decision." Derek didn't answer that. He stood by the front door, waiting for Beth.

She turned to me, her expression revealing how torn she was, how tempted she was to run.

"But he's right, Jim, we can't leave Chloe. Oh God, if that was me trapped somewhere in there, I don't know what I'd do except pray you'd all keep looking for me."

"We need more people. We need supplies. More batteries, torches and lamps. We searched the whole damn place and we didn't find her. We need help!"

Derek said, "I can't leave until I know for sure she's not still in the house."

"Fuck!" I said, hopelessly frustrated. I took a step away from the car.

That step probably saved my life.

There was a crash above our heads. We all looked up, but the car lights didn't extend upwards to the second floor so it was shrouded in darkness. Time seemed to slow down. I was aware of glass raining down around us—I could see it sparkling as it fell through the beams of light, like deadly snowflakes. I turned towards Beth, curiously calm, watching everything in slow motion.

And then the car exploded.

Not in a ball of flame, but still an explosion is the only way to describe it.

One moment the car was there, its reassuring headlights giving us much needed respite from the suffocating darkness, and the next there was a huge bang and the lights went out. The impact knocked us from our feet.

I had no idea what had happened. We were plunged into darkness again. I fumbled in my pocket for my torch and flicked it on, struggling to my feet. I searched for Beth until my torch beam settled on her.

"Beth, are you okay?"

"Yes, yes I'm all right."

Derek shone his own torch at the car. After I reassured myself that Beth was still in one piece, I directed mine the same way.

The back of the vehicle was unscathed. The front half was flattened. The front wheels splayed in unnatural directions. Steam poured from the crushed radiator. The windscreen was buckled and cracked. The remains of the engine hung out from the car's twisted metal shell. It was mangled beyond repair.

Sat atop the ruined vehicle was the bookcase from the library.

CHAPTER 7

We stood and stared, dumbfounded. The bookcase from the library, the one that had inexplicably moved across the room, had just crushed our car. It had *fallen* on our car.

Something had picked it up and thrown it out the window.

We all looked up. My torch beam met with Derek's to light up the shattered window of the library above our heads.

If we'd been any closer to the car... If we'd been *in* the car...

"Shit," whispered Derek.

I couldn't say anything. The despair of losing our escape and the realization that we were dealing with something with immeasurable power—it was more than I could bear.

"It's trying to kill us!" Beth said, barely audible.

I moved closer to the car. I don't know why. Maybe there was something salvageable. The bookcase had so utterly destroyed the engine and the battery that not even the car alarm could function. It was dead, its chassis broken and its wheels bent. It was a useless hunk of twisted metal.

I was out of ideas. Soon our last two torches would lose power and fade away. It was still hours till dawn and there was no other source of light available to us, save the book of matches in my pocket. They would most likely burn, one after the other, for about ten minutes tops. By my reckoning, we'd be without any light in under an hour. And even if we did find Chloe, what then? Where would we go? It was too cold out here to just go sit in the garden until morning. We probably wouldn't die from exposure but we might get hypothermia. Who knew what state Chloe was in? She might be injured or bleeding. If we went back in the house to find her, what if the *thing* in there decided to throw another bookcase at us?

"We still have to find Chloe," Derek said. "I'm going back inside."

"No," I said. "No, Derek. We're not going back in that house. Your torch is fading already and mine can't be far behind. We need more light and something to protect ourselves with."

"Where are we going to find that?"

Beth spoke up. "How about the lodge?"

I nodded. "Right, that's what I was thinking. Maybe there are candles in there. Maybe even torches with fresh batteries. Maybe there's some warmer clothing. Perhaps the phone works or we could get a signal on our mobiles.

"That's a lot of maybes," Derek said, unconvinced.

"We can't find Chloe in the dark."

"He's right, Derek. I'm sorry." Beth hung her head.

Derek paused for a moment longer and then nodded.

As we set off down the driveway, he kept looking back towards the house and shining his torch in that direction. It didn't reveal very much, in fact the light was looking so yellow and dim that Derek finally decided to turn it off and conserve what little battery he had left.

My torch was now the only light source. I swung it back and forth to show the edges of the path, and then aimed it forward into the darkness. Now even this was growing dimmer. The light was so weak, it showed us nothing but our immediate vicinity. It was starting to look very yellow.

"Oh shit," I said. "We need to hurry."

We started running, the light bouncing over the path and our feet crunching on the gravel.

Then the torch went out.

We all stopped. Without the sound of our footsteps, it was eerily quiet.

And of course, completely dark.

I held a hand in front of my face and couldn't see it. I looked up to the sky, but the moon and the stars were nowhere to be seen. Too much cloud cover. I couldn't even see the tops of the tall conifers where they should have contrasted with the sky. There was a flurry of squeaking and fluttering from above our heads but of course we couldn't see what was causing it. Bats, most likely.

I suddenly had no idea which way I was facing. Surely it was still towards the lodge and the gate. I hadn't turned around at any point, had I?

"You two still there?" I asked tentatively. I half expected to be completely alone.

"Yeah," Beth said.

"Me too," said Derek.

"Okay hold out your hands."

The first hand I connected with was soft and had a couple of rings on it. I hugged Beth tight, really hoping this was her and Derek didn't just have unusually feminine hands. Someone else placed his hands on our arms.

"There you are," Derek said. "Thought you might have left me."

All his bravado in the house, his go-off-on-his-own-and-find-Chloe spirit, had dissipated. He seemed deeply disturbed, at least from what I could tell from his voice and the way he clutched hold of my sleeve.

"Which way is the lodge?" he asked shakily.

It was amazing how fast we had completely lost our sense of direction without the light.

"Oh, my cell!" Beth cried, surprising us.

Seconds later, a glow appeared in front of my face. Her smart phone was on.

"I turned it off earlier to save battery. Hmm, there's not much left. Still, better than nothing."

The glow was barely perceptible when she shined the light on the path, but it gave our eyes something to get used to and we could just about see each other.

"I have a flashlight app," Beth said.

"Leave it off for now. That thing drains the battery too fast."

"Okay."

We stumbled on, holding onto each other, using the dim glow of Beth's phone to guide us. The crunch of gravel beneath our feet reassured us that we were still on the path. We kept on going, desperately hoping there was nothing following us that we couldn't see. It was a long driveway but I was sure it was taking too much time to reach the end. Then, finally, the dim light revealed the gate.

"Okay the lodge is over here," I said. I led the others towards the wooden front door of the little cottage. We stumbled down a couple of steps and felt our way along the deep porch before congregating at the door.

I pulled the ring of keys from my pocket while Beth found her flashlight app and turned it on.

The light was so bright I couldn't see anything for a moment. But after blinking a few times I was able to choose a suitable key and find the lock.

Moments later, we were inside and with the door closed. Beth had switched off the flashlight on her phone, so we were back to the dull glow again.

I noticed an aroma that pervaded the lodge.

Lavender.

"I'm not the only one smelling that, right?" Derek asked.

"What the hell?" Beth said. "Are the ghosts camping out down here instead of the house?"

"Maybe they're scared," I ventured. It seemed ridiculous.

"We need to find lights," Derek said.

"Okay, let's start in here." From the soft glow of Beth's phone, we could make out a cozy living room with a fireplace and well used seats gathered around it. There was a dining table and chairs by the windows and a desk on the far wall. We moved over to that. I opened the desk and rifled through the contents. There was nothing in the top part, but in one of the drawers was a torch.

I clicked it on. It worked! We could see much better by the torchlight, and we soon located the door that led to the rest of the lodge. I lifted the latch and swung the door open. The torch revealed a narrow corridor with a red-tiled floor. There were two doors on either side with another one at the end, opening into a bathroom. The first two on either side were bedrooms, as was the furthest on the left. The second door on the right had a step up into the kitchen.

We filed in, the torch revealing worn counters and ancient looking appliances. A kettle sat on the stove and cabinets lined the walls. There wasn't much the others could do without the torch, so they left it to me to go through the draws and cupboards. I found a packet of biscuits that were unopened and hadn't passed their sell-by date.

"Anyone hungry?" I asked.

We tore into the packet. It had been hours since we had eaten our takeaway and now we were ravenous. I found glasses and poured us all some water. With the terror and adrenaline now fading from my system, I felt like I could just stumble into one of the bedrooms and fall asleep in seconds. Instead I kept looking and found a candle with a holder. I took the matches from my pocket and lit the candle. Now the kitchen was bright enough for the others to join in the search. We found a packet of cream crackers, again within its sell-by date, not that soft crackers would have put us off. Derek found another candle and also a bunch of batteries. Beth sat at the little kitchen table and took apart her torch, replaced the batteries and screwed it back together again. To our relief, the torch was working fine. Derek did the same with his torch and we were back in action again.

"I'm going to check the bedrooms and the living room again. See if we missed anything," said Derek. He stepped down into the corridor and walked away.

"Christ I need to pee," Beth said. I went with her. Not that we were scared of anything, the atmosphere in the lodge was so much lighter than that of the house, it was much easier to breathe and we could almost relax. The smell of lavender was actually quite pleasant, if a little musty. But I still wasn't willing to let her go anywhere without me. If I lost her, I'd never forgive myself.

We reconvened in the living room and checked our haul. Some more matches, two candles and a holder, three working torches, some extra batteries and a very small toolkit.

I didn't want to leave. I knew we had to, but for the first time in hours I felt safe.

"Guys, I've got a signal!"

We hurried to Beth's side. She was holding her phone in the air. The time read two-thirty in the morning, which wasn't as late as I was hoping. Dawn was still a good four hours away and it would remain pitch black outside until then.

I pulled out Arthur's card, handed it to her and she dialed the number. She tried it again but it wouldn't connect. "I guess the signal's not strong enough."

"Try texting him."

Beth typed a message and pressed send. We watched the little progress bar as the phone tried to send the message. It stalled and didn't resume. Then the signal disappeared completely and the message popped up, asking if she wanted to try again.

"Any other suggestions?" Beth asked. "Hey wait a minute, that's not right."

"What?" I asked.

"Well, the phone was connected long enough to update the time."

"Update the time?" Derek said. "What do you mean?"

"I mean, the phone synched with local time."

I laughed without any trace of humour. "But we didn't cross a date line. Why would it…?"

Beth sounded distraught now. "No, that can't be right."

I leaned over her shoulder and checked the display. The date showing was yesterday's date, the day we arrived here. The time was ten-thirty-two pm.

"It must be a glitch. How can it only be ten-thirty?" I asked.

"It's not a glitch," Derek said. "The phone got a signal long enough to resynch the time and updated itself. It would be tough to get that wrong."

I shook my head. "The last time I checked my phone it was past midnight!"

Beth sat down on one of the comfy old chairs around the fireplace. "Oh God, Jim, the kitchen counter, the drawing room, remember?"

"What was it you said? Like we'd never been there."

"Or like we'd not been there *yet.*"

"What are you talking about?" Derek asked.

I explained, "Remember when you came down from the apartment and you thought we'd cleaned up the kitchen?"

"Yeah, I remember. So?"

"While we were upstairs it's like time must have moved backwards," Beth said. "The time moved to earlier in the night, maybe to a time before we set up all our stuff in the drawing room or ate anything in the kitchen."

"Then why wasn't our stuff still in the car?" Derek asked.

"Whoah!" I held up my hands. "How is this even possible? Nobody can just wind back time."

"Maybe the ghost can."

"Do we have to call it a ghost?"

Derek scoffed. "What would you like to call it? We've all seen it now. I think we can say that this is a fucking ghost we're dealing with. No parlour trick could explain what we saw in the cellar."

I circled the room, trying to wrap my head around what Beth and Derek were telling me.

"Why is this so hard for you to accept?" Beth asked.

"Oh so now you're ganging up on me?"

"No, Jim, I just think it's time to abandon any preconceived notions of what's possible and just deal with the fact that there's something in that house that wants to hurt us."

"It's a fucking ghost," Derek insisted.

"What I want to know is," Beth said, "why is the lavender lady haunting the lodge? Why didn't we smell any hint of lavender in the house?"

"Maybe this is her holiday home," I suggested weakly.

Derek let out a string of expletives. "This is a waste of time. My wife is still in there, all alone and probably scared out of her mind. And I abandoned her. We've got what we came for. It's time to go back." Derek switched on his torch and aimed it at the fireplace. "Ah ha," he said. He walked over and picked up an iron poker.

"What good is that going to do?" I asked.

"It makes me feel better." He headed for the door.

"We can't go back yet," I said.

"I'm not going to sit around chatting with you. I've wasted enough time as it is."

"We searched the whole house, Derek," Beth said. It was a relief that she seemed to be taking my side on this one.

"There's that other locked door in the ballroom. There might be another basement under the hall that isn't connected to the wine cellar. We didn't try to get into the attic…"

I shuddered at that thought. The wine cellar had been creepy enough. For some reason, attics terrified me even more.

"Beth's right," I said. "You might find her but chances are she's somewhere we can't get to."

"What? Like a secret room or something?"

"Maybe," Beth said. "Or, I was thinking something else."

She had Derek's attention, and mine.

"Go on," he prompted.

"I'm thinking it's connected to that clock," she said. "There were five faces, right? Maybe each clock represents one of us. Maybe there's one for each of us and one for the ghost."

I frowned. "That clock is probably two hundred years old. How could it be connected to us?"

"I've no idea, but it's weird how three of the clocks were moving forward and the other two were stopped. The top one started moving backwards and moments later we saw the... thing." She shivered. I did too. "Maybe the fourth clock relates somehow to Chloe."

"So what does it mean that it was stopped?" I asked.

"I don't know, but if we could get Chloe's clock to move, maybe she'd come back into synch with us and we'd be able to see her."

"You want to go back into that basement?" I felt slightly panicked at that prospect.

"I think we may have to."

"So we start her clock, and then what? She slips back into our time zone?"

"This is ridiculous," Derek spluttered. "This isn't Doctor-fucking-Who! This is my wife and I have to find her."

"We're trying to help," Beth insisted.

"No, you're wasting time while she's stuck in there. I thought you might be on to something important but talking about mystery clocks and time travel isn't going to bring Chloe back."

I reached out to put a hand on his shoulder. "It's okay, we know you're worried."

"Don't you fucking touch me," Derek spat, raising the poker. I took a step back and raised my hands.

"Okay, sorry."

"I'm not listening to any more of this. I'm going back now."

"Without a game plan we're just going to be wasting time once we get there," Beth said, throwing up her arms in frustration. "Think about what you've seen tonight, Derek. You saw the thing in the cellar. You can see what time my cell phone shows after resynching with the network. You saw the clock in the cellar move backwards until it matched the three going forwards, and then all hell broke loose. I don't have all the answers, I'm just guessing, but it strikes me we have a much better chance of beating this thing and getting Chloe back if we have a single clue about what it wants and what it's capable of."

I wanted to applaud her speech. Instead I kept my mouth shut and watched Derek's face for any indication that he was about to murder the two of us with the iron poker.

Instead his features softened and he slumped down into one of the wooden chairs at the dining table.

"I just can't do it alone, you know? I can't lose her. If I lose her I have to raise them on my own and I just don't have a fucking clue. It's so easy for her, she always knows what to say and what to dress them in and when to be strict and I love my kids but sometimes I get so... frustrated and I just want to scream."

Beth and I watched him silently, unsure of how to respond to the sudden admission. What was telling, at least to me, was that he didn't seem to be worried about losing Chloe because he loved her, but instead was worried about how he would cope in her absence. It confirmed what I had suspected since I first heard they were getting married.

"Sorry," he said after a moment. "I don't know why I'm telling you all this."

"We're the only ones here," I said.

There was a loud crash from somewhere behind the interior door. We all turned. Derek stood up, clicked on his torch and came with us to the far side of the room. Derek hefted the poker and I lifted the latch.

"Do you think it's followed us?" Beth hissed.

I raised a finger to my lips and swung open the door. The corridor beyond was empty, but another crash came from the far end.

The three of us rushed to the kitchen to find the kettle on the floor, several cupboard doors open and the tap running.

I immediately assumed the ghost had followed us down here. Fear gnawed at my nerve-endings and I envied Derek for having a solid, iron poker to wave around. Any kind of weapon would have made me feel an awful lot braver right now.

Derek used the poker to close the cupboards while Beth picked up the kettle.

"Is that the best you've got?" Derek yelled, much to my surprise.

Silence.

"I want my wife back. Give her back, you fucker!"

The entity, whatever it was, clearly didn't like being called names. A drawer to Derek's right flew open with such force that its contents jumped in the air, a few odds and ends spilling out onto the floor. The drawer stopped about five inches from Derek's right hip. If he'd been standing any closer it might have crippled him.

Derek slammed the drawer closed with the poker.

"Come on, you bastard."

"Derek, calm down, I don't think this is helping," Beth said.

I disagreed. "You tell him, Derek!"

Beth was staring daggers at me but I pretended I couldn't see her in the gloom.

Derek didn't seem to care what either of us thought. He slammed the poker down on the counter, putting a sizeable dent in it.

"You can't hurt me, you've got nothing that can hurt me!" he screamed. I thought he was acting mad to get a rise out of the entity, but maybe I was wrong. I saw the look on his face, his fury accentuated by the torchlight. It looked real to me. Derek was never much of an actor, it had to be said. I could hardly blame him. If someone laid a finger on Beth I'd be ready to drive a poker through a few skulls to vent my anger too.

There was a loud, distinct cough from the corner of the room behind the door. Immediately all three of us snapped our torches round to cover the area. There was nothing there, but obviously we'd all heard it and it wasn't one of us.

We stood stock still, listening. Waiting for the next occurrence.

"Ask it something!" I urged Derek.

"How is it going to answer?"

"One cough for yes, two coughs for no!"

"That's crazy," Beth said. "This isn't that damn ghost hunting show."

"Any other suggestions?"

"Shut up both of you," Derek snapped. Beth and I dutifully fell silent.

"All right, you cock-sucking wanker, let's talk. One knock or cough or whatever for yes and two for no, okay?"

No.

We all heard it. It came from the same corner of the room as the cough. Everyone took a step backwards.

"Fucking hell!" I said. "It talks."

Even Derek seemed cowed by this revelation. It was the weirdest thing I'd ever heard. It wasn't spoken aloud; we didn't hear it with our ears. Instead we were aware of the word, like having a memory of a recent event without actually experiencing it. If the others hadn't reacted I would swear it was simply my imagination.

"Do you have my wife? Do you have Chloe?" Derek asked, regaining some of his lost courage.

No.

"Where is she?"

In the. House.

Something about that voice, even though I wasn't hearing it directly, made my teeth vibrate unbearably and caused beads of cold sweat to form on my brow.

"Did you follow us from the house?" I asked.

No.

Now Beth spoke up. "Do you... live in the house?"

Yeees.

"Why are you here in the lodge?" she asked.

Pushed. Out.

The sound, if you could call it that, was like skinning my eyes with a vegetable peeler. It was profoundly uncomfortable. It seemed to resonate on the same frequency as unease, setting every nerve in my body on edge. I had to fight the urge to break down the back door and run screaming into the night.

Whatever it was we were talking to, it wasn't the black mass from the house. I was certain of that. As certain as I could be. Unless it was just playing games with us.

"Did you destroy the car?" I asked.

No.

"Do you want your house back?"

The entity didn't answer directly. Instead, the room began to shake, almost imperceptibly at first. Then a pencil in a glass jar up on a shelf began to clink. The drawers and cupboard doors bumped gently against the woodwork. The water pipes groaned ever so slightly. The metal latch on the back door rattled. It wasn't violent but it was everywhere, like a mini-earthquake.

"I'll take that as a yes."

Beth asked, "Are you Percy's grandfather?"

The room shook again.

Disappointing... Boneidle... Littleshit...

I shivered. I didn't think I could take much more of this. Beth moved to my side and slipped her hand into mine. I guessed she felt much the same way.

Derek looked shaken too, but he did what Beth and I couldn't do and pressed on with the questions.

"Did Percy push you out of the house?"

No. Trapped. Me. Littleshit.

"He tried to trap you in the house?"

Yeees.

"The clock!" Beth said, so suddenly it made us jump. "Did he try to use the clock?"

Yeeeeeeees.

There was an audible sigh, like a wounded animal moaning in pain. It lasted just a few seconds. Again we felt it more than heard it.

We smelled the lavender again. For a moment it was so strong that it was hard to breathe. We all coughed and choked, drowning in the overpowering scent.

And as fast as it came, it was gone. The air was still, the room was quiet, and all we could hear, far off in the distance, was the muted sound of someone beating a toy drum.

CHAPTER 8

I suggested to Beth that she stay at the lodge to see if she could get a signal long enough to call for help. She was having none of it of course. I assured her it wasn't because I was being sexist. I acknowledged she was more capable than me. Honestly, I didn't want to put her in harm's way. Is that love? Perhaps. Is it telling that I was more worried about her well-being than my own? I could have elected to stay at the lodge instead, but I doubted I could ever face her again if I acted like such a coward. Besides, her battery was so low now it would struggle to send a text message, never mind make a phone call.

Derek was eager to get back to the house of course. I'd lost track of time, it was kind of irrelevant anyway, but Chloe had been gone for hours now. I hardly knew her but I felt desperately sorry for the poor woman. Guiltily, I also felt damn glad it wasn't me or Beth trapped alone in the house.

I managed to persuade Derek to give Beth and me a moment alone before we set out. He stomped off to the kitchen while I took Beth to the furthest corner of the living room, by the windows that during the day would have afforded us a view of the gate and the lower driveway.

Once I was sure he was not listening in, I pulled her close and whispered in her ear.

"This is our chance. Let's just go."

Beth pulled away from me like I'd slapped her.

"That's pretty low, Jim. You'd leave Derek to find Chloe alone?"

"It's not about being heroes. We could lose each other forever in that house. We could even die!"

"Yeah we could, but an innocent woman is trapped in that house and we can't just leave her. And don't forget she's here because we invited her. I'm kind of shocked at you, I've got to say it. I thought you were made of stronger stuff."

"Oh please, can you blame me for being scared? I worry about your safety. Do you really think if the roles were reversed, if you were trapped in there and I was alone with Derek and Chloe, that they wouldn't take the first opportunity to get as far away from here as possible?"

"Chloe wouldn't. Derek might I guess. I don't know him well enough to say. But you? I expected more from you."

"I don't want to go back in that house, Beth. I don't want you to either."

"Then stay here and try to get a signal. Keep Percy's grandfather company. I'm going to look for Chloe."

"You barely know her!"

"What difference does that make? She's stuck in a terrifying situation. We have no idea what state she's in. And you're okay to just abandon her to save yourself?"

"Ourselves, you and me."

"Well now I know why Derek called you an asshole."

I blinked. "He did? When?"

"He said it behind your back in the drawing room. I don't remember what you were talking about, but he said 'asshole' behind your back and you didn't hear. I didn't say anything because I didn't want to kick up a shitstorm."

"Good to know."

"So what did you do to him, Jim? Did you abandon him to die when you were kids? Did you push his mother over a cliff?"

"No of course not!"

"Then what? Derek's known you much longer than I have. Maybe he's seen more sides to you. Maybe he's right and you *are* an asshole. Right now I kind of see where he's coming from. And don't think I've forgotten about that photo of Anna."

"It wasn't my photo! Please don't do this, not now. We need to be united."

"We'll be united, don't worry. I need you as much as you need me. After this is over we need to have a talk. I'm going to get Derek and we're all going back, the three of us, and we're not leaving without Chloe, okay?"

"Okay, I get it."

She left the room. For the first time since dusk I was glad to be alone. I was angry that Beth couldn't see that I had both our best interests at heart, that I wasn't just being a coward. I suddenly felt very tired and disoriented. I hated not knowing what time it was. Maybe if I curled up on the sofa and fell asleep, I'd wake up the next morning with sunlight flooding through the windows to find Derek, Beth and Chloe all packed and ready to leave. We'd laugh, we'd reminisce, then we'd put as much distance between ourselves and this hateful fucking place as humanly possible.

The return of Derek and Beth interrupted my dreaming.

"Let's go," she said. End of discussion.

And before my better judgment could stop me, I was outside again in the crushing darkness. This time I had a torch, spare batteries, matches and a candle. It didn't make me feel much more confident.

"You want to hear my theory?" Beth said as we trudged up the gravel pathway.

"Sure," said Derek. I kept quiet, afraid that I might not be able to keep sarcasm from my response, which would only land me in more trouble. She would come around, she always did after I'd done or said something stupid. But I knew there was a cooling period where it wasn't wise to push, and right now I was mayor of the cooling period.

"I reckon Percy was haunted by his grandfather. You heard what the ghost said, Percy was a disappointment. What if Grandpa haunts Percy's every waking moment, and a good number of the sleeping ones? What if Percy gets sick of this and decides to do something about it?"

"Like what?" I asked, keeping my tone even. Christ it was cold out here now. Focusing on Beth's words was helping me keep my teeth from chattering.

"What if he decides to trap the spirits somehow?"

"So he's a fucking Ghostbuster now, is he?" I was glad Derek said that and not me. I may have been persona non grata but Derek got a free pass.

"No but what if he sets a trap for the ghost and snags all three of our long term tenants plus something else, something much more dangerous. So dangerous that the other three ghosts abandoned the house and took refuge in the lodge?"

Derek scoffed. "Well then they're not trapped, are they? If they can leave the house."

"Maybe they're not trapped in space, they're trapped in time."

"More Doctor Who crap," said Derek, clearly done with the talking and eager to introduce his poker to the phantom wife-stealer.

I kept quiet. I knew what was coming. I dreaded those words more than I'd ever dreaded any words before. Worse even than, *I'm leaving you.* Even worse in some cases than, *I love you.* Here they came...

"I want to get another look at that clock," Beth said.

Derek agreed with her. "I want to see what was under that second pile of dust sheets."

I couldn't stay quiet any longer. I halted and shone my torch at the backs of their heads. A moment later they stopped and turned.

"Are you forgetting what happened in the wine cellar?"

Derek shrugged. "This time I'm ready."

"Oh, because you have a poker? Whoop-di-doo!"

"This time I'm not going to panic and run away," he insisted. I'd believe it when I saw it.

The air of foreboding seemed to return at that moment. Despite our encounters in the lodge, it had almost been possible to forget the events in the house, or at least to put them out of mind for a short while. But now we were heading back into the lion's den. As we started walking again it was almost like wading through deep water. I would have given anything at that moment to see Chloe coming down the path towards us, so we could all just turn around and go back to the relative peace of the lodge.

As we rounded the bend, the side of the dreaded house became visible at the extreme edge of our torch beams. I halted again. Beth stopped too but this time Derek kept walking.

"If you're too scared then go back to the lodge," he said. "I'll go in there alone if I have to."

"I'm not running away," I insisted. "I just want to know what the game plan is."

Derek sounded about ready to hit me. "We go back to the basement. We can go back in by the side door if you like. Beth wants to see the clock and I want to make sure there's nothing underneath that pile of covers. We've been through this. Quit stalling and let's go."

"Do you want to go back to the lodge?" Beth asked me in a warning tone.

"I guess not."

"Glad to hear it. Get your keys ready."

I pulled out the small ring of keys and used my torch to find the one for the side door. Beth and Derek had already reached the wreck of the car. I hurried to keep up, shoes crunching loudly on the gravel. As I passed the remains of our escape, I shone the torch into the back seat, which was more or less intact. The engine, windscreen and front seats had taken most of the impact. I pressed my face and the torch up to the glass, looking for any equipment we'd missed lying in the foot well. I was suddenly aware that this was what characters in horror films do right before a face suddenly appears behind the glass. I backed off hurriedly. I hadn't seen anything, but I was so on edge by this point that every shadow cast by my torch beam made me nervous.

The others were well ahead now.

"Come on, Jim! Either give me the keys and fuck off, or get a bloody move on!"

"Shhh!" I hissed at Derek.

"Oh, you don't think it knows we're coming?"

If I'd been holding the poker, Derek would have met with a pointy reckoning at that moment. I didn't say a word as I trudged onwards, eventually catching up with them as they reached the side door opposite the garage. I slotted the key into the lock and turned it.

Derek opened the door and aimed his torch inside. Beth's beam joined Derek's. The corridor seemed empty. Both beams converged on the door to the wine cellar, now closed. I was pretty sure we'd left it open in our rush to escape. We crept inside and I closed the outside door behind us. I didn't lock it. If we needed to beat a hasty retreat I didn't want to be fumbling for keys again.

Derek opened the door to the wine cellar, which creaked appropriately, doing its best to add to the creepy atmosphere. The offbeat ticking greeted us, just as understated as before and no less unsettling. It was cold again in this part of the house. The air outside was pretty chilly, but in here it wasn't refreshing or bracing. It was a stifling cold, like being inside a tomb of ice.

Derek was already descending by the time I reached the doorway. Beth was at the top of the stairs, about to follow. I hesitated, struggling to cope with going down there again. I tried to think happy, comforting thoughts as I followed Beth. It didn't work. I wanted to sit down on the steps and close my eyes. Fuck that, I wanted to run out into the fresh night air. I guessed Beth was feeling the same way. She may not show it, but I suspected she drew strength from her anger at my willingness to abandon Chloe. So be it.

The wine cellar was just as it was when we'd first come down, except for the broken lamp on the floor and the single pile of dust covers instead of two. The uncovered clock stood in the centre of the space still ticking away. As we approached it I could see that the three faces in synch with each other all said it was nearly midnight. Beth switched on her phone and checked the time, showing it to me. I could see that they did indeed match.

"So I think these three are us," said Beth, pointing to the three clocks running at normal speed. She indicated the top face, currently showing a time of 3.30 AM. "That one is our murky friend, given that it ran backwards."

"So the fourth one must be Chloe," said Derek. The last clock still wasn't moving but was now showing 1.15 AM.

Beth nodded. "So all we have to do is wait for an hour or so and we'll catch up to her."

"No way am I just going to sit here and wait. What if she moves again?"

That was a good point and Beth didn't have an answer. Perhaps the entity was moving Chloe back and forth in time to keep her away from us. That's assuming we weren't all insane for even contemplating a time-travelling ghost in the first place.

Maybe this was all a drug-induced hallucination.

Derek was prodding the pile of dust covers with his foot. Eventually he plucked up the courage to lift them. There was nothing of note underneath, just more covers. I didn't know whether to be relieved or disappointed.

"Look at this!" Beth said. She was behind the clock now and had opened a hatch at the back so she could access the inner workings. The wooden backing swung on little brass hinges. The ticking was louder with the mechanism exposed. The letters *AW* were clearly etched into the brass frame of the uppermost clock.

We peered inside. There was a piece of paper tucked in between the outer casing and the brass frame of the clock itself. Beth used her nails to tease the edge of the paper, slowly working it free until she held it in her hand. It was a neatly folded piece of notepaper. When she opened it out, one side revealed handwriting in neat rows.

The writing was in English, but much of it didn't make any sense. It seemed to be instructions for using the clock, but for what purpose it was hard to tell. There was no context to the writing, so if you didn't know what you were trying to achieve it was impossible to tell from these instructions.

Beth read them aloud. *"Ensure the clock base is connected directly to the foundations of the building. Wind the clock, set all five faces to the same time, some five minutes hence. Then wait for that time to arrive. Just remember, only the last in has mastery over the others."*

"What does that mean, *last in?*" Derek asked.

I didn't have a clue. Clearly neither did Beth.

"Now we know why the clock is in the wine cellar though," she said. "So that it can be connected to the foundations of the house."

I took the paper from Beth. *"Only the last in has mastery.* That's an odd statement. So whoever is last in will have mastery over... which others?"

"Those who were first in?" Beth said.

"First in where?" I asked, peering inside the clock. "It's pretty cramped in there."

"Maybe we should try setting the time ourselves," Beth said.

We stood in silence and let that sink in for a moment.

Slowly, we all moved around to the front of the clock. Nobody made the first move.

"Are you going to do it then?" I asked Beth.

"The one that hasn't moved is the fourth clock, right?" Derek said, his hand reaching out to touch the immobile face. "If the top one is our friendly visitor, and the first three are us, then the fourth one must be Chloe."

I nodded. "Makes sense. Also, it fits with what's on the paper. *The last in has control,* which is true if *the last in* is represented by the top clock, which corresponds to the ghost and…"

"I'd say he's in control of all of us," said Derek.

"Assuming it's a 'he'," Beth said.

"Didn't you say you thought the other ghosts were trapped in the clock?" I asked Beth.

"It was just a theory. I'm just guessing. Maybe the clock isn't anything to do with what's happening."

I coughed. "Whatever it is, it's got us where it wants us down here. So let's try this and then get out of here."

Beth reached out and tried to change the time on the fourth face. She pushed the hands as hard as she could but they would not move. I gave it a try, and then Derek, but impossibly the hands didn't shift by a millisecond.

I tried preventing the hands of the other clocks from moving and they were just as stubborn. "I guess the only thing that's moving these clocks is time."

Beth returned to the back of the clock and shone her torch inside. "I don't see a pendulum," she said. "I could stick something in and try to jam the mechanism."

We searched our pockets but none of us had anything suitable.

"Maybe if we could remove the clock…" Beth suggested.

"Chop it down?" I said.

Derek was hesitant. "We could lose Chloe forever."

"We're never going to find her while that thing is in control," Beth said. "I say we try."

I glanced nervously at the fifth clock, as if expecting the very mention of such a thing would bring the entity hurtling towards us.

"Okay," said Derek. "Let's do it."

The three of us hurried up the stairs and went outside. The night air and the lack of ticking was a relief. I locked the outer door behind us so nothing could come through and then we crossed the path to the garage. The access door was locked too so I fumbled with the keys before settling on a longer one I'd not used for anything else. It was the right key.

The door came open with a tug. The hinges creaked so loudly the sound carried out over the grounds and the lake, echoing into the distance. It was agonizingly loud.

We'd not had a chance to look inside during the day. Now it occurred to me that there might be a vehicle in here. Unfortunately, the garage was empty of cars or motorbikes. I would have settled for a mobility scooter at this point. There was a bicycle in one corner but it looked pretty old and both tires were flat. It was better than nothing. A wheelbarrow stood upended against one wall.

There was a large amount of gardening equipment. No ride-on mower, unfortunately, though that would make a useless getaway vehicle anyway.

Derek went straight to the equipment. I saw him pick up a large axe and examine it with his torch. Then he spotted an item that made him drop the axe and hurry over to it. It was a chainsaw.

"This should work," he said, hefting it. It was big and powerful-looking, but also old. I'd noticed a chainsaw on the back of Arthur's truck as he left the grounds, so likely this one had sat unused for a while.

Derek checked there was gas in the tank and then tried it. He yanked on the chain several times but produced only a cloud of debris and the smell of burnt oil.

He didn't give up though. On about his fifteenth try, amazingly, the saw roared into life. The noise was staggering, like a bunch of cats thrown into an industrial blender. The air filled with the acrid smell of ozone and more burning oil.

Derek turned it off and the blade sputtered to a stop. The garage hung heavy with dust, soot and sudden silence.

"Let's get back to that clock," Derek said.

I was extremely nervous about entering the house with potentially deadly weapons. There likely wasn't much we could do to the entity, and if it could throw a heavy bookcase out of a window then there was plenty it could do to us. I hefted the axe anyway and dutifully followed. Disconnecting the clock from the house really did seem like our best option. I just hoped it wouldn't result in poor Chloe being even further removed from us in the process. I shuddered again when I thought about her. Assuming she was conscious, she must be going out of her mind with terror. The only thing keeping me sane was that I had Beth and Derek here with me. I still didn't know why Derek was so pissed at me, but at least I felt more secure as part of a group.

We crossed the path and paused at the door to the house as I took out my keys. With the axe in one hand it was hard to select the right key with my free hand, so Beth took the keys from me and quickly found the right one. She opened the door.

That cold dread gripped me again as we walked back into the house. Derek went first, the chainsaw empowering him somehow, like he was now the one in control. Good luck to him. His attitude wasn't rubbing off on me. Beth too seemed more determined, now that we had a mission and a possible end to this nightmare in sight.

I was more skeptical. I'd come face to face with this thing twice now and I knew what we were doing was going to bring it back for a third go around. I didn't want to see it again. Already I knew that for the rest of my life, should I survive the night, I would see that thing every single time I closed my eyes. I would never get a good night's sleep again. Right now though, that was the least of my worries. If the ghost wanted us dead it probably would have finished us off hours ago, but who the hell knew what it wanted?

We descended the steps once more, torches sweeping the wine cellar for any possible appearance from the entity. I illuminated the clock and noted that the time shown by the top clock face had not changed much since we were last down here. The ticking was as bad as always and it set my teeth on edge. For the moment at least, we had not attracted the entity's attention.

I had a feeling this was about to change.

"Are you sure about this?" I asked.

Derek answered by firing up the chainsaw. If the machine was deafening in the garage, down here it was ear-bleedingly loud. I clutched my hands to my head as the roar of the power tool reverberated in the confined space. Beth staggered back, hands also clamped to her ears. Derek was laughing. I couldn't hear him, but my torch lit up his face enough to know he was almost maniacal. Beth managed to keep her torch on the clock long enough for Derek to aim the roaring blade.

As he connected with the clock though, something in the chainsaw went *CLUNK* and it whirred to a halt.

"Shit," said Derek. He tried to start it again but it was having none of that. "Shit shit shit!"

"Is something jamming it?" I said, struggling to hear anything over the roaring in my ears. .

"No I don't think so." Derek's voice strained with frustration. "Fucking thing is just old. As soon as it hit resistance…" He tossed the power tool to the floor where it clattered loudly.

"Try the axe," Beth said.

Before I could protest, Derek grabbed the long-handled weapon from me. He directed Beth to shine her light at the clock again, then planted his feet and made ready to swing.

"Hello?"

It was very distant, but we all heard it.

"Hello, is anyone here?"

Someone else was in the house. It was a man's voice, but so soft and muffled I could only just make out what it was saying over the incessant sound of the clock and the ringing in my ears. We strained to hear for a moment longer.

"Who is that?" Beth asked.

Derek dropped the axe and pulled out his torch. "Come on," he said, switching it on.

He and Beth headed to the stairs. I lingered for just a moment, wondering. I shone my light at the clock face. To my horror, the fifth clock face was showing the same time as the first three. I knew what that meant.

"Guys, wait!"

I ran after them, taking the steps two at a time. Already they were hurrying through the corridor.

"Stay together," I pleaded with them. "Wait up, please."

But Derek was too busy calling out, Beth right behind him.

"We're here," Derek yelled. "We're coming."

"Guys, there's nobody there. It's a trick. Guys?"

I was at least three seconds behind them. I had to catch up before they crossed the ballroom. Why were they ignoring me? Did they think I was calling out to the new arrival too?

"Derek? Beth? Wait up."

Beth turned back to me, not slowing her pace. Both had reached the door to the conservatory. They were about to step over the threshold.

"Hurry up, Jim," she called, and then turned to face forward again, never once slowing.

I burst into the conservatory and halted, my torch flicking this way and that.

The room was empty.

Sure there were plants everywhere, and the air was thick with humidity, but there was no sign of Beth and Derek.

I had known it, deep in my heart. I dreaded this. I told them we needed to stay together at all times but here I was, alone anyway. I knew that nobody had come to rescue us, and I cursed Derek and Beth for falling for such an obvious trick. But then they'd not heard the entity mimic someone else before. I couldn't be certain that's what had happened, but it seemed likely. Clearly it had been a trick when I'd heard Derek screaming in the kitchen and I lost the girls upstairs, and now we'd fallen for it again.

And here I was, in the conservatory, alone. The entity had pulled his time switcheroo on us when for just a second we were in different rooms. And now Beth and Derek were as lost to me as Chloe. I had no idea what time it was, or even if it was the same night. I didn't know if the entity was in here with me or terrorizing Beth and Derek somewhere—or sometime—else.

I started crying. I hadn't cried in a long time but at that moment I couldn't help it. I sank to my knees and sobbed.

I'd lost Beth. I was on my own.

CHAPTER 9

There was only one thing to do.

I wiped my face on my sleeve and stood up. I wasn't beaten yet. I charged back to the ballroom, crossing the room as fast as I could. I didn't look back. I didn't look to the sides. I kept my torch beam focused on the door to the back corridor and I kept running. I passed through the doorway, ran to the stairs and plunged down into the wine cellar again.

And stopped at the bottom.

I searched furiously with my torch, shining it into every corner. The broken chainsaw was gone. The axe was gone. A dust sheet covered the clock, which was still ticking like an explosive device, ready to go off. I pulled the sheet away and shone my light on the plinth. There was no sign of any damage inflicted by the chainsaw. I moved to the back of the clock, forcing it open and reaching inside. Sure enough, my fingers connected with the piece of paper. I pulled it out and unfolded it, and saw the exact same message as before.

Again it was like we'd never been there. The entity must have sent me back in time, to a point before we found the wine cellar.

I really was alone.

Quickly I checked the clock faces. The first three clocks still all read the same time, which I found surprising. Maybe they didn't represent the three of us after all. The top clock was showing a different time from the others. That meant the entity wasn't around right now, but I knew all too well how quickly that could change.

I had to get out.

I turned and ran back up the stairs. Once in the corridor I turned and practically fell upon the outer door.

Locked.

We hadn't locked it when we arrived here. We left it unlocked in case we needed to make a quick getaway. How come it was locked now?

Of course, I was in an earlier time *before* we unlocked it.

I reached for my keys, but they weren't there.

I'd given them to Beth.

I turned very slowly, my torch shining down the corridor and my breath coming in ragged gasps.

My grip on sanity lost a couple of fingers at that point. I had intended to return to the lodge. There I would wait the night out until the sun came up, and only then return to the house or try to get help. But with this door locked, my escape route was gone. I'd lay odds that all the other doors were locked too.

I could still try the front door. Maybe I could unlock it from the inside without the key. I struggled to remember the configuration of the lock from the inside of the door, but I hadn't paid enough attention earlier and now I couldn't recall if I needed a key or not.

I hurried back into the ballroom at a brisk walk. It was as fast as I dared go. If I ran I might trip, and the idea of twisting my ankle all alone in this place made me sick to my stomach. I could not resist shining my torch around the room and wished I could stop. The shadows lurched as my torch beam moved, and with every single movement I thought something was coming at me.

I couldn't take much more of this. My nerves were already in tatters and now I had to find a way out of here on my own? It was too much for me to take. I felt dizzy and nauseous. As I reached out to grasp the door handle to enter the conservatory, my hand trembled so much it was hard to grip.

I fumbled with the door handle and nearly fell into the conservatory. Maybe Derek and Beth would jump out at me any moment, now that their little joke was over. We could all have a good laugh and go find Chloe and get the fuck out of here. But they didn't. I dared not even call their names in case something else heard me. That was ridiculous, because whatever was in control here likely knew exactly where I was and how pant-wettingly terrified I felt.

I entered the kitchen. My torch beam swept over the counter to find it still completely clear of debris. I had to assume my stuff was still missing from the drawing room too, which sucked because I still didn't have my mobile phone.

I did have a torch, a candle, matches and spare batteries, so at least I wasn't about to find myself in the dark.

One with a light, one with a stick, and one with the shivers.

Make that just one, all alone with the shivers.

I tried singing to myself. The tune of *Ode to Joy* sounded ragged and breathless.

"Oh God please I am so sorry,

"That I don't believe in you."

I stepped gingerly into the hallway, aware that the staircase loomed to my right as I headed for the front door.

I didn't look back. Instead I sang the next line so I wouldn't think about the stairs.

"If you get me out of here,

"Then maybe I'll believe you're true…"

It seemed to take forever to reach the door, but as soon as I did I flipped the latch, grasped the handle and pulled.

It wouldn't open. Perhaps I'd gone back in time to a point before we had unlocked it. But Beth and I had entered the house while it was still light, so why was it dark outside?

I ducked into the drawing room and shone my light around. Dust covers still on, no sign of our equipment. The room appeared just as it was when we first arrived. So what time was it now? Why wasn't I running into myself and the others?

And then it hit me. I'd been assuming the entity was shifting us around in time *during the same night*. Why should that be the case? Right now could be last night, in relation to when we arrived. It could be last week! If I really had gone back to a time before we arrived, then it made sense that the kitchen was tidy and the drawing room was missing all our stuff. Hell, I could have travelled a year into the past for all I knew.

So that's why we couldn't find Chloe! She'd moved to a night when we weren't even here yet. So she really was all on her own in the house. And now so was I. It was unlikely I was here on the same night as Chloe. There was little hope of finding her if I went looking. At least, that's how I rationalized my decision to get out of the house by any means necessary. I didn't care if I ended up in the 1980s, I just needed to get out.

I returned to the hall and stood at the foot of the staircase. Upstairs was so dark my torchlight barely illuminated anything.

I was shaking again, so badly I couldn't keep the torch steady. As I ascended I quietly continued my ridiculous ditty.

"Why the hell would I go up here?

"I must be a lunatic…"

On the third step up, I paused. I was heading to the library to see if I could climb out of the window broken by the flying bookcase. But of course, that had happened on the night we arrived, not *tonight*. If I was in the past, the bookcase would still be standing opposite the shelves along the wall and the window would still be intact. No way out. I wanted to look anyway but the impenetrable darkness upstairs made me falter. No amount of silly lyrics to Beethoven tunes would muster the courage to go further. So I went back downstairs again. It was still dark as all hell down here, but at least it was a little more open concept and there were fewer places for things to be lying in wait for me.

I stepped back into the hall, wondering where in this wretched place was safest for me to hole up and wait for dawn, if it ever arrived. The answer was nowhere. I still had to get out. I could feel panic rising now, my breathing becoming ragged and urgent again. The hopelessness of my situation tore chunks from my resolve.

"I need to get out of here,

"Before I spray the walls with sick…"

I hurried to the living room and closed the door behind me. I checked that the door to the dining room was also closed and that there was nothing in the room with me. Then I moved to the nearest window and threw open the shutters. Of course, I couldn't see a thing outside, but it wasn't the view I was interested in. I examined the window frame in the torchlight, hoping it was made of wood, preferably rotten. The windows comprised of three tall panes anchored in stone. The glass itself looked tough to break. No way out here.

Each part of the house had different architecture. Surely the window frames would be different in other rooms.

Steeling myself, I opened the door to the dining room and entered cautiously. Again I checked the doors and then moved to the windows. The frames here were wooden but unfortunately in good condition. However, the individual panes in the huge windows were much larger and the glass was less thick. I tried to size one of them up, wondering if my body could fit through. I decided it was worth a try so I stepped down from the recessed window sill and chose the biggest, heaviest chair I could find. It was the only dining chair that had arms, which added considerable weight to the solid oak piece. I placed the torch on the table, pointing at the window. Then I picked up the heavy chair. I got a good swing going, once, twice, three times, all without connecting with the glass. On the fourth swing, I'd built up some velocity and managed to crash the chair into the window with some force.

The sound was like a gunshot and made my ears ring again. The glass did not shatter, but the chair might not stand up to a second blow. Still, there were plenty of chairs and I had to keep trying.

So I swung the chair again. This time the glass gave way and blew outwards, followed by bits of exploded furniture. I was left holding a severed chair leg in each hand. I used them to clear out the remaining shards of glass still stuck in the frame. It wouldn't be smart to slice myself open and bleed out before I reached the lodge. I tossed the chair legs outside.

I was halfway out the window when I heard the voice.

It was unmistakably Derek. He sounded desperate, perhaps even in pain. I paused, one leg out of the window and one leg still in. For a moment I considered running anyway. Most likely I was hearing the ghost play yet another trick. If it had just been Derek I was abandoning, I probably would have kept on going and not looked back. The miserable bastard seemed to have nothing but contempt for me, as if I was somehow responsible for his sucky existence and the crappy choices he made.

But the problem was, as far as I knew, Beth was still with Derek.

And I couldn't leave her.

"Please! Oh God help me," cried Derek's voice again. It was definitely coming from upstairs.

This was a trick. I *knew* it was a trick. But if there was the slightest possibility Beth was genuinely upstairs and in trouble, then I couldn't leave her, could I? Surely if the entity was trying to trick me, I'd be hearing Beth's voice call to me. No?

In that moment, I am ashamed to say, I very nearly left the house. My scrambled brain tried to justify my cowardice by telling me if I couldn't hear Beth, I had no reason to believe she was still with Derek. I decided I could live with myself if I left him behind, but not if I failed to check in case Beth was with him.

Reluctantly I climbed back into the room. Thumps and bangs came from the ceiling now. As I entered the living room, I noticed the chandelier swayed dramatically. I had no desire to know what was going on upstairs. I only wanted to run and keep running. The instinct for self-preservation was so strong it was almost overwhelming.

Yet I found myself once again at the foot of the stairs, peering upwards, using my torch beam to try to see into the gloom.

There was a bang so loud, so damn loud, I jumped and started whimpering. I shrank down against the wall at the bottom of the stairs, almost sobbing with terror.

But it was about to get so much worse.

Something small, something solid, was rolling down the stairs towards me. It bounced on each step.

Bounce bounce bounce.

It rolled past me and came to rest against the far wall opposite the staircase.

It was a torch. It was switched off. I couldn't tell if it was Derek's or Beth's.

I had to hand it to the entity, this was a nice touch. Compelling.

I stood up, mustering courage I didn't possess and forcing down the urge to throw up. Somehow the inclusion of a solid object to entice me into going upstairs felt like an insult, like I was being toyed with. I was angry about it, and the anger bolstered my resolve. I wanted to yell at something, so I did.

"Very convincing," I said, directing my anger up the stairs. "I like the torch. Bit over the top though."

I wasn't trying to antagonize it, or make it reveal itself. I had absolutely no desire to see the fucker ever again. The outburst helped suppress the urgent desire to run away. Also I wanted to know if Derek was really up there or not.

"Jim? Is that you? *Please. Help me.*"

I went over and picked up the torch. I wasn't going to let it disappear on me as soon as I left the hall.

"Is Beth with you?" I called up.

"What? Jesus Christ, Jim! What difference does it make? Fucking help me!"

I didn't move a step.

"Is Beth with you?"

"Yes! Oh Christ, yes, she's here. It's got her. Help me!"

I ascended the stairs in about five seconds.

At the top, my torch showed me the corridor in both directions, but didn't stretch far enough to reveal the far end.

"Where are you?" I called.

Silence.

Definitely a trick. There was no question now. Derek and Beth weren't up here. The fucker could pretend to be any one of us. I wondered if it was luring Beth to a terrible fate right now by pretending to be me, calling out to her. I wondered if it threw a torch at her too.

I let my anger boil over. I allowed myself to be enraged at this manipulative bastard son-of-a-bitch. I wanted it dead, or even more dead. I wanted to find out exactly what it was and I wanted to hurt it. Maybe there was someone it loved while it was alive and I could hurt *them*. Either way, I would make it pay.

"Why are you doing this?" I called into the darkness.

Again no response.

I'd had enough. I was more angry than scared right now. I had a chance to walk down those stairs and leave via the dining room window. I didn't take it. I was so angry about that. If I'd still just been scared I might have done the sensible thing, gone back downstairs and escaped through the window.

Instead I switched on the dropped torch. Now two beams sliced through the darkness, clear and strong. Neither was on the verge of cutting out. Neither was dimming. Neither was about to switch itself off mysteriously. And if one did, I had the other. It gave me strength. It gave me determination to do something about this. For the first time in my life, I didn't feel like a coward. This was my chance to prove I had some balls, to myself, to my girlfriend, to the old schoolmate who had lost all respect for me, and to the entity that sought to make my life hell.

I advanced down the corridor. I didn't look in any rooms. I was heading for the library. Always the damn library. When I reached it, I pushed the door open and shone one of the torches inside. The other I directed down the corridor.

There was nothing odd about the library. The window was intact, the bookshelf was back in its original position, my laptop and tripod were nowhere to be seen, and the furniture was still covered.

I moved on. I kept going until I reached the door to Percy's room, the bedroom right at the end of the corridor. Ahead was the games room. I must have been standing directly above the ballroom now.

I heard a noise behind me.

I turned, my false courage evaporating like warm breath on a winter's morning. I aimed both my torches down the long corridor, back the way I had come. They picked out nothing.

The lights came on.

The brightness was so intense I couldn't stand it. I cried out, my arms flying up to cover my face. The electric lights had come on, all the way down the corridor. It lasted for maybe a second, but the impact on my vision was crippling.

I cried out and dropped to my knees, dropping both torches as my hands came up instinctively to protect my eyes. The lights had gone out yet fireworks flashed across my vision. My optic nerves burned. I scrambled for either torch, searching blindly, desperately in the darkness. I couldn't see anything, even if the torches were still on. My hand grasped one of them, the other lay somewhere to my left. One was enough. I stood up and shone the light down the corridor again. I blinked, trying to focus. Slowly, my eyesight returned to something near normal, even though tears streaked down my face. I blinked a few more times, trying to work out in the gloom if I had suffered permanent damage.

Boom, it happened again. The whole length of the corridor lit up. For a split second I could see every door, every picture hanging on the wall, the stairs at the far end, and something else before I was plunged back into the dark. My assaulted eyes struggled to adjust back to torchlight.

It didn't hurt so much this time, but it still left me disoriented. Every hair on my body stood on end. I was rooted to the spot, utterly incapable of processing what I'd seen.

Standing at the top of the stairs.

Not standing.

Just *there*.

It. The thing. The entity. Black as night, absorbing light like a black hole. Staring at me. A face distorted beyond recognition. Suggestions of limbs, rolling like thunder clouds in the mass that shouldn't have existed at all. I aimed my torch at it but the beam didn't even reach the stairs.

Footsteps now, booming, coming towards me. I felt panic rising. It was coming. It was coming for me.

The electric lights flickered on and off again, several times, showing me a stop motion image of the thing coming closer and closer, moving with impossible speed... at the library door, next to the wall of the apartment, just three doors away from me.

I screamed and hurled myself sideways, pushing into Percy's room in panicked desperation. It was instinct more than anything. I don't remember making the decision. I slammed the door behind me and just a second later felt a bang as something collided with the other side of it. I stumbled forward at the impact, trying to regain my balance as the door came open. I threw myself backwards, my back slamming into the wood and forcing it closed, knocking all the wind out my lungs and sending a jolt of pain though my spine.

Bang. Against the door again, nearly pitching me forward into the room.

Oh God, why didn't I leave this fucking house when I had the chance? What the fuck was I trying to prove? That I'm brave? That I'm somehow a big man who can cope in the face of terrifying opposition? I was an idiot.

I braced myself for the next assault but it didn't come. I shone the torch to one side and saw a chair, just three feet away from me.

Taking a deep breath I lunged at the chair, moving away from the door for a precious couple of seconds. I grabbed the heavy wingback and dragged it, using my body to brace the door again. Gasping for air and trying to think straight I took a moment to think, listen and recover. Then I spun around and rammed the chair up under the door handle.

Checking that it was secure, I retreated a few steps into the room and stood watching the door, ready to leap forward and brace it again if the chair didn't hold.

There was no sound from outside the room. Had it given up?

I was breathing so heavily, I can't imagine it couldn't hear me. My heart pounded and my eyes stung with tears. I did not for one moment think I was safe. I knew it would come back. It was toying with me, seeing how much I could take. I knew at that moment that there was no way this thing was going to let me leave. Even if I had not advanced down the corridor, even if I had run back down the stairs to the hall, it would have slammed the door to the living room and sealed me in. I just knew with a sense of crushing dread that my last chance to escape had been when I was halfway out of that window. From the moment both feet landed back inside I was toast.

But I wasn't defeated, not yet. Maybe I could get the window open in this room and escape across the roof?

I shone the torch further around the room and jumped with fright, crying out in shock.

A man was sitting on the bed.

CHAPTER 10

I had no idea who he was. He was staring at me, clear as day, his eyes blinking in the light of the torch. He'd just been sitting here in the fucking dark this entire time.

He was old, clearly, with white hair and a heavily lined face. He was clean shaven and wore neatly pressed white clothes.

I retreated, standing up against the wall right next to the door. I kept the torch trained on him, wondering what the hell he was going to do to me.

He simply put a finger to his lips and said, "Shhhhhh."

That was about as much as I could take. I started whimpering again, making odd noises I wasn't in control of. I wanted so badly to pee I was surprised I'd not pissed myself already. I broke out in a cold sweat and felt dizzy. I think my body was shutting down from the stress.

"Shhhh," the man said again.

He pressed his wrists together and held up both fists, like his hands were bound together. One hand dropped and the other held up four fingers. Without a word, he pointed to his nightstand and vanished.

The nightstand popped open, unlocked.

I was completely alone in the room. The only sound was my urgent breathing and a soft, sobbing sound I realized was also coming from me.

I tried focusing on making sense of what I had seen. Four fingers? Four what? What did that mean? Number four... Four four four. The significance eluded me. I wondered if it wasn't conveying the number at all but was instead some obscure message in sign language.

My curiousity was helping to calm my fear. The old man's disappearance had weirdly cancelled out some of my panic. Clearly he'd been trying to tell me something, and by focusing on the puzzle I was able to gain some sanity back. I risked leaving the door and went over to the nightstand. Carefully I pulled open the drawer. There were a few odds and ends inside, but my eyes were drawn to a journal with a rubber band around it.

I lifted it out and took it to the bed. Before sitting down, I was careful to make sure I was the only one there. I removed the band and opened the first page.

The paper had, "Percy Logan's Journal", written on the cover. I recognized the handwriting from the library earlier.

Was the man I'd seen Percy? If it was, that meant the entity outside the room was someone else. So if it wasn't Percy and it wasn't his grandfather then who the hell was it?

I wanted to read some of the journal, but not here. Escape was still foremost in my mind.

I put the book down on the bed and moved to the casement window. I tried sliding the bottom frame upwards but it wouldn't budge. I strained against it for about a minute but only succeeded in wearing myself out more. I checked all around the edge of the frame but I hadn't missed a latch anywhere. The window was stuck closed. I looked around for something heavy enough to break the glass, or bludgeon the frame with, but all I could see that might do the trick was the chair wedged under the door handle. I wasn't about to remove that.

Clearly I wasn't going anywhere right now. I sat down on the bed again, took out the candle and matches, wedged the candle into a standing position between a small bedside lamp and an empty vase, and lit it. The candle sputtered and then filled the room with a soft, flickering glow.

I turned off my torch. No sense in wasting the battery.

Then I picked up the journal again. I glanced nervously at the door before starting to read. I was hoping Percy would mention the entity or the clock, or the number four. It might shed some light on how to find the others or even get rid of the entity. Knowledge is power and all that. Clearly Percy, if it was really him, had wanted me to read this. I wasn't going anywhere for the time being. I had all the time in the world.

That's when the connection hit me. Number four. The clock. The fourth clock face didn't correspond to Chloe. Instead it was tuned to Percy's ghost. Percy was number four. When Percy held his wrists together he was trying to tell me that he was a prisoner. Percy was as trapped here as me. The old man was number four! So that meant the first three clock faces must represent the drummer, the lavender woman, and Percy's grandfather. The fourth was Percy himself. And that left one more. The fifth ghost. The black mass. The entity that could mimic voices, could crush a car with a bookcase hurled out of the window, and could make people and things move around in time. It was the last one in.

It was in control.

I opened at a random page and started reading. Percy's handwriting was very neat, almost serial-killer-neat in fact.

Sunday, December 5th

I can't sleep. The banging keeps me awake every night now. It drives me to distraction. I am tired all the time, I cannot get any rest. As soon as my eyes close, Grandpa starts up his racket again. The old bastard will not leave me alone. He's been dead for forty-five years and he still will not leave me alone. Some nights I wake up and he's sitting by my bed, staring at me. He calls me useless, tells me I've wasted my life and amounted to nothing. The family line will die with me and he's ashamed I've not found a woman to help me pass on my cursed genes. He never lets up.

I rubbed my eyes, which were still stinging from the burst of light. It was hard to read by the candlelight but this was fascinating stuff. It seemed the original ghosts of Binsham House were not as benign as Arthur had made out.

Many entries said much the same thing, they outnumbered the mundane accounts of Percy's participation in the village choral society or his outspoken opinions on tourism in the area (he was dead against it, refusing to open the house and grounds to visitors even to raise money for his church).

But most of the entries were about the regular torture Percy suffered at the ghostly hands of his dead grandfather. Before tonight I would have assumed his writing was that of a delusional geriatric, but now…?

Monday, February 15th

I spoke to Father Jeremy again today about my predicament. He is friendly but young, and thinks me a doddering old fool. I asked him to come up to the house, to see for himself what goes on here and the nightly abuse inflicted upon me. He simply smiles and says of course, but not tonight. Always not tonight. Always got something more important to do. I hate his smugness and his youth. He thinks he's above everyone in this village despite the fact that the estate makes me worth one hundred times his value. Nobody wants to hear my opinion these days. All in too much of a hurry to modernize everything.

And Grandpa? Yes he visited me again last night. I am not afraid of him. He does not usually try to hurt me. But he is disruptive. He shines lights in my eyes. He bangs things in my room. He shouts and yells and screams at me. He even once threw a glass at me. I told him he could have killed me and if he did, I would haunt his buggering arse for the rest of eternity. He didn't like the sound of that but he didn't throw anything at me again.

But as I grow older I know inevitably I will be joining him one day. My Lord in Heaven, I beseech thee not to abandon me to such a fate as this.

As time went on, it was obvious the lack of sleep and peace was affecting Percy's sanity. His entries became less coherent and more sporadic. Months would go by with no update, followed by rambling pages cursing everyone he came into contact with and calling his grandfather dirty names that belied his intellect and education.

What I held in my hands was quite simply an account of one man's descent into madness. Before tonight I would have dismissed it as the ramblings of a deranged lunatic, conjuring the image of his dead grandfather in order to focus and justify his rage.

Now I knew better. I'd heard his grandfather in the lodge, confirming what Percy himself recounted in the book. After my encounters with the entity tonight, I was ready to believe anything.

I flicked through more pages, scanning the odd sentence here and there and finding much the same, yet making even less sense as time went on.

And then suddenly, one year ago, everything changed. The journal entries became lucid, much more mundane and far less disturbing to read. There was not a single mention of the abusive grandfather. When had everything changed?

I flicked back some pages, then some more, until I found the last rambling account of sheer hell at the hands of his ghostly ancestor. And one word leapt from the page immediately.

Clock.

I scanned to the start of the entry and began to read.

Thursday, July 3rd

My salvation is at hand. Greg from the antique shop called me. He says he has something that can help me. He has no idea if it will work, but he's been worried about me for months, especially after Father Jeremy told him about my story.

I headed down there after lunch. It is hard for me to drive these days, my eyesight is deteriorating, but this was worth it. As soon as I saw the clock I wanted it, regardless of its more unusual properties. I have never liked clocks that much, don't keep many around the house, but this one spoke to me. It is beautiful. It stands on a tall column and has five clock faces all grouped together on one side. It is quite exquisite, unlike anything I've ever seen before.

And this clock is going to save me.

Greg explained how it works. There are five faces, he said, and the clock is able to 'capture' five spirits. The final spirit, the fifth one, would gain control over the other four, and over the entire house, able to control every aspect of it. I found this fascinating. It had been sold to him by a traveller who had unwittingly released its previous occupants and had tried to recapture them within the clock. He had failed, so instead he moved on, but he took the clock with him. He said the part he got wrong was to not physically connect the clock to the house itself. The clock must become part of the very foundations. He had ignored that part and he had released five very angry spirits in his house.

I brought the clock home and have read the little note he placed inside it over and over again. This could be my salvation.

Monday, November 18th

Construction on my new wine cellar is nearly complete. Grandfather is mad as hell at me about it, but I do not care. This whole house has been torn down, rebuilt, burned down, reorganized, rearranged and rearchitected so many times in its potted history, digging a cellar will make no difference. I have bought a case of wine and intend to order more. It is something I have a passing interest in. The real trick is connecting the clock directly to the foundations of the house. This is a unique building, in that what still stands today is not what originally stood on these foundations, so I pray this will work and will bring me peace.

Thursday, November 28th

Tonight I started the clock. There are three ghosts in this house. When I die, I need to be the fifth. I am missing one. If I am not the fifth, I will not be in control. I must be in control. Grandpa is asking about the clock. I don't know or care if he understands what it is for. It is part of the house now. There is nothing he can do about it. Maybe he sees the future. Maybe he knows what's coming. All I know is, as soon as I have a fourth ghost, I can send my grandfather away and never suffer another night's unrest for the remainder of my years.

Tuesday, December 1st

I have done what I needed to do. Last Sunday I finally convinced Father Jeremy to come to the house tonight. I told him to tell nobody, lest they fill his head with more stories of my insanity. I told him that only he could save me, and as his parishioner it was his duty to attend to me. If he saw or heard nothing unusual I promised never to mention this again. Reluctantly he agreed, probably just to shut me up.

I am not proud of what I did tonight, but I did what I must do. I now have my fourth spirit. I regret that I did not have time to give Father Jeremy last rites nor did I bury him on sacred ground. But thanks to his sacrifice, when I die, I will be the fifth ghost and I will be in control. I will shut my grandfather out of the house and I will reach back through time and ensure that from the moment the clock is started, he can no longer bother me. I will not suffer his abuse any longer!

Seeing Father Jeremy's spirit absorbed into the clock was truly remarkable. It took time for the good priest to find his way to it, and all that time the clock remained open to receiving new guests. But after about an hour of searching, the spirit found its way to the clock and was safely ensconced within. It was fascinating and disturbing. I hope that I will not have to carry this guilt for much longer.

Perhaps, once I am gone, someone will discover this diary and remove Father Jeremy's remains from the hidden space behind the wine racks, accessible from the corridor to the left of the ballroom stage. His body is safe there until such time as our spirits are released from this realm. I apologize to his parishioners. He was a good man, if naïve, and he did not deserve what happened to him. I am a desperate, old man and I need to ensure that I do not end up in this house with my grandfather for all eternity. I will make my peace with Father Jeremy on the other side.

And that was it. After this entry there was no more mention of Percy's grandfather, or the terrible thing he had done. It was just Percy's regular everyday life for several months following the starting of the clock and then no more. The last entry was from just over a month ago. And now Percy was dead.

I reread December 1st's entry again and shuddered. Percy had created his own ghost in the house. Was he really admitting to murder?

Was there a *sixth* ghost in the house?

And that's what didn't make sense. If Father Jeremy had become the fourth ghost because Percy murdered him, then Percy should be the fifth ghost. Why then, was the black mass so firmly in control? Why had Percy held up four fingers to me? Why did he hold up his wrists as if they were bound? Why had his plan failed so spectacularly?

Maybe time was mixed up in this hell house and Percy had occupied the fourth slot while the priest he murdered became number five. Was the black mass, the entity that had been terrorizing the four of us all night, the ghost of a murdered priest?

I'd be pretty pissed too, if I'd taken the time to visit a parishioner's house late one evening and then been murdered. I might take it out on the next four people to spend the night at the house.

Frankly, Percy's ghost scared the shit out of me too. He'd sat right here beside where I was sitting now, and shown me where his journal was and complained mutely that he was a prisoner of the man he killed. And that was the point, he'd killed a man. I saw no remorse in the words of the journal. I saw no begging for forgiveness from the phantom locked away in this room. It was as if the murder was just something that he'd been forced to do to rid himself of Grandpa's spirit. Maybe Percy's grandfather was right to be pissed at his descendant. Maybe the real monster in this house wasn't the entity after all. What hell would Percy have unleashed if he had ended up linked to the fifth clock face? I still didn't quite understand why that had gone wrong for him, but maybe I was glad it had.

"Ghost number four, your time is up," I muttered to myself. I switched on one of my torches and blew out the candle. Cooling the wick with wetted fingers, I made sure it wasn't going to ignite anything. Then I put the candle back in my pocket.

I removed the chair from the door, took a deep breath and stepped out into the corridor.

CHAPTER 11

My fear mounted as I moved towards the stairs, torch beam swinging from side to side. But at least now I understood the entity's pain and why it was lashing out.

I had no idea whether I was in the past or the future relative to Beth and Derek. The library window was not yet broken so it appeared as though our group had not yet arrived, which in theory meant I could leave a message for when we did get here. Perhaps I could wipe out this time stream altogether and find myself in the car leaving the house before night fell, having received a clear and precise warning not to stay the night.

To do that I needed something to write with and I needed to leave the journal somewhere we would find it as soon as possible after arriving.

I knew exactly where to place it.

I entered the library with trepidation. After all, this was the first place I encountered the entity. Or perhaps it was Percy who had walked in, crossed the room and walked out again while I was cowering under the table. Either way, I knew I would be there, and I knew it would be a good place to leave the journal.

I hurried over to the unbroken window and looked down at the driveway, angling my torch to try to see if the car was there.

It wasn't.

It made sense. Either we'd left or we hadn't arrived yet. Either way, the car wasn't there tonight, whenever tonight was.

But here was concrete evidence that we had moved in time, more compelling than the disappearance of the others, or Beth's phone showing an impossible time. The car would take a lot of work to move from the driveway in its wrecked state. It would have taken heavy equipment. Loud equipment.

If I thought about it, the entity had been moving us around in time all night. How else to explain why Derek didn't hear Chloe just before she disappeared? It had been playing games with us from the moment we arrived.

It wasn't hard to get disoriented, especially if different parts of the house could move around to different points in time. This was just too weird. I needed a white board to work it all out. Or perhaps a whole bunch of string.

I noticed there were no other clocks in the house. I hadn't really thought about it before, but it was true. The only clock we'd seen was in the wine cellar, and clearly that one wasn't keeping regular time on any of its five faces. Percy had said in his journal he didn't like the things, but without them it was impossible to tell where and when he was.

Everything, it seemed, was intended to put us off guard, make us unsure and scare us shitless. Ghosts usually wanted to move on, or to get intruders off their territory. This entity seemed to want neither of those things. It just wanted to fuck with us. Maybe it wanted revenge but had selected the wrong targets. Maybe confining Percy's ghost to his room for all eternity wasn't enough for it.

The library had a small bureau tucked in behind the door. I opened it and quickly found a pen. I started writing in the front of the journal.

The ghost is a priest murdered by Percy! I wrote. Then I listed the dates of the pertinent entries. Then I added, *Do NOT stay in this house after dark. Weird shit will happen. Jim from the future signing off (don't ask!)*

I looked at what I'd written and it bothered me. If I read this note, I'd have more questions. Was I really writing it in the future? I'd want to stay and find out the answers. Maybe this was a really bad idea. Maybe I was in the future anyway, so leaving the journal for me to find soon after arriving here was a waste of time.

Too late to worry about that now. I heard footsteps coming down the corridor outside. They were different from the entity's steps. It was hard to put my finger on why. Were they lighter? They were certainly irregular, almost shambling. I didn't know who this was but it was abundantly clear to me that this was not the entity walking towards the library.

I stepped back, away from the door. Was this Derek coming? Or Beth or Chloe? It didn't sound like them. Was the entity screwing with me again? I kind of hoped it was. I wanted to talk to it, tell it I understood how unfair it was that Percy had murdered this innocent clergyman who was simply doing his duty.

I stood with my back to the centre table, light shining towards the open door. Whatever it was would see the beam illuminating the landing wall opposite, but I wasn't about to turn it off. I had a feeling it would find me anyway, and I wanted to see what I was facing.

Thump, thump, thump.

Was that my heart or the stranger?

Finally, a figure appeared in the doorway. I gasped, nearly dropping the torch. Somehow I managed to keep hold of it. The figure turned and I saw its face. Fear gripped me like never before. My guts twisted and a low whimper escaped my lips.

The figure was that of a man, tall and thin. He wore a blank expression, regarding me with hollow eyes. His neck was slashed open, causing his head to loll unnaturally to one side. The cut was deep and ran from one side of his neck to the other. There was no blood. The torchlight caught fragments of internal muscles, arteries, windpipe.

The gash was just above his dog collar.

I backed away, moving around the table, never letting my torchlight leave the figure for a second as it stumbled into the library. It stared at me, making some godforsaken hissing sound as it tried to speak. It could not. Its vocal chords were cut. I could not tear my eyes away.

It reached out to me. I had run out of space to retreat. My back was now against the window. I started to move to the side as it lurched around the table. It wanted to get to me, I didn't know why, but I knew with absolute certainty that I did not want those pale, lifeless hands to touch me.

I was in the corner now, with no escape. I started to sob, couldn't help but think about how it would kill me. I didn't want to die.

Oh God, those hands on me. Cold, so cold. I kicked out, struggled to get free but it would not let go.

"Get off me!"

Still it held on. The dead priest's face was just inches from mine, its cold dead hands clamped against my arms, pinning them to my sides, the torchlight angled upwards making its face and neck wound even more horrific. The smell was rank like rotten meat left in the sun for days. It pushed its dead face even closer. I felt like I was going to black out.

And then it spoke.

It managed to say just one word. One simple word was all it could manage. It rasped and gargled the word, mangling it almost beyond comprehension as its torn throat tried to spit it out.

"Three."

And then it let me go. I huddled in the corner, crying and gasping for air. The dead priest turned and walked from the room. Once out in the corridor it turned left, heading back towards the stairs. Then it disappeared from view.

I gasped and choked in the corner, listening to its receding footsteps in between my own uncontrollable heaving for breath. I threw up against the wall, violently. Then I crashed into one of the chairs, unable to remove the dust cover before I fell into it. I sat there for some time, the acid taste of sick in my mouth and the smell of the dead priest lingering in my nostrils. My arms hurt like hell where it had grabbed me, and I was shaking uncontrollably.

It took me a long time to regain any semblance of composure. For a moment I considered following the priest to see where he was returning to, but the thought of that vile corpse coming anywhere near me a second time... it made me want to throw up again.

Eventually I stopped hyperventilating. I needed water so badly, but I didn't really want to go downstairs right now. I could make my way to the bathroom along the corridor.

Drinking could wait a minute.

I kept the torch focused on the doorway, but there was no sign of movement. I couldn't hear anything now, except my own breathing, which was a relief.

Concentrate on putting it all together.

I worked hard to slow my breathing and tried to think about that one word the priest had said. Clearly I had been wrong. The fifth ghost, the one in control, wasn't the priest after all. Father Jeremy was trapped by the clock before Percy had died. The dead priest was number three. Percy was number four.

So who was in control? Who was making my life such hell? Who was number five?

I heard the distant drumming again, just like before when we were in the lodge. I shone my torch out the window but I couldn't see anything. It definitely sounded like it was coming from outside. So I tried something else. I switched off the torch and just stared into the darkness.

There, down in the herb garden, a small figure moved along the path, casting a faint glow on the plants on either side. A little boy with a tin drum.

And then I realized Percy's mistake.

The old man assumed he would take the fifth face of the clock when he died. He thought he would be the one to take control of the house and of the other ghosts. The original three ghosts, plus the dead priest, and finally Percy himself.

But the mistake was easy to see in hindsight. While the lavender lady and Percy's grandfather both haunted the house, the little boy with his toy drum was only ever seen *outside* the house.

The little boy was free. He wasn't held in the thrall of the clock. The entity had no power over him. Percy had miscounted, and when he died there was still one more space in the clock's rogues' gallery.

Somebody else had died in this house. Between Percy's death and our arrival, someone else had passed away in the house and was rewarded with mastery over everything.

So I was back to square one. I had no idea who or what I was dealing with.

But the priest's visit to the library wasn't a coincidence. The entity had wanted me to see it. It had wanted me to hear its torn throat struggle to tell me it was ghost number three. It wanted me to work out who it was.

Somehow, that chilled me even more. It shouldn't have been a surprise—the entity had been toying with us all night. Knowing however that this thing, this being, was intelligent, insane and powerful... I realized there was no way for me to win. My only option was to try and escape again.

So I rose shakily to my feet. I stumbled out into the corridor, trying to keep my balance. By the time I made it to the top of the stairs, I was ready to collapse. The encounter in the library had drained my strength and whatever resolve I still had left. It was a struggle just to put one foot in front of the other. So I stopped for a moment and listened. There was no sound of footsteps. No signs of movement at all.

I hurried down the stairs, turning right at the bottom into the living room. I didn't stop to look around, just went quickly into the dining room.

My heart sank. The window was unbroken again. I would have to try to break it once more. The heavy chair I had used wasn't there either, just leaving the lighter ones. I might be able to break a window using one of those, but it would take a few tries. So this room, the dining room, had moved in time to a point either before the window was broken, or after it was repaired. Since the big chair was gone, that implied that my breaking of the window was in the past. If it hadn't been broken yet, the chair would still be here.

I remembered back to when Beth and I spoke to Arthur. He had warned us about recent events when vandals had broken a window at the back of the house. Could this be what he was talking about? Was I the vandal?

I moved over to the window and felt around the edges. The caulking was dry but pliant, which confirmed the recent replacement of the window.

So now I knew two things. This room was now in the future, after the breaking of the window. It was also in the past, relative to our arrival at the house. Since Arthur said the vandalism was recent, that meant the chunk of time between my breaking the window and our arrival was likely not very long.

So all I had to do was break another window and then leave the room. The entity would then move the room forward in time again to a point where Arthur had called in the repair people to replace the glass, so at least one day closer to the day of our arrival.

Eventually, the entity would take me back to Beth and Derek. Of course that was assuming it didn't work out what I was doing and send me back to 1966. It also assumed that Beth and Derek were still in the house on the same night of our first arrival.

I took a deep breath. Too many assumptions...

Arthur had said that the vandals broke the window on Wednesday. That meant that today was probably Thursday. I had to get back to Saturday, which meant two more time jumps. I figured the rest of our equipment had been moved to Friday, so I could assume the entity would skip that day and I only needed one more time jump to get back to Saturday. This theory included a whole heap of guesswork, and it made my head hurt, but it was all I had to go on. Chloe was hidden somewhere in all these days as well, and I had no clue where she was.

I froze. I could hear something. It was so faint I almost dismissed it. A moment's pause confirmed what it was: the ticking of the clock. It was gnawing at my brain again, seeming to grow louder now that I was aware of it. Could I really hear it from here? That irritating anti-rhythm, setting my teeth on edge and unsettling my frazzled nerves.

I closed my eyes and tried to shut out the incessant noise. I had to concentrate. Trying to work out how to get back to Beth was making my head spin, and the unnatural ticking was freaking me out. I tried to concentrate on the task at hand. All I had to do was trick the entity into making me jump in time. Simple, right? But what could I do to prompt the entity to make me time travel?

As far as I could tell, the entity would cause a time jump for three reasons. The first reason was to split us up. Since there was nobody else to split me up *from*, I couldn't exploit this to trigger a new jump.

The second reason was to prevent an escape. I could go smash another window, but Arthur said there was only one recent case of vandalism. If I caused another, would I change history? Would the entity send me into next year to avoid a contradiction? If I did enough damage, would the police come?

Should I set a fire? What if nobody saw the fire and called for help before I had burned to death? Yeah, maybe not. Feigning escape was an option, but perhaps not a very good one.

So that meant I would try the third method and see how that went. The third reason for a time jump was to separate us from our equipment.

I was about to take a huge gamble. Just thinking about it made me nauseous. But if I got this right, I'd be back with Beth. Perhaps I'd be back in Chloe's time instead, or back with all the equipment. My mobile phone, the camera, the charger, the lamps...

If I got it wrong, I'd end up in the middle of an entirely different night, all alone, with no light. Or worse. The entity seemed to be able to move parts of the house forwards and backwards in time. Perhaps only the room with my equipment would jump and I'd be left exactly where I started.

I could still escape. I could smash another window and leave immediately. I could hide out in the lodge until dawn. Then I could run away and never come back.

But what about Beth? I'd spent my life running away from women as soon as they got close, treating them like shit. Before, it didn't bother me. Now I cared. I cared about Beth. She was everything I could possibly hope for and then some. She was smarter than me, better looking than me, yet she wanted to be with me. How could I let her go? The old me would feel threatened, would feel that there was too much pressure. I would throw it all away because of some misguided sense of self-importance. That was the old me. I wasn't like that anymore. I had changed.

Or at least I told myself I had changed. If I ran away now, I would simply prove that the selfish, egotistical little shit I used to be had not changed one bit.

If I ran away now, Beth and I would be over – assuming she ever got out too. If I didn't at least try to rescue her, there would be no future for us. To leave her here, to make her suffer when I could have at least tried to find her, I just couldn't do it. She had probably also worked out the triggers for the time jumps— maybe she was in the process of trying them out herself. I knew she wouldn't give up on me, so I wasn't going to give up on her.

I left the dining room and returned to the hall via the living room. Once again I didn't let my torch waver from the direction I was heading in. I even resisted looking up the stairs as I passed by. I hummed *Ode To Joy* under my breath, mostly to drown out the ticking.

I headed straight for the drawing room.

As I entered, I looked around, just in case all our equipment had magically returned. It had not. The room was as untouched as it was the first time we'd entered the house.

I checked that I still had my matches and candle stowed away. Then I placed both torches on the table in the middle of the room, both still on.

Then I left the room.

I stood in the hallway, the light from the drawing room casting a dim glow. I closed the door.

And I waited.

There was no sound. No movement. I was alone in the dark

I could see the outline of the door in front of me, lit from behind. It was pretty faint and cast no light into the hallway.

"Come on. Come on!"

I was waiting for the light around the door frame to go out. When that happened, either the room had jumped in time or I had.

The glow refused to disappear. It stubbornly stayed on.

I banged my fist against the door.

"Come on, you fucker," I yelled.

Still nothing.

I turned towards the stairs, or where I thought they lay.

"I know you can't resist this. Take my torches you bastard. Leave me in the dark. You can do it. Go on."

I turned back. The glow was still there.

And then something occurred to me.

Every time there had been a time jump—that I was aware of—we had been in a separate part of the house. Not just in the next room but a different section. The house was a mish-mash of different architectures, built in different eras. Perhaps the entity was able to make sections of the house jump but not individual rooms. Perhaps the very fragmentary nature of the house itself was what gave the entity the ability to move pieces of it around in time, rather than the whole building jumping together.

It was just a guess but it fit with my experience.

The drawing room, hall and living room were all in one section of the house. The oldest part built in the Gothic style. The kitchen and dining room were in the part of the house that had burned down and been rebuilt.

I had to leave the oldest section of the house. And that meant going further from the torches and the meager light.

I wanted to light my candle. I didn't though. If the entity knew I still had light, it might not bother to separate me from the torches. It probably knew anyway but I couldn't bring myself to give everything up just yet.

Tentatively, my ears straining to hear any unusual sound while my eyes showed me absolutely nothing, I walked away from the drawing room. I moved slowly, mindful that I could veer off course and walk into a wall. Or, worse, I might bump into the stumbling corpse of a dead priest wandering about in the dark. But there was no sound, just my own footsteps and the creaking of the boards beneath my feet. I kept going, assuming I was walking towards the kitchen. I couldn't see a damn thing. It was absolutely, completely and utterly dark.

I struggled to control my breathing. With every step I felt more and more panicked. I fought down the urge to turn and run back to the drawing room as fast as I could, to grab the torches and to find something to smash a window with, to run and run and never come back. I thought of Beth. I pictured her in my mind. I stopped, turned and checked that the glow around the drawing room door was still there. It was, and my eyes drank in the light greedily. I had to tear my gaze away from the dim rectangle. I positioned myself once more so that the drawing room was behind me and I kept moving forward.

Eventually, I stumbled down the slight step into the kitchen.

I felt the air change behind me. The hairs on my neck stood up. It was a feeling I was familiar with, even though I'd not noticed it before because I'd been running or shouting or just plain terrified. It was a feeling that seemed to accompany shifts in time, or at least that was my guess.

I turned.

The light around the drawing room door was gone.

The entity had taken the bait.

And now I was in the dark, with no torches, and still completely on my own.

I strained to listen. Not a sound.

I could resist no longer. I pulled out the matches and I struck one. I expected a spectral face to loom out of the darkness but none came. Instead I could make out the parts of the kitchen nearest to me, and I could see the reflection of the flickering match in the window. I couldn't see very far into the hallway. I took out the candle and lit it, shaking the match out before it could burn my finger.

Now I could see further. There was no light coming from the drawing room, so that part of the house must have time-jumped. A day—maybe more—separated me from my torches.

But the ghost wanted more. It wanted every source of light I had. I could feel it. I knew that my strategizing about numbers of days and how many jumps it would take to get back to Beth were completely worthless. What mattered was whether or not I was willing to trigger the jump. Could I really go through with it? Could I take that final step and leave myself completely vulnerable.

I'd come this far. I wasn't going to run away now.

I found a stand in one of the cupboards and placed the candle into it. Then I put the only source of light down on the floor of the kitchen. The flame glowed against the tiles, casting a flickering pool of light across the floor. I put my matches down nearby, not close enough for the candle to light them, but near enough that I could find them in the dark if I had to.

I took a deep breath.

I stepped over the threshold, back into the hallway.

The atmosphere shifted again.

I was plunged into darkness and thrown into hell.

CHAPTER 12

This latest jump changed everything. I could hear it coming from above. I stepped back into the kitchen; the room felt different now than just moments ago. The candle and my matches were gone and it was pitch black again, but above my head there was noise. Creaking floorboards. Running feet. Wailing and screaming. Something bad was happening, upstairs in the apartment.

I wanted to run away and hide somewhere. Instead I stumbled forwards, hands outstretched, blindly making my way towards the apartment door. I scuffed my shoulder and elbow against the wall first, then moved along until I felt the indentations of the door frame. I located the handle and opened the door.

A gust of cold air blew outwards, surprising me. I took a step back, my hand still holding the door, straining to see anything at all. I heard someone at the top of the stairs crying in pain. The sound twisted my guts with anxiety. It could be Beth. It sounded a bit like her, though I'd never heard anyone make such a twisted, tortured noise as this before.

I put my foot on the bottom step and squinted upwards towards the crying. The stairs turned around a bend half way up, so even if there had been light I wouldn't have been able to see the source of the sobbing. I hesitated, not wanting to go further.

The entity had tricked me several times now, I was not about to be tricked again.

"Beth?" I whispered. The crying continued. "Beth," I said a little louder.

The person at the top of the stairs held back their crying for a moment.

"Jim?"

Oh my God, it was Beth.

"Beth, it's me, I'm here." I started moving up the stairs, still hesitant. How good an impression of Beth could the entity make? Was she real? Did I dare hope?

"Oh God, Jim." I heard her rise, start coming down the stairs towards me. We crashed into each other half way up. It was her! It was really her! I held her tightly in the darkness. Her long hair felt so soft beneath my fingers as I stroked it. We sought out each other's mouths and kissed desperately.

We parted, breathless. I was crying. I reached out to touch her face, feeling her cheeks beneath my fingers. They were wet with tears, just like mine.

"I thought I'd lost you," I said, holding her close again.

"Jim, where did you go?"

"We got parted. I let you get ahead of me and I was taken to another time. I was all alone. I thought I'd never see you again."

"Oh Christ, Jim, I've been all alone too!"

"Where's Derek? Did he leave you?"

"Yes. He said he heard Chloe and he ran ahead. Then he disappeared just like you did!"

I vowed to punch Derek hard in the face if I ever saw him again. Leaving Beth was unforgivable. Right now though, I didn't intend to spend one more second in this house than was absolutely necessary.

"Where's your torch?" Beth asked, panic in her voice.

"I gave it up to get back to you," I explained.

"What? Why? What were you thinking? You mean we're stuck in the dark?" The questions came faster than I could answer them. She sounded like she was about to lose her sanity. "I've been alone for hours, Jim. Please tell me you have a candle or something, please!"

"I don't, I'm sorry. Where's your torch?"

"It was ripped out of my hands hours ago. I've been searching for it ever since."

"And your cell phone?"

"Battery's dead."

"Shit. Why were you up in the apartment?"

As Beth answered, we descended carefully, still clutching hold of each other for fear of something pulling us apart and sending us tumbling through time.

"The ghost has been taunting me with voices. I heard you, I heard Derek, but whenever I moved towards the voice there was nothing."

We emerged into the kitchen. My plan was to return to the living room and try to break a window again. Unless...

"Beth, do you have the keys?"

"No, Derek had them."

"Okay well never mind. We can break a window. I did it earlier, I was going to escape."

"Why didn't you?"

"Because I couldn't leave you!" It felt good to tell her that, especially because it was true. I couldn't believe I had even contemplated leaving without her. She would still be here, sitting on the stairs crying, waiting for rescue, and I would be hiding out in the lodge, feeling guilty. Despite everything, I was glad I was here right now. I was glad she was here too.

She held me a little tighter. She didn't have to say thanks, her body pressed tightly against mine showed her appreciation. She kissed me and I felt like ripping off her clothes and fucking her right there in the kitchen. The stress and terror of this night culminating in a passionate release of two bodies in the dark.

But that could wait for later. Right now we had to get out of here.

I think she felt the same way. She didn't move away from me, didn't stop leaning in and keeping me as close as possible. Maybe she just didn't want any chance she might lose me again. She seemed to have forgotten her previous animosity towards me. Nothing like a night of terror in a haunted house to settle a domestic dispute.

"Did it hurt you?" I asked as we stumbled through the kitchen in the dark.

"Yeah, it pushed me down the stairs. I don't think anything's broken but it fucking hurt." I held her a little tighter. "And my eyes hurt from all the crying. I'm such a flake."

"No, God no. It sounds like you were alone even longer than I was. I think I'd have gone insane."

"Where are we going?"

"To the dining room. It's got the largest window panes. I should be able to break one with a chair."

"You said you broke one already though."

"Yeah I did, and when I came back it was fixed."

"The ghost moved the room through time?"

"Or me, who knows? Remember Arthur talking about the broken window?"

"Yeah."

"Well there you go, that was me. I'm the vandal."

Beth didn't respond to that, but given all she'd been through I hardly expected her to appreciate an ironic aside. We had just entered the living room, going entirely by memory because it was still pitch black of course. I stumbled over a chair I swore wasn't there before, but then the last time I was in here might have been a week ago for all I knew. It was too awkward to hold each other close as we passed through doorways so we simply held hands, but tightly so we didn't accidentally slip apart. I turned and crashed into another chair, bruising my leg.

"Fuck! What happened in here?"

"Derek and I were trying to escape the... ghost. We made a mess."

Finally, with much crashing and stumbling, we made it into the dining room.

"The window is to our left," I said. The heaviest chair fell apart, but I should be able to use one of the others."

"Okay."

"Now listen, you have to trust me. I have to let go of you now or I won't be able to break the window."

"No, don't leave me!"

"I'm not leaving you. Just stay right here." I led her over to the table, feeling the polished wood with my free hand. I guided her over so that she could feel the surface too. "Now as long as you keep your hand on the table right here, we'll be fine."

"But what if the ghost separates us again?"

"It can't. It can only move us around if we're in different parts of the house. This room is in the oldest part of the house. I think the entity can move pieces of the house around in time like a giant Rubik's cube, but it can't split the rooms themselves. If one of us leaves the dining room to go to the conservatory, we're walking into a different section of the house, a newer part. Then we could get separated. Okay?"

"Okay, if you say so. My head still hurts and I can't stop crying."

"Once we're outside, we'll head to the lodge. There might be more candles we missed, you never know. Or we can just wait it out until dawn. It has to come eventually."

"All right, my hand is on the table. I'm letting go of you, okay?"

We let go. I hurried around the table looking for the nearest chair, not wanting to be apart from Beth for any longer than necessary. Oddly, there were no chairs on the side of the dining table furthest from the window. I moved around to the head of the table, feeling my way. No chairs here either. Now to the window side.

"Where the fuck are all the chairs?" I said, widening my search away from the table now in the hopes that someone had pushed the chairs up against the walls.

"Oh, I forgot to tell you," Beth said. I stopped in the darkness, turning towards the sound of her voice. "They're all in the living room. They got moved."

"Moved?" I asked. "Who moved them?"

"Well I helped."

An icy chill slowly crawled up my spine.

"Why would you do that?"

"I don't know," Beth replied. "I'm a bit confused. Must be the bump to my head."

"*Who* did you help?"

"Derek and I moved all the chairs."

A terrible feeling came over me then.

"Don't you want to escape?" I asked, moving very quietly towards her.

"Of course."

"Then why move the chairs, Beth? Why take the heaviest chairs in the house out of the one room with window panes big enough for us to climb through?

I reached her now. I took her hand in mine again and put my other hand up to her face and hair. Her cheeks were still wet with tears.

"Let me see what's wrong with your eyes," I told her soothingly.

"But we can't see anything," Beth replied.

"Just keep still." I raised my fingers, tracing a damp path from her cheek to her lower eyelid. My hand trembled as I placed my index finger on the surface of her eye. And felt nothing. With mounting horror, I gently moved my finger forward. It met no resistance. Her eye wasn't there.

Suddenly a torch snapped on. Beth's face was illuminated. The dampness was not tears, it was blood. Both her eyes were missing, empty sockets gaping at me in the sudden burst of light. I closed my eyes against the glare and recoiled, smashing into the table and sprawling to the ground.

When I stood up, Beth was still bathed in a pool of torchlight. Sickened, I stared first at my girlfriend's ruined face and then back to the source of the light, blinking furiously as my eyes adjusted to the glare.

"What the fuck? What happened to Beth? Jesus, what the fuck happened to her?"

"She fell down the stairs," Derek explained. "She was pushed."

"Did you push her?"

"What? God no! Not as such."

"What does that mean?"

"I didn't push her."

I turned my horrified gaze back to Beth's beautiful face. "Baby?" I said. "Your eyes…"

"What's wrong with them?" she asked.

Oh God, she thought she was still in the dark.

"Beth." I stepped forward and took her hands in mine, staring directly into the black pits in her skull.

"There's no sense trying to tell her," Derek said, coldly.

"Why?"

"Because she's dead."

"What?"

"She banged her head halfway down the apartment stairs. The ghost pushed her so hard she died when her head slammed into the wall."

I still held her hands in mine. She seemed so innocent somehow. The kind of innocence that comes with lack of understanding. An ebbing away of her intelligence, like her brain was shutting down.

I stepped away from her.

"Jim? Where are you?" she implored, breaking my heart just a little bit more with each word.

"You're very calm about this," I accused Derek. "She's dead and yet she's still walking around."

"I'm guessing she's possessed by the ghost. Jim, I'm sorry—I really am. She's been tormenting me for hours. I kind of got used to the idea that she's dead. Sorry if that sounds callous."

I rounded on him. I still couldn't see his face behind the torch, but I hoped he could see how incensed I was.

"Sounds callous? She's fucking dead, Derek!" Hot tears coursed down my cheeks. I felt my legs weaken and I had to reach out to the table for support. "She's dead and now she's a fucking puppet."

Derek stepped forward and stood the torch upright on the table. The light diffused throughout the room, casting everything in an eerie gloom.

"I'm sorry, Jim, I don't know what else to say. She's been following me around since she died, like she expects me to protect her. I had to lie to her about losing my torch to explain why she couldn't see anything. If I sound indifferent about it, well I'm trying to stay sane while a corpse traipses after me in a dark, haunted house in the middle of the night, when I'm the only living person left in the whole building."

"Don't call her that."

"What? A corpse? She is, Jim, she's a corpse. She's gone. She's not in there anymore."

I propped myself up on the table to prevent myself from falling. The movement caused the torch to roll off and clatter onto the hardwood floor. The light flickered for a moment but didn't go out.

My stomach was heaving like I was going to throw up. Somehow I managed to keep it in check.

"Then why is she talking like Beth?" I managed to say between gasps.

"I think the ghost is just providing the power. Her brain is still connected and sort of working, so you know, turn the handle and the music comes out."

"Why are you saying I'm dead?" Beth asked. "I'm not dead! Jim! Tell him I'm not dead!"

"Sorry, Beth," said Derek. "You're very very dead. I checked your pulse after you fell and you didn't have one. When you stood up, once I got the courage to come anywhere near you, I checked it again and you still didn't have one."

I went around the table, pushed past Derek and grabbed the torch. Then I returned to Beth and moved around her, shining the light at the back of her head. I saw a tangled mass of hair near the top of her skull at the back, and the clear protrusion of skull bone.

She really was dead.

"And her eyes?"

"Huh?" said Derek.

I spoke very quietly, almost too softly for him to hear. Beth may have been dead, but I didn't want to alarm what was left of her. "What happened to her eyes?"

"Oh, I did that."

I felt like I'd been kicked in the throat. All the breath escaped my body and I couldn't draw any new air in. I just stared at him open mouthed. Eventually I managed to say something. "You did this to her? Why?"

"Every time my light shone on her I saw those dead eyes staring at me. I went a bit crazy after the fifth straight hour, or at least that's what it felt like. Hard to tell, but it was a long time. She wouldn't leave me alone so in the end I put her eyes out with a kitchen knife."

I couldn't believe what I was hearing. Amazingly, Derek was still talking. "Think of it this way. You get to do what most people don't when they lose a loved one. You can ask her all the questions you always wanted to, and she'll answer. All those things you wish you'd asked when she was alive and you never did."

I threw myself at him, launching myself across the table and slamming into him. I swung a punch at his face but it was wild and he dodged it easily.

"You defiled her," I screamed, lashing out at him uncontrollably.

He threw me off and stood up. Even in the gloom I could see him backing away, his hands held out to try and placate me.

"Hey, Jim, look I know how it sounds but you've got to understand, I was alone in the dark with a fucking corpse following me around. I couldn't get rid of her. She kept staring at me, it was driving me crazy. I had to do something!"

"You could have covered her head or something. You didn't need to ruin her eyes!"

"She would have taken off anything I tried to put on her. I tried shutting her in a room but she managed to get out, and then she stared at me like I'd betrayed her. I couldn't take it anymore."

I lay on the floor where he had thrown me. All the fight had gone. I started sobbing.

"Don't cry, Jim," said Beth. "It'll all be okay."

Somehow that just made it worse.

Weird trivial shit went through my head then. How was I going to get her body back to the US for burial if she wouldn't lie down and stop moving? When her brother died, her parents had insisted on an open casket. That was going to be tough to do for Beth's wake. And oh God, the police! How the hell was I going to explain this to them? Could I blame it on Derek?

Shit, none of that mattered. The woman I loved was dead, yet she was still walking about the place. It was beyond sick. It was beyond wrong.

I wished she wasn't dead. I wished I could have done something to save her. But what could I have done, trapped in a different time?

Derek picked up the torch and put it back on the table standing up. The light it cast upon Beth's face caused her eye sockets to resemble yawning mouths, the shadows extending the size of the pits. She still looked beautiful but in a twisted way. Derek was right about one thing. I did have the chance to ask her stuff I'd always wanted to.

"Beth," I said, trying to be brave and taking her hands in mine again.

"Hi honey," she said. "I'm cold."

"I know. I'll get you a blanket in a minute. Beth, I have a question for you."

"Okay, go ahead. Ask me."

"Beth, I love you more than any other woman I've ever known."

"Do you want me to leave the room?" Derek asked.

"Yes," I snapped. Then I hastily corrected myself. "No! Don't fucking go anywhere. I don't want to be alone again."

I turned back to Beth, trying hard to pretend her beautiful brown eyes were still gazing at me.

"Beth, will you marry me?"

She giggled and gripped my hands so tightly.

"Oh God, oh wow. Yes! Yes I'll marry you. Oh Jim!"

She threw herself at me, her arms around my neck. For just a moment I felt that her death wasn't real. For just a moment I believed she was still alive.

And then I pulled away from her.

"I'm sorry, my love, but you're dead. You died on the stairs."

"Why are you saying these things?"

"Because it's true, hon." I stroked the hair beside her face. Fresh tears rolled down my face. I didn't want to let her go, but I had to.

"I thought we were going to get married."

"Yes, hon, of course we'll get married. We'll get married in the States, yeah? When we go back? You'll look lovely in white."

I picked up the torch and shone it at her one last time. She really would have looked lovely on our wedding day.

"Stay there please, Love. Derek and I are just going to the next room for a moment. We'll be right back, okay?"

"Okay, I trust you, Jim. You won't leave me, right? I'm scared of the dark."

"No, Beth, I won't leave you."

"Okay. Have fun!"

It was like talking with a child. Clearly her brain was breaking down, making her revert to childhood. It broke my heart to leave her there.

Derek and I quietly left the room. Softly I closed the door behind us. I was crying so hard it was tough to keep my eyes focused. We were standing now in the short passageway with the rear doors at the far end. I wondered if I could break them down if I ran at them hard enough. Or maybe I could convince Derek to unlock them with his keys. I had an important question to ask him first.

"Did you find Chloe?"

"No."

"Shit."

"She's probably dead."

"What makes you say that?"

I wasn't aiming the torch at him but Derek's whole demeanor told me he was shrugging.

"I've had a lot of time to get used to the idea. I did my crying and I'm done now. I'm more worried about what I'm going to tell the kids."

"If you didn't love her, why did you marry her?"

Derek didn't deny my blunt question. "I got her pregnant. I did the honourable thing."

"You were an idiot for getting her pregnant when you had no money."

"Yeah, well shit happens. We can't all have the perfect life like you."

I paused before answering, refusing to let him get to me. "My life doesn't feel very perfect right now."

We stayed there in silence for a full minute.

"So what do we do now?" I asked.

"I can't leave," said Derek, "not until I'm sure. Besides, if we can find a body I can at least claim on her insurance."

"That's pretty cold," I said sourly.

"Don't worry. I'm not going to get rich off her death. I'm thinking of my kids, believe it or not."

I changed the subject. "There's ways to force a time change. We can try it if you want. Maybe we'll jump to a day where Chloe is. Maybe she's still alive."

I was hoping he would tell me it was okay, I could leave and he would carry on looking. Instead he seemed interested until I told him we'd have to give up the torch.

He shook his head, becoming more animated than at any point since our reunion. "I can't cope with the dark again! I was in the dark with your dead girlfriend for well over an hour before I remembered she was carrying spare batteries."

"So what do you suggest we do?"

"We should talk to the ghost. Ask it what it wants. If we give it what it wants it might let us go and give us Chloe back."

"I'd rather lose the torch and be in the dark again."

"We only have one torch and I'm not leaving it."

"But I have the torch," I pointed out.

"And I have the keys."

"Want to swap?"

We handed over the precious items warily, like Cold War enemies exchanging captured spies on neutral ground. I half expected Derek to grab both items and run, but then he'd be in the same situation he was before I arrived. He may not like me, but at least he was with another live person again. I guessed that must be the deciding factor.

Immediately I went to the back door and unlocked it. I swung it open and was about to take a step over the threshold when I hesitated. Did outside count as a different part of the house? If I was out and Derek was in, could a time change occur, leaving me alone again?

"Leaving so soon?" Derek asked. There wasn't much humour in his voice.

"No, just getting some air." It was very pleasant to breathe in the cool night breeze. I gazed at where I assumed the horizon was, looking for any faint sign that the sun might be rising. I had no idea how many hours remained until dawn but there was no doubt it was way overdue.

I wiped away my tears and realized I was desperate to pee. So I unzipped my fly and relieved myself out the back door, into the dark. It felt oddly liberating, after all the stress and heartache and pain. Here I was, pissing out the back door of a posh manor house.

"Are you taking a leak?" Derek asked with disbelief.

"I recommend it. I'm not gonna go find the toilet in the dark." Once I was done I zipped myself up and stepped back inside. "Just don't step over the threshold, okay?"

Derek followed my lead while I held the torch. I avoided lighting him up and instead shone the torch towards the conservatory door. I suddenly felt ravenous and thirsty. It was amazing what you didn't notice when you were under stress. Right now I felt almost relaxed. I realized with a heavy heart that

I didn't have much left to lose. Beth was dead. I no longer had to worry about finding her, or escaping with her. Without her, I couldn't think of much point in fighting to keep myself alive. There was a time when I burned through girlfriends like mobile phones, upgrading to a fancier model every year or so when I got bored of the old one or something cooler came along. But Beth was different. I couldn't live without her. That was a stupid statement. Of course I *could* live without her. I was still capable of maintaining myself. I just didn't *want* to. I felt it more keenly now than when she was alive. I missed her so much already. I wanted to go back into the dining room, turn off the light and hold her close, pretend that everything was okay. Even in this brief respite I was still under stress and probably not thinking straight. If I made it to morning, how bad was it going to be when the full impact of her loss hit me? Could I really cope with all that hurt after going through so much already?

So what did I want now? What was left? I wanted Derek to find Chloe so we could all leave. I also wanted something else first. Something that seethed within me now, boiling up like heart burn.

I wanted revenge.

I rolled that last word around in my head for a while. It sounded right. It was as good a cause as any.

It implied fighting, instead of just stumbling around in the dark. It implied that the entity might have some weakness, which so far it had not revealed. It demanded I grow a pair.

"Where are you going to confront it?" I asked Derek as he came back in.

He took the torch from me and said, "In the wine cellar, where else?"

Of course. The wine cellar.

"Do you still have matches?"

"No."

"Shame."

"Are you planning on burning down the house?"

"No, just the clock."

"There might be matches somewhere we've not looked. Or you could try sawing through the clock's base with kitchen knives."

"Okay, let's go get them."

CHAPTER 13

Together, Derek and I stepped into the conservatory, being careful not to get separated again. Once we were in I let him go ahead. He had the torch so he didn't object to leading the way. I wanted him where I could see him, however dimly. After all, here was a guy who had put out the eyes of a corpse with a kitchen knife. Even if Beth wasn't my girlfriend, I don't think I could have done that. If I was crazy enough to do it I certainly wouldn't be calm and rational afterwards. I shuddered. Derek gave me the creeps. Whatever his justification, I could never forgive him for what he'd done.

But I wouldn't need to. After I had my revenge on the entity, once we'd found Chloe and escaped from this house, once all this was done, then I'd cut off all ties with Derek and never see him again. Not a problem when you live in different countries.

We entered the kitchen, again trying not to get separated. Once inside I hung back by the conservatory door. A weight had descended on me, a depression so profound it was hard to breathe. There was no point in returning to the US, not now Beth was gone. Without her, I had few ties in the States. I had no job besides working for my dad, which took me all over the place. It didn't matter where I was based. All my friends over there I knew through Beth, so we would likely drift apart too.

She was my world. And she was gone.

Derek pulled the knife block from the kitchen counter, but it took him both hands to hold it so he put the torch down.

"Come and take the torch, will you?"

In a daze I walked over and picked up the torch, grateful that he wasn't asking me to carry the knives. In my current mental state I might use them on myself. Now of course I had the problem that I would be leading the way with a heavily armed psychopath right behind me. I would have to try hard not to piss him off.

I shone the light around the kitchen in case there was anything else we could use.

"Have you noticed something," I asked as the light moved over the central counter.

"What?"

"The food debris is back." I walked over to the counter and ran a finger over its surface in the torchlight. My finger gathered fragments of the meal we had shared together on the night we had arrived here. That meant we were now either in the same night, or one soon after. Was this "tomorrow" night? I hurried over to the rubbish bin. Inside were take-away bags and containers.

"This time someone really did clean up."

"So?" said Derek.

"Well think about it. On the night we arrived, we ate our meal then abandoned it when we heard the banging upstairs. Later we came back to the kitchen and found everything was gone, no leftovers, no bags, no crumbs. So at that point the kitchen had moved back to a time before we arrived. Now the crumbs are still here, but someone put the big stuff, the bags and containers, in the bin. Did you do that?"

"Of course not."

"Well then it must have been done in the morning, on the day we left this place. The morning after the night we arrived."

"Which means we make it to morning?"

"I think so. If Arthur had done it, he would surely have cleaned the counter too. We obviously left in a hurry but stayed long enough to pack up our stuff and chuck this crap away."

"So why is this important right now?"

I wished Beth was here, she was much better at getting her head around this stuff than I was.

"Because it means this is the night *after* the night we arrived. We've moved forward in time."

"So what? Maybe Arthur does come in the morning after we arrived, and maybe he only has time to put away the big stuff. Maybe he has no idea what happened to us and is just pissed we left everything in a mess. Maybe it doesn't mean we get out of here alive."

I didn't answer him. He was right, but what he was missing was the significance of *when* we were. Something was nagging at my brain, something vital. I led the way from the kitchen and Derek followed. He was eager to get down to the wine cellar. As we walked, something important occurred to me.

Beth was dead. Was she the fifth ghost? Was it her? It didn't feel like her, and it was highly unlikely she would put us all through hell. Unless she was still really pissed at me. But I couldn't see her taking it out on Chloe and Derek too, even after death. I'd been looking for the identity of the fifth ghost, assuming Father Jeremy was number three as his corpse had told me, and Percy was number four. Beth had died in the house, she could be number five. As I understood it, the clock—once installed—sucked in any "available" spirits and then waited for more people to die. That meant Beth was number five. But I honestly didn't believe the entity could be Beth. She was mad at me when we parted, for sure, but not crazy enough to put us all through this.

So if Beth wasn't the fifth ghost, who was?

I was aware of Derek walking behind me as we passed through the conservatory. His breathing was ragged with exhaustion and from hefting the heavy knife block. I thought about how much damage he could do to me with those knives. Of course he could have killed me already, but what if one of those knives ended up killing him instead?

"Derek," I asked as the two of us crossed into the ballroom.

"What?"

"How much do you hate me?"

He stopped in his tracks. A few steps further into the room I stopped too. I covered him with the torch beam. He dumped the knife block on a nearby table and dusted his hands down.

"We're going to do this now, are we?"

"Do what?"

"Have it out. You and me. I wanted to deal with the fucking Amityville Horror first but as usual it's all about you. We need to work together to survive this, you and me, so I was going to play nice. I've been biting my tongue this whole damn time and now you just want to bring it all out in the open and deal with our issues, is that it?"

"I need to know what you're capable of," I said.

"I'm not going to knife you in the back, Jim. Jesus, there's been enough death already. What the hell do you take me for?"

"You took out her eyes, Derek."

"She was *dead*!"

"I know that, but… I don't understand how…"

"I went a bit crazy, I admit it. I went nuts because she kept staring at me every time I looked at her. I lost it, I went nuts." He was repeating himself. My eyes flicked towards the knife block, and I wished I'd confronted him before we'd picked it up from the kitchen. "But there's a world of difference between taking out a corpse's eyes and hurting a living person, Jim."

"So you say."

"So I say. I'm not going to hurt you, as much as I'd like to."

I took a step away from him. "Why? Why do you want to hurt me?"

"Because I fucking hate you, Jim. I don't know why I ever accepted your friend request. When you moved away I thought I was rid of you. You're an insufferable prick and I never wanted to see you again!"

I was stunned. I thought I might have inadvertently pissed him off at some point. This was a profound hatred. This was deep shit. But what shook me more than Derek's words was the movement I heard upstairs. Creaking floorboards and the like. Something above our heads was waking up. I raised my eyes skywards.

"Uh, Derek," I began, but he was in mid-rant now and wasn't going to be silenced.

"Look at you, you smug bastard. You've never done a hard day's work in your life. Everything you have was handed to you. You live off your dad's money, jetting about the world looking at cool places and then back to your luxury apartment in Chicago, which Daddy paid for no doubt."

The movement upstairs had faded but was still audible. Whatever was overhead was heading away from us, likely making for the staircase...

"And boo hoo about your fucking girlfriend, Jim. I'm sure you'll miss her for the five minutes it will take to find the next poor bitch that comes along."

"I asked her to marry me," I said.

"She was fucking dead when you asked her, you dickwad. You could have told her you were signing up for the army and shipping off to Afghanistan for all the difference it would have made. It's piss easy to ask someone a tough question when there are no consequences to the answer."

In the distance I could hear those footsteps. They sounded like they were on the stairs already.

"Derek, we have to leave."

"No! Fuck you, trying to run away again. Just because your bitch is dead doesn't mean you don't owe me. You're going to help me find my wife, you miserable shit. It's your fault she's here."

"I was trying to be nice."

The footsteps were getting louder again and I could swear I heard a door burst open. It wasn't overhead anymore; it was coming from behind Derek, on the ground floor.

"Nice? Yeah you've always been nice, haven't you Jim."

I didn't stop to listen to him. I took off at a run, heading for the door to the right of the stage.

"Come back here," Derek yelled.

I opened the door and was about to pass through when I realized the entity was already here. It stood in a black cloud of hate just behind Derek. My former friend didn't seem at all fazed by the presence.

"You are not allowed to leave."

The door slammed shut with such force it propelled me back into the ballroom and I nearly dropped the torch. I stood quaking in fear. If I hadn't relieved myself at the back door, I'd be pissing myself right now.

My voice sounded small and squeaky. "So I was right."

"We had a little chat while I was on my own in the dark," Derek said. "We realized that our hatred towards you is entirely mutual. We have so much in common it's scary."

"I know why you get on so well, Derek," I stammered, having problems forming words. "It's because you're the same person. Derek, you're going to die and you're going to become the last spirit trapped in the clock. You are the fifth ghost!"

"That's not true. I'm not in any danger. The entity likes me. You're the one who's going to die, Jim."

"Think about it, Derek. If that were true then I'd be trapped in the clock and I'd be the entity. Or if neither of us then Beth! Either way, I don't think the ghost would have murdered her."

Derek faltered somewhat. "That's not true," he insisted.

"It is true," I said. "But you don't need to hate me."

"Why not?"

I had the germ of an idea, but I needed to be back in the same time zone as all of our equipment.

"We need to return to the night we arrived here. I need to show you pictures on my phone."

"Pictures of what?"

"Derek, you don't know me. You don't know the real me. There's stuff I do, it's not on Facebook and I don't go around shouting about it. I only work a third of each year for my dad, so in my time off I volunteer. I know I was a lazy bastard before, I know you resent that, but I've changed, I swear."

"Bullshit!"

"Then let me show you. Ask your friend to take us back to the night we arrived and I'll show you."

There was a long pause. I hardly dared to breathe. Then, without another word, the entity disappeared into the conservatory. There was a shift in the atmosphere, and I knew we had jumped in time again.

"It's done."

I breathed out heavily, sweat running down my face and neck. Were we really back to the same day we'd arrived? Was all our equipment sitting in the drawing room? Was Chloe here?

"Okay," I said. "Come on. I'll show you the real me. I'll show you the pictures of the kids I help, and the shelter I work at."

As we were leaving the ballroom, I casually shone the torch at Derek's face. For just a second as I passed the knife block, I blinded him. In that moment, I grabbed one of the knives and slid it under my belt behind my back. I prayed I hadn't just stabbed myself in the arse with it. Adrenaline was pumping so hard through my system I doubt I would have felt it cut me. Thankfully, Derek didn't notice that I now had a weapon.

There was no sign of the entity now. Derek seemed more at ease, though I kept him permanently in my torchlight so I could keep tabs on where he was.

"I'm so glad it's gone," he said, rubbing the bridge of his nose. "I don't know what comes over me when that thing is around."

"So you don't hate me?" I asked hopefully.

"Oh I still hate you, but that thing scares the crap out of me. It kind of takes over. All I can think about is hurting you."

"That's reassuring," I said. If Derek found that funny, I didn't catch him smiling. I was trying to get a handle on just how far gone he was. After all that time alone with a corpse for company, after whatever the hell the entity said and did to him, and after putting out my girlfriend's eyes with a kitchen knife, I guessed he wasn't too far from the ragged edge. I was about to send him even further over.

We were about to enter the kitchen when I stopped. Derek turned.

"What is it?"

"I can hear something," I said. I shone my light at the other door, the one leading to the backdoor hallway. "I think Beth's still in the dining room."

"But we've moved back a night. She shouldn't be there."

"Can I check? Do you mind? I want to be sure. Then we can go get my phone from the drawing room."

Derek eyed me suspiciously and then nodded. I led the way, uncomfortably aware that Derek was right behind me. If he'd had a torch, he'd have seen the blade tucked into my belt. But he didn't, so as far as I knew he was unaware of it. My heart hammered again. Did he know what I was going to do? Did I know? I was just taking this one step at a time. Right now I just had to get Derek away from the house.

I stumbled as we reached the doorway to the corridor beyond the conservatory. I deliberately fumbled the torch and let it roll away. As I dropped, I stopped myself from falling by grabbing hold of a large porcelain urn. There was nothing in it but it looked heavy nonetheless. I prayed it wasn't too heavy to lift.

"What is it?" Derek said, sounding very unconcerned for my wellbeing.

"Just tripped. I'm tired."

Derek reached for the torch. I saw his hand go for it. I took my chance.

I hefted the urn. It was just the right weight. I brought it crashing down on Derek's head. It didn't break. Instead it bounced off with a hollow thunk. Derek crashed to the floor and didn't move. I grabbed the torch and put it between my teeth. Then I turned him over and checked he was still alive. He was, thankfully. I didn't want him to die in the house. I had no idea how quickly he would recover, so I summoned every last ounce of strength, placed my hands under his arms and heaved him towards the back door. I was lucky Derek was skinny and didn't weigh very much, but even so the strain of pulling him to the back door was nearly too much for me.

The door was locked of course, so I dumped Derek on the floor and scrambled for the key. I was glad I'd opened the door *tomorrow* because now I knew exactly which key was the right one. I got it first try. I could hear footsteps coming. Loud, violently loud. The light fixture above my head creaked as it swung. The walls reverberated with the crashing of something very angry.

There was no doubt in my mind now. Derek and the entity were one and the same. It knew he was injured and it wanted to make sure I didn't leave the house.

I threw open the door and reached down to grab Derek again. The entity's crashing footsteps were so close now, it could only be in the next room. I hurled myself towards the open back door, expecting it to slam closed any moment. Instead, both inner doors, to the conservatory and the dining room, burst open with a bang that startled me.

I didn't stop to look, I didn't use the torch to see where it was, I just pulled and pulled and somehow managed to get Derek outside and out of the way just before the outer door slammed shut.

CHAPTER 14

Still I didn't look back. I dragged Derek's prone body away from the house as fast as I could. The wheelbarrow was still on the opposite side of the courtyard. When I reached it I dumped Derek in, grabbed the handles and took off as fast as I could, heading towards the lake. The torch was hurting my jaw and my teeth. The blade at my back was uncomfortable as hell, my legs were like jelly and my arms felt like they were going to fall apart, but I kept going. I had to get as far away from the house as possible.

I must have looked quite a sight, bouncing over the lawn with a bloke in a wheelbarrow. At one point I hit a bump and the barrow lurched, hurling Derek out onto the ground. I cursed, gathering him up and shoving him back in again. As I set off again, I realized I'd passed up my one opportunity to get my phone back, and maybe get my hands on a fresh lantern. But I'd made my decision and I wasn't going to waste my hard-fought opportunity.

It took a long time to reach the lake. When we got there I was beyond exhausted.

I dumped Derek out of the wheelbarrow unceremoniously. He was waking up. I had to do this now.

Breathing so hard I thought my lungs would explode and my heart would give out, I tore the knife from my belt. I almost hoped I'd fumble the blade and send it flying into the lake. Then the decision would be made for me. But no, not today.

No excuses.

I held the torch in one hand and the blade in the other, and I stood above Derek as he slowly woke up. I had to do this now.

Right now.

Derek groaned but had not lifted his head yet. I was running out of time.

One with a torch, one with a knife...

I had to kill him. I had to plunge the blade deep into the soft tissue between his neck and his shoulder and then rip it out. I had to sever a major artery and let him bleed out onto the grass.

He'd be dead in seconds, here by the lake. Then he couldn't die in the house, and the entity would never come into being. Here, on this night when we first arrived in the house, Derek would die and maybe Beth might live. It was a brilliant plan with just one tiny drawback.

I couldn't do it.

I tried. I thought I might be capable, if push came to shove. I believed that if I ever had to kill someone to save myself or someone I loved, I wouldn't hesitate to get the job done. And here I was, with a prime opportunity to deny the entity its existence, to kill its origin before it could be born within the walls of the house, and I couldn't go through with it.

I sat sobbing on the ground, the torch and knife still in my hands. I was exhausted, beaten and defeated. I had one shot at ending this insanity and I had not taken it.

I thought of Percy, driven so insane by the constant abuse from his grandfather's ghost, who had murdered an innocent priest in cold blood just for a chance to be free from the torture. Now here I was with a similar chance.

I was either a better man than Percy, or a bigger idiot.

"Where the fuck am I?" Derek moaned, rubbing the back of his head and wincing.

He must have seen the knife in my hand by the light of the torch because he sat up in a hurry.

"Why do you have a knife? Did you hit me?"

"Yes. I'm sorry. I was going to kill you."

He sounded understandably pissed. "Was it something I said?"

"Believe it or not I was trying to stop you from becoming the entity."

"By killing me?" I couldn't see his face. He could come at me and take the knife if he wanted to. I wouldn't blame him. I didn't shine the light at him, just kept it by my side as I sat slumped by the lake.

"If you were going to die and become that *thing*, I figured I'd make sure you didn't die in the house. That way the clock wouldn't suck you in and you wouldn't be the one in control. Maybe Beth's entity could take that spot, since she dies in the house tomorrow night. Maybe she wouldn't die at all."

"If you'd asked me I might have volunteered."

"I was hardly going to tell you what I was planning. The entity would have stopped us since you and it were getting along so well."

"Fuck that… Bloody thing crept into my head. Whispered things. Told me to do and say stuff. I feel free now, for the first time in hours I can think clearly. Made me cut Beth's eyes out. Oh God… I couldn't stop myself…"

At first I thought he was choking but instead he was vomiting onto the lawn.

Had I misjudged him? Was he under the influence of the entity when he'd done and said those things? Ironically, if I'd known that, I wouldn't have dragged him down here to kill him. His behaviour was fuel to my anger and desperation. I had *wanted* him to die. At least, some part of me had. Not enough to actually go through with it.

"I'm sorry," I said.

"It's okay," he said in between hawking and spitting. "I've not been myself since I stepped into that house. If you cut out my girlfriend's eyes I'd cut your throat too."

Well that was a reassuring thought.

"I'm just glad you didn't go through with it," he said.

"Me too. I'd never forgive myself."

"Yeah I'd hate to have made you feel bad by letting you stab me to death."

He was starting to sound like the old Derek I used to know. I even smiled a little, despite my exhaustion and my increasingly slim grip on sanity. For the first time in a while, I felt like I had someone on my side.

"So what do we do now?" I asked.

"I have to go back in," said Derek. In the gloom I saw him rise to his feet.

I turned off the torch, but we were plunged into total darkness again. There was no hint of dawn's arrival. I had no idea what time it was. I turned the torch back on. It seemed a little dimmer than before.

"If you go back in, it'll just cloud your mind again," I said as I reached into my pocket. My spirits lifted a little as my fingers curled around a handful of spare batteries. I took out two and turned the torch off again.

"What choice do I have? I still haven't found Chloe." His voice sounded different in the darkness. More ethereal. Like I was hearing him inside my head.

I unscrewed the end of the torch. "I'm not going in there with you."

"Then I'll go in alone. You don't have to go back in. Why don't you stay out here and wait for dawn?"

I emptied the nearly-spent batteries into my lap and then slotted in two new ones, hoping they weren't already dead. I felt like a Hollywood action hero, battered but determined, loading new cartridges into my shotgun before heading back into the fight. Right now though, a torch was so much more useful than a shotgun. If I couldn't see, how could I shoot? *What* would I shoot? It would feel reassuring though, carrying a gun. I needed one of those rifles with a torch attached to the barrel.

Christ! I was falling asleep. My body was at breaking point. I needed rest so badly. I felt like curling up in the grass and taking a nap. I'd wake with the sun and only then would I go back in the house to get my phone, and then I'd get the fuck away from this hell hole.

I screwed the back of the torch together and clicked it on. The light shone bright and strong. This time I did smile.

Derek was standing close to me, his hand outstretched.

"I'm not going in there in the dark!" he said.

The last thing I wanted to do was give him the torch. I had made up my mind. What else could I do?

"You're not going in at all."

"Jim, I have to."

"I'm going."

"I appreciate it, Jim, but you don't have to do that."

I clicked off the torch to save the batteries. "Yes I do. If you go in, you'll die and become that *thing*. If you go in, it'll get control of your head again. If you go in, I have to give you the torch, and I don't think I can do that."

There was a long, silent pause.

Derek spoke first.

"I'll walk you to the back door then."

"Okay."

I clicked the torch back on and he reached out to help me up. I shone the light towards him just to double check he still had eyes or wasn't missing his head or something. He seemed normal but tired. His eyes were sunken and his face was drawn. He seemed even thinner now than when he'd arrived.

Then I swung the light around where I had been sitting to make sure I'd not left anything behind, save for the two spent batteries. The torch glinted off the knife, which I'd forgotten about. I picked it up, electing to carry it rather than risk stuffing it into my belt again.

Then the light settled on the wheelbarrow.

"I'm going to need that," I said.

"The wheelbarrow?"

"Yeah. Push it will you?"

Derek dutifully raised the wheelbarrow and moved back towards the house with it. I walked alongside him, keeping the torch off to save power and only occasionally flicking it back on for a moment to ensure we hadn't veered off course.

"The photo of Anna," I said as we walked in pitch blackness. "You brought it, didn't you?"

Derek spoke his admission without emotion. "Yeah."

"Beth was really pissed at me about that. Why do you have it?"

"I've no idea how it got out of my wallet. It's inside a hidden flap, there's no way it could fall out."

"So you were in love with her?"

"Obviously."

"I wish you'd said something to Beth before she died."

"I'm sorry."

"So what's the story?" I asked. "When did you fall in love with her?"

"While she was still dating you. No, earlier than that, when she and I met at that stupid convention thing I was working at. She was working there too. We hit it off. I invited her to come out with me and some friends…"

"And then she met me."

"Yeah."

"Shit."

"Yeah." Derek sighed. We listened to the sound of the wheelbarrow trundling over the lawn and our soft footsteps on the grass.

"So you must have been pissed at me," I guessed after a time.

"I was already pissed at you. That was the final straw. I only stayed around you to be around her, but she never noticed me after that. And then you fucking dumped her."

"What can I say? I was an arsehole back then. She had a chance to go to Australia and I was a lazy fuck and didn't want to go with her. I told her to stay with me or it was over. We argued. I dumped her."

"She was *crushed* by what you did. For some reason I can't fathom she really loved you."

"How do you know? She left the country a couple of weeks after we split up."

"Because I went to see her. I begged her to stay. I told her how I felt. She said I was sweet and she loved me like a brother and blah blah blah. After what you did to her, it's hardly surprising she didn't want to be with anyone else."

We were quiet again. I was stunned. I had no idea Derek felt that way about Anna. I'd even run it by him before I asked her out, in case he intended to do it first. Still, what could he say to me but yes it was okay? What would I say in his situation?

"Why didn't you go after her?"

"To Australia? Oh sure, nothing says boyfriend material more than following someone halfway around the world on the vague hope she'll fall in love with you."

I did laugh at that. It felt good, cathartic.

"Laugh at my pain, you bastard."

"If I get Chloe out, are we going to call it quits?"

"Will I stop being mad at you, you mean?"

"Yeah."

"Jim, you're the most arrogant, lazy, freeloading, oblivious fuckwitted wanker I've ever met."

"I guess I deserve that."

"Yes you bloody do. And you tried to kill me!"

"Sorry."

"Apology not accepted."

"Glad to hear it."

We were silent for a while after that. We were close to the house now. We could tell without turning the light on. The walls exuded an air of hostility.

"You got a plan?" Derek asked.

"Yeah."

"Gonna share it with me?"

"Hell no. I don't want that thing in there having any idea of what I'm up to."

Truth was, I was making this up as I went along. I had a theory, but if I was wrong I didn't want to have to explain to Derek why it hadn't worked.

"Do me a favour though," I said.

"What's that?"

"Go to the garage and get a couple of shovels, put them in the wheelbarrow and meet me back here."

"Are we going to bury something?"

"Yeah."

"It's not me is it?"

"No, Derek, I'm past the whole murdering you thing. Just remember, don't step inside the house, okay?"

"Like I need reminding."

"I mean it. This thing will do anything to get you inside. Maybe you shouldn't stay here at all."

"Listen, I don't relish standing around outside in the dark, but I'm not going inside again."

"Okay, wish me luck."

He didn't. I clicked on the torch, stepped forward, and opened the back door.

CHAPTER 15

As soon as I stepped inside the atmosphere changed. More than just going from the fresh air to stuffy confinement. The environment seemed wrong, foreboding. It didn't feel like I'd time travelled, but it did feel like stepping into another world. The silence felt artificial. I remember visiting a science museum many years ago and walking through a sound-deadening tunnel. Hundreds of tiny holes lined the walls, which absorbed sound and made the centre of the tunnel utterly silent. It was so unnatural, to hear nothing at all, it hurt my ears. That's how it felt at that moment.

There was an odour as well. Like something had died. Which of course, it had. Today? Tomorrow? Months ago? It was hard to be sure, but the smell was old and decayed.

My torch lit up the short corridor and the two doors on either side. Both were closed. I expected the entity to send me back and forth in time, and to be honest I had no clue if Derek would still be there when I returned. *If* I returned. Right now it was the same night as it was when Derek, Beth, Chloe and I arrived at this house. *If* I got out of here, it might be the middle of next week and Derek would be long gone.

Nothing for it but to press on. I couldn't go back to Derek and tell him I'd given up. Beth's spirit was probably in this house somewhere, lost and afraid. The clock may not have her trapped, but maybe the entity was torturing her. And poor Chloe, innocent Chloe, who I had invited to come here. She was still lost somewhere, somewhen. She wasn't my wife but she was my responsibility.

I paused at the end of the corridor. In front of me was the conservatory door. To get to the drawing room would be faster through the dining room, but I couldn't bring myself to go back in there after we left Beth's corpse alone. I knew she wasn't there *now*, but somehow I couldn't bring myself to open the door.

So I went through the conservatory. My torchlight made terrible shadows from the branches and leaves of the plants. They moved as my torch moved, as I moved, so they lurched and leered. I tried to put such thoughts out of my head. I knew what I had to do and I wanted it done quickly.

But first, the drawing room. I had to get there before the ghost time-shifted me. So I hurried into the kitchen. I shone the torch over the counter and saw the reassuring presence of our meal's detritus, including the shopping bags and food containers. This was the same night that we arrived. I hadn't shifted yet, and if I could make it to the hallway without a time jump, I should be able to get our stuff from the drawing room.

I crossed the threshold into the hall. I didn't feel any shifting in time. If I'd moved in time, there was nothing to indicate it. Perhaps the ghost was busy haunting tomorrow. But it must have known I was here. Was it toying with me? Did I not pose a threat? Was it bored with me?

I tried not to think about the stairs as I passed by. The entity could be anywhere, but the stairs filled me with more dread than anything else, perhaps with the exception of the wine cellar.

I could hear something now. I held my breath and stood in place, listening. At first I thought it was footsteps, but the pattern was irregular. With a shock I realized I was hearing the ticking of the clock. How the hell was I hearing that? Was I going crazy? I had to get this done and get out of here quickly.

I crossed to the drawing room, took a deep breath and pushed open the door.

The room was silent, mercifully free of ticking sounds. I pushed my torch beam into the corners of the dark, poking and prodding with the light, chasing the shadows away only to have them crowd back into place when I moved on. To my delight, all our equipment was here. The lamps were present too, though they were both dark. I hurried over to the first one and tried to light it, but the valve was already open, the canister spent. I moved to the other lamp and this time was rewarded with room-filling light.

The shadows scurried and receded. It took my eyes a little time to adjust, and I turned around in place examining every corner, every nook, and especially the ceiling. I was alone in here. I turned off my torch and closed the door to the drawing room.

I went to the mobile charger and pulled out my phone and Derek's. While the charger itself was dead, our phones had full power. I switched both of them on but of course there was no signal. It was reassuring just to hold them though. I could leave right now through the front door with my key, and Derek and I could walk away from this place until we were back in range and we could call for help. It was so tempting, I felt like abandoning my elaborate and doomed-to-fail plan and just doing that instead.

I had no idea how much gas the lamp held, so I spent a minute replacing the canister on the second lamp. It was awkward to do, but once done I fired it up. The room was brighter than it had been since before dusk. It felt almost safe in here now, but I knew it was anything but. Memories of falling bookcases and Beth's empty eye sockets chipped away at my fragile resolve.

I picked up another spare torch, put the phones in my pocket, and abandoned everything else. I didn't need the laptop or the video and digital cameras either. They would just slow me down.

With the lantern in one hand, I reached out with the other and pulled on the door. I opened it slowly, not knowing what I would find on the other side.

I jumped in shock.

Derek was standing there.

"Holy shit! You nearly gave me a heart attack!"

"Sorry," said Derek.

"Why are you here? I told you to stay outside."

"Yeah, you did. It was dark. I got scared."

I retreated into the room and let him enter. I closed the door behind him.

"I don't want you here, Derek. What if your head gets screwed with again?"

I turned around to face him but he wasn't there. The room was empty.

I was alone.

My heart pounded, my skin crawled and I shivered.

What. The. Fuck?

"Derek?" Maybe he was playing a prank on me. I opened the door again and looked outside into the hall. There was nobody there either.

I turned back into the drawing room and there he was, standing two feet from me. I jumped again.

"Derek what are you doing? Where did you go?"

"Did you miss me?" he asked. His voice was wrong. It sounded like it was coming from another room, like a distant call. It didn't quite match the movement of his lips.

Derek exploded into a mass of blackness.

I screamed and fell backwards into the hall landing hard on my back.

The thing with Derek's face charged after me.

"Where is he?" it screeched.

I scrambled away from it, unable to get up.

"Where is who?" My voice was breaking up. I pushed myself away, scrambling to keep from letting it touch me, never taking my eyes from it.

"Where am I?"

"You mean Derek?"

The entity stopped. It coalesced for a moment, the lamp light from the drawing room framing its dark mass, making it appear much larger.

"I must be here. I must be here."

And then it was gone. In the blink of an eye it disappeared.

I lay there breathing hard. More than ever I just wanted to flee. The front door was just metres from me.

I rose to a sitting position, but before I could stand up I fell back again. I was moving along the floor, feet first.

Something was dragging me.

Oh God, I couldn't stop it. It was pulling me towards the stairs. It was going to drag me *up* the stairs. I fought and twisted, lashed out as it took me away from the light. I couldn't see anything pulling me, felt no tugging on my clothes, but something held my left foot and I couldn't stop moving.

The stairs were agony, each step digging into my spine as the invisible something yanked me upwards. I felt utterly helpless. I cried out, scrabbling to gain a hand hold on one of the railings.

"Get off me!" I yelled, over and over. Panic took over. I thrashed about, kicking out with my free foot, hard enough to split one of the wooden railings.

And then it let go.

I tumbled down the staircase, banging my head at least twice on the way down. I landed in a heap at the bottom, groaning in pain and struggling to move. I had to move.

Shakily I stood up. Nothing seemed to be broken but my head throbbed and my arms, legs and back ached and smarted from a hundred bruises.

I didn't stop to check myself for further damage. I lurched back into the drawing room, staggering against the door frame and forcing myself forward.

It wasn't a change in the air or the hairs on my neck standing on end that confirmed that I'd moved through time, though I experienced them as before. Instead it was the sudden, blinding daylight streaming through the windows of the drawing room.

I fell to my knees and blinked repeatedly. I felt battered and confused. The sudden daylight made my head spin. I couldn't grasp it. Was I being released? Could I walk out the front door? Were the others outside? Had I just woken up and dreamed the whole thing?

I stood shakily, determined to seize the opportunity and leave the house while I might have a chance. The lamp had time travelled with me. It was no match for daylight though. I should take it with me in case I time shifted back into night again.

I reached out for it but something outside the window caught my eye.

Someone.

It was a man, approaching a window from the outside as he neared the house. I stared at him, my head tilting at an angle as I tried to take it in.

It was me.

I moved towards the window, my mouth open like a zombie, staring at my own face as I approached from the outside. I seemed so undamaged, so clean.

Oh shit! This was me arriving! I was seeing what I thought was a reflection, except it wasn't. It was really me! I wanted to scream and wave my arms at the other me, staring in with a confused expression on his—on *my* face. Instead I just stared back, unable to process what I was seeing.

And then the other me was gone and I was plunged back into the dark.

CHAPTER 16

The window went black as the atmosphere shifted and my skin tingled. It was night again. I'd been given just a torturous glimpse of where I'd been just hours ago, when I still had the chance to turn around and walk away. But I already knew that the sight of my battered and bloodied face through that window had not been enough to deter me. The entity was fucking with me, pure and simple.

I grabbed the lamp, made sure I still had the house keys, torches and phones, and then headed back to the bottom of the staircase.

The fall had shaken me. The time jump had assaulted my sanity. But I knew what I had to do. For this all to be over, I knew I had to go up. I stood rooted at the bottom step, unable to continue. Dread filled me. Palpable fear locked my feet to the ground. I stared at the shattered railing, broken by my tumble down the stairs, splintered wood sticking out at an angle. It was a visceral reminder of what had happened to me and might well happen again.

I told myself I had to be brave, and yet my head turned and my eyes gazed longingly at the front door. I wanted to be the other me again, the me that walked carefree in the daylight, the me that was bruise and wound free, the me that could reach out and touch Beth whenever I wanted to.

I held the image of Beth in my mind. Not dead-Beth with no eyes, but living, lovely Beth, spinning on the lawn of the gardens, loving her surroundings as I loved her. I missed her so much it hurt me deeper than any of my injuries. Taking her away from me was crushing my soul, and there wasn't much the entity could do to me that was worse than that.

I held up my lamp and I took my first step upwards. The roof didn't cave in, nothing appeared at the top of the stairs and I wasn't dragged into hell.

So I kept going. In no time I reached the top. It was just as it was the last time I was up here.

I walked on. I wanted to be done with this and gone as soon as possible.

When I reached the library that feeling of dread took hold again. Given what had happened the last time I was in here, I felt like a moron for voluntarily coming back.

But in I went. This time at least I had more light.

The air was fresher in here, mostly due to the broken window letting in the night breeze. It occurred to me that what I was looking for might well be in the bookcase embedded in the four-by-four outside the window, but I trusted my memory and moved over to the shelves covering one entire wall. Sure enough, the Bibles were here. But tucked in beside them was what I was really after. Like a good Catholic, Percy had exactly what I was looking for. *Rites of the Catholic Church Volume 1.* I didn't see volume two anywhere so I had to hope this would be sufficient. And there it was, Rites of Christian burial.

I turned around and nearly walked straight into Derek again.

"What are you doing?" he said in that weird, shifted voice.

I backed away, bumping into the bookshelf.

"You're not Derek," I stammered.

"I look like him." He moved closer until he was just inches from my face. I felt a wave of extreme cold that sucked the air from my lungs. "I sound like him. Are you sure, Jim?"

"Yes I'm sure." I could barely breathe, never mind speak.

Not-Derek backed away suddenly, seeming to phase in and out of reality, moving to the door with impossible speed. "What will you do next?"

And then he was gone. I clutched hold of my book and my lamp and I made for the door, gritting my teeth to stop them from chattering.

One with a lamp, one with a book, one with the shivers...

Something struck the back of my head. I turned in surprise as something else collided with my chin.

It fell to the floor. It was a book.

"Oh no."

A torrent of books flew off the shelves. I raised my arms to protect my head and they clattered against me with astonishing force. I struggled to stay upright against the onslaught, pushing towards the door, my back turned on the flying books. I refused to let go of my lamp and book of rites, but the volumes hitting me were so heavy I was worried the lamp would shatter.

I made it to the corridor outside. The library door slammed behind me and I collapsed against the far wall. The lamp was dented but intact and still alight. My other hand still clutched the book of Rites.

I wanted to sit there for a moment to at least calm myself down and get my breath back, but I knew I had to keep moving. I hauled myself to my feet and staggered back down the corridor. It could throw books at me, it could drag me up the stairs, it could murder my girlfriend, but it would not stop me. I was absolutely determined, more than I ever had been in my life. So Derek thought I was lazy? I would show him I was a survivor and I could get the job done.

I stood up, clutching the far wall for support. I felt dizzy but still conscious. I took a step towards the stairs, then another. Derek was waiting for me at the top, except it wasn't really Derek. It was dead-Derek.

"You won't believe what I'm going to do next," he said. The words settled on me like freezing rain down my back. I wanted to run at him and punch him and shove him down the stairs. I wanted him dead. Of course this thing was *already* dead, but I knew that whatever happened tonight, I would see this through and I would send this hateful, vile, rancid creature screaming into hell if it cost me my life.

But I kept calm. I kept myself composed somehow. I didn't rise to its taunts. It did not frighten me anymore. It could be violent, it could be devious and it could send me hurtling through time like a spinning top in a TARDIS, but it had already taken away the only thing in this world I truly cared about and it had nothing left with which to hurt me.

So I walked up to dead-Derek and I calmly, deliberately, spat in his face. To my surprise, the sputum landed on solid flesh. I reached out and poked him with a finger.

"You're real," I said.

"I am anything I want to be. When I died and woke up a ghost, I thought I was doomed to wander these halls forever. It took a good hour of stumbling around before the clock sucked me in, or at least it felt like an hour. And when that happened, everything changed. Such power! It felt amazing. And you, my dear friend Jim, you made it happen. You killed me, and you will still kill me, and there's nothing you can do to stop it happening."

"I'm not going to stab you with a kitchen knife," I said.

"No, that's true. It's going to happen just as it was supposed to happen. I don't know what you've got in mind, but it doesn't matter now."

"Why doesn't it matter now?"

"Events are already in motion."

"What the fuck are you talking about?"

And then I heard a voice that chilled me even more than dead-Derek's unearthly tones. I heard a single word called, cried out into the night that made my mind unravel with dread.

"Derek!"

The voice was female, utterly terrified, beyond sanity almost. It came from the library and that voice echoed in a way that voices didn't echo in these upstairs rooms. It echoed around a walled-in area. It echoed because it was shouting and screaming out of a broken window into the cool night air outside.

It was Chloe.

It was the one thing, the one word said by the one person absolutely guaranteed to get Derek, the living Derek, to set foot in this house.

"No. No no no. No, Derek no!"

I was torn. Should I rush in and stop Chloe shouting, or should I run downstairs and try to intercept Derek before he inevitably entered the house in search of his wife?

Indecision gripped me. But in the end, the choice wasn't mine to make.

"Chloe! Is that you?" Derek's voice was distant, muted, but it was unmistakably him calling back from outside.

"Oh God, Derek?" Chloe screeched. "Please help me! It's so dark! I can't see. I'm so scared. Derek, please!"

"I'm coming, just stay there!"

It was too late to silence Chloe. In her current state I couldn't explain to her fast enough that she had to tell her husband to stay outside. In the distance I heard the crashing of doors as Derek entered the house by the back door and tried to find his way to us in the dark. I had no other choice. I had to get him out before he was possessed again. I turned back to the stairs.

Derek, dead-Derek, blocked my way. He looked less solid now, more gaseous like the time I had seen him on the ceiling of the drawing room. I lunged at him, desperate to get past.

Something strange happened.

I halted at the top of the stairs. A weird feeling came over me. It was like the world shimmered around my head. For a moment I thought I was time jumping again, but this felt different. What the hell was going on? Now, terrifyingly, I couldn't move. I was stuck in one place, unable to even move a finger. What was it doing to me?

Then I started walking.

I cried out in shock, but my words sounded muffled and unreal. I wasn't in control of my legs or my arms or any part of me. I was walking back to the library. I couldn't stop myself. Visions crowded my head of pushing Chloe out of the window, or stabbing her with my knife, or some other terrible thing the entity was going to make me do to her. I couldn't stop it. I was on a roller coaster just before the first big drop and I'd changed my mind, I wanted to get off. I felt sick, overcome with disgust at the lack of control over my own body. I was lurching like a fucking zombie and I couldn't stop myself.

"I'm coming, Baby" I said. Except, I didn't say it. The entity surrounded me, I was sure of it. I felt like something evil, something utterly *wrong*, had invaded every cell of my body. I couldn't stop talking.

"Follow my lamplight, I'm here."

I raised the lamp to illuminate the library door as I approached. Behind me, I could hear Derek, still downstairs but close, trying to locate the staircase in the faint light from the drawing room.

Chloe appeared in the doorway of the library.

"It's me," I said, involuntarily. "It's Derek! Oh my God, Chloe, you're alive!"

"Jesus, Derek, oh thank God, thank God."

Chloe rushed forward. I tried to scream, tried to tell her to keep away. I wanted to yell at her, I'm not Derek, I'm not him! Keep away! Keep away! Please...

Chloe hurled herself into my arms. I enfolded her in a tight embrace, all the while saying things like, "Oh baby, oh my love, oh I'm so sorry I lost you."

And then she kissed me. She kissed me like she hadn't seen me in years. Like she loved me more than anything else in the world at that exact moment. And despite everything, I sank into that kiss. I don't think I had a choice, I couldn't have resisted if I wanted to. But to have a living, breathing woman kiss me felt so good, it eased my panic and calmed my nerves.

We parted. I parted from her. I felt myself in control. The lantern lit up our faces. The entity was gone. Chloe was staring at me in confusion, clearly shocked to see that my face had changed, from her perspective.

I swung the lamp around.

Derek stood at the top of the stairs. The real Derek. The living Derek. His expression was dumbfounded, totally blown away.

"Oh no," I said. "No, Derek, no. Derek it's not what it looks like."

"You fucking bastard."

"No, Derek, no!"

I could only keep protesting. I didn't know which words would convince him. I didn't know what to say. I felt guilt and self-revulsion and anger and hatred towards myself and the entity that made me do this.

"I fucking *hate* you," he screamed.

And then he charged.

CHAPTER 17

He hit me so hard I couldn't breathe. I slammed into the carpet, burning my elbows and nearly knocking myself senseless. The lamp rolled out of my grasp.

"Derek, please," I wheezed, my gasps barely audible. "You've been tricked!"

But he didn't listen. He rained punches on my face and chest like a man possessed. Pain exploded in my punished skull. I struggled to bring my arms up to defend myself.

"No, Derek!" Chloe said, rushing forward.

Derek ignored her. He hauled me to my feet.

"So that's why you were being so brave, eh? Couldn't wait for a little alone time with my wife. Maybe you've spent hours with her up here, have you? You told me I was the ghost, well perhaps it's you. Perhaps I murder you right now and you become the fucking entity, so you can get me out of the picture and give your living self a little time with my woman."

He was ranting, out of control, but at least he wasn't hitting me. My ears rang and I saw stars. I wanted to go to sleep and let it all be over.

Derek hit me again and I heard something crack. It might have been my nose. I couldn't feel anything anymore.

"Oh God, Derek, please stop hitting him!"

"And you!" Derek roared, rounding on Chloe. "I can't believe I actually risked my life to find you. I don't even fucking love you, you bitch! But I'm your husband, and I stayed faithful to you all these fucking miserable years, and you repay me by sleeping with this loathsome pile of shit?"

"It's not true, Derek, please don't say these things." Chloe was a mess. I could see it even in my shell-shocked state.

Derek raised a hand to strike her.

From out of nowhere, I yelled something incoherent. Somehow I managed to get to my feet. Derek halted the punch and turned to me, a sneer of contempt writ large across his face.

"Well look at that," he said, pushing Chloe away. "Finally Jim-boy grows a pair. At last he takes a stand. Nobody to spoon feed you now. Nobody to tell you how awesome you are while you squander everything the good Lord gave you. You lazy sack of shit. Come on then. She's my wife but you tainted her. Who knows what the hell you did to her while I wasn't around."

I'd heard enough. My vision was clearing and my face was starting to hurt like daggers had been plunged into my eyes. It fuelled my rage. This fucker had to be taken down before he killed me and then turned on Chloe.

I roared at him, like a wounded animal, and hurled myself forward with everything I could muster. He seemed surprised by the ferocity of my attack, stumbling backwards as I swung my fists at his face. I don't think any connected. I was far too uncoordinated to avoid striking his arms as he raised them to protect his head. But it pushed him back, away from Chloe and down the corridor.

He blocked one of my punches, grabbed my overextended arm and slammed me into the wall. I discovered that there were areas of my body that hadn't been hurting before, because they hurt like fuck now. He punched me in the stomach four times. On the fourth punch, I heaved and would have vomited if there was anything in my stomach. I collapsed, gasping and choking. He kicked me, sending me rolling down the hall. I changed my tactics at that point. Escape seemed pretty sensible, before my brains were dashed against the wall.

Dead-Derek stood at the top of the stairs. If the others could see him, they didn't react. I guessed Chloe was too distressed and living-Derek was too rage-fuelled, but I saw him.

"I have to go now," he said. "I'll see you later."

And he vanished.

"You're not going anywhere," Derek growled, clearly thinking I was the one saying I had to go.

He picked me up and hurled me down the corridor, slamming me into the railing at the top of the stairs. The wood was already slippery with my blood. I felt consciousness slipping away. I couldn't stand up, I couldn't drag myself away. All I could do was wrap an arm around the railing and pull myself down onto the top step. Maybe I could slide down the stairs head first. Maybe I could haul myself up. Maybe I was a dead man. Maybe I would become the fifth ghost after all. Maybe I deserved Derek's wrath. Maybe I actually enjoyed that kiss with Chloe. Maybe I didn't deserve to live.

I forced my head to turn towards him. Lights flashed around my peripheral vision.

"Derek, please, you have to believe me." I gasped. I spat out blood and perhaps a tooth. "It's a trick! It wasn't me kissing Chloe!"

"How convenient," Derek said as he approached. He grabbed a handful of my hair, forcing my head up. It occurred to me that with the entity gone, Derek probably wasn't under any influence. This really was how much he loathed me. Years of boiling, bubbling, seething hatred finally surfacing in one moment of catharsis. He didn't blame his father for beating him, he blamed me for causing him to fail, which led to the beatings. And now it was my turn.

I knew I couldn't take much more. Consciousness was slipping away again. The pain morphed into a throbbing pressure around my skull. I had no idea if I was even capable of standing.

I saw the foot come at my face. I don't know how, pure self-preservation perhaps, but I managed to reach out and grab his ankle, deflecting the blow and causing him to stumble. He struggled to place his foot on something stable but I was in the way.

At that moment my strength gave out. I let go of the railing.

We tumbled down the stairs, he and I. There was a terrible crunch and then a sickening, ripping sound as we went down. I had no idea what the noise was.

I landed in a heap at the bottom of the stairs for the second time that night. I couldn't move. Everything hurt. I latched onto the pain again, using it to keep myself awake. I lay there, gasping and trying to spit the pooling blood from my mouth. The glow of the lamp from the drawing room cast an eerie pallour through the hallway. From my twisted position on the floor I could see the door. Maybe I could somehow get in there and barricade it before Derek finished me off.

But Derek hadn't reached the bottom of the stairs.

And then Chloe screamed and didn't stop screaming.

She stood at the top of the stairs, my lamp in her hand, shining yellow light down the staircase.

Half way down, suspended on the railing I had broken earlier, was Derek. His lifeless eyes stared out over the hallway as he swung slowly back and forth. I peered at him, trying to focus in the half light. Chloe descended, whimpering in shock, desperately hoping he was still alive. As her lamp neared him, I could see that the broken railing had penetrated Derek's back as he fell and had burst through the top of his skull.

Blood dripped from his open mouth. His limbs twitched as his body caught up with the death of his brain. After a time his limbs went still but his body carried on swinging back and forth where it hung from the shattered railing.

CHAPTER 18

Chloe collapsed on the stairs, sobbing bitterly, the lamp forgotten on the step beside her.

I couldn't move. All I could think about was that I had killed him. I killed Derek. I made the entity. I was the ultimate cause of all the horror that we had been through tonight.

And that meant I was responsible for Beth dying.

I'd invited Derek here, and now he was dead because of me. I'd brought Beth along to keep me company on my assignment and now she was dead because of me. Poor Chloe was now a widow because of me.

I felt like shit. I'd been beaten to within an inch of my life but it wasn't punishment enough.

I struggled to find something, anything, worth pulling myself out of this puddle of blood for.

Chloe. She was alive and her kids needed her. Maybe I could pay my penance by helping Chloe.

I tried to get up but my body was too exhausted and too battered to respond. I managed to move my free arm a little, and it hurt to do so. I dropped my hand back into the puddle of blood slowly forming there. Some part of my brain was alarmed at my blood loss, but as far as I could tell I wasn't bleeding out. The blood was mostly coming from a gash on the back of my hand. It should have hurt but so many alarms crowded my brain it was hard to discern where any of the pain was coming from.

"Chloe," I said weakly.

She ignored me, still sobbing over Derek's corpse. I couldn't blame her.

"Chloe, please," I said. "Help me! We don't have much time."

In fact we had no time at all.

The entity was forming before our eyes. It poured from Derek's eyes, nose and mouth like someone had pumped him full of black smoke. In the lantern light, the fog looked like a lightning cloud as it reflected the glow from its billowing surface.

Chloe recoiled in horror. I still couldn't move. I just stared at it, watched as it issued from Derek's broken body. It was like the house was on fire. The smoke collected around the chandelier in the centre of the hall ceiling, enveloping and obscuring it. Just like it had done in the drawing room the first time I had seen it. It looked formless, aimless, and I wondered if it was trying to work out what had happened to it. Regardless, I didn't have long before it found the clock, gained control and came after me with a vengeance.

I realized that at any time, Derek's ghost from the future could return. But it told me it had to go, as if it didn't want to be here at the same time as its own "birth". If I was lucky, that meant I had around an hour before the clock sucked the new entity inside. Just an hour to find a way to destroy it. And the future entity shouldn't bother me during that time. If I was lucky.

"Chloe," I croaked.

She looked up, her eyes puffy and her cheeks streaked with tears upon dried tears upon ruined makeup. She'd clearly been pushed to the absolute limit of her sanity and was faced with the impossible knowledge that her husband didn't love her and was also very, very dead. And also a violent, evil spirit.

"Chloe, he didn't mean what he said," I lied. "The entity, the ghost, it possessed him. It possessed me when we kissed. It tricked Derek and it made him do nasty things to you. He loved you, Chloe, he told me. He cried out for you when he was scared. Chloe, please." I was lying to her, but I didn't have time for lengthy explanations and she was hardly in the mood to hear them. She needed to hang on to the one truth that might help her cope with Derek's death, at least in the short term.

"He loved you, Chloe. He wasn't himself when he said those things."

She stood very slowly, turned to me and then descended the staircase. I tried to sit up without much success, wondering if she was going to pick up where Derek left off and start kicking me.

She didn't.

Instead she helped me up. I leant heavily on her but I managed to stand. My spine felt like it had been run through a mangle. My head throbbed, my nose was probably broken and I was sure that more of my skin was covered in bruises than was left unblemished. The gash on my hand dripped more blood onto the carpet and I was pretty sure I'd cracked some ribs. But I was standing—with help—and I was able to talk.

"When I kissed you, I thought it was Derek. I saw Derek."

"It was the entity tricking us. It had control of me for a time. I couldn't stop myself from talking to you and kissing you back. I'm so sorry."

"No, it's not your fault. None of this is your fault."

It *was* my fault but I wasn't going to argue with her.

"Chloe, you have to help me. We don't have much time and we have work to do. We have a chance to finish the entity off for good but I need you. Will you help me?"

She nodded, her expression blank. She seemed utterly numb, devoid of emotion now. At least she was functioning and responding to instructions. I could use her.

"Go upstairs and fetch the book I dropped on the landing when Derek attacked me."

She nodded and, lamp still in hand, ascended the staircase. Her eyes flicked between her dead husband and the mass still swirling around the chandelier on the ceiling. If she realized now that Derek had *become* the entity, she didn't say anything. She was likely too shocked to put two and two together. The foggy mass was sinking slowly to the floor now, still swirling but moving downwards.

As Chloe ascended, I dragged myself to the drawing room, all the while clutching hold of the wall to keep me upright. With luck I didn't have to worry about being time shifted and losing both Chloe and the book. With the entity staying away from its own creation, for the time being I believed we were safe. All that would change when the clock absorbed Derek's ghost.

I pushed myself into the drawing room and struggled my way over to the second lamp. I picked it up and headed back out to the hall. The entity was nearly at floor level, still unfocused and shapeless.

Chloe met me at the bottom of the stairs. She handed me the book and then gave me a hug, clearly relieved to see that I hadn't been whisked off to another time, leaving her all alone again. She had taken a big risk by leaving me to go back upstairs. I knew we were unlikely to be separated, but she probably didn't. I admired her faith in me.

"How much time do we have?" she asked, her voice still lacking emotion. Perhaps she had shut off that part of her brain and was dealing just with facts and instructions right now.

"Not long. Soon the clock will turn that thing into Super-Specter and we'll be in serious trouble."

"What clock, what are you talking about?"

"In the wine cellar. I guess you've not seen it yet. It has five clock faces, like one of those airport clocks showing different time zones, but it's old. When we first saw it, I think we were in the future, so the fifth face was already occupied. Right now it's empty and about to receive its final guest. I think the clock is in a state of flux but I'm really only guessing."

"None of what you're saying makes sense."

I wished Beth was here. She'd get it. Hell, she would have understood way faster than me and might have sorted this mess out hours ago.

Chloe must have read my mind.

"Where's Beth?" she asked. "Is she lost too?"

I didn't answer. I couldn't. I didn't need to. She could read my face even through the mess it was in. She gave me a hug and didn't pursue the question. "Just tell me what to do," she said. I had no idea how long she had been alone but she was clearly happy to be with another living person again, regardless of what happened to her husband. I guessed that she was thinking about her children, determined to prevent the loss of *both* their parents.

"Come with me," I said.

Still leaning on her for support, I led her into the living room. It would be faster through the kitchen, but I didn't want to go anywhere near the entity still swirling in the middle of the hall.

Not saying a word, the two of us entered the dining room. I hesitated after entering, wondering who I would find in here. But the room was empty and the chairs were all back where they belonged. I felt a pang of loss.

Chloe was looking at me. "Do you need to rest?" she asked.

"Yes," I said, "but later. I need to see the clock."

"The weird one in the wine cellar?"

"Yeah."

We passed through the conservatory and into the ballroom. I limped to the right of the stage and unlocked the door so we could get to the corridor. I tried to move quickly but my body was having none of it. I hurt everywhere and my progress was painfully slow.

I almost fell down the steps into the wine cellar. Thankfully, Chloe helped me down. I sat on the bottom step while she moved further into the room, her lamp held out to illuminate the clock.

The lid was open. Hopefully this meant it was waiting to receive the fifth spirit, a spirit no doubt following us towards the phantasmagorical vacuum cleaner of lost souls.

I had my answer. If we were going to do this it had to be right now.

"Chloe, we need to go back upstairs. We need to move quickly." It was getting hard to talk through the swelling in my face. One eye was bruised shut and I could feel pressure building around my jaw. I must have looked like shit.

"I think you should take it easy," she said.

I smiled. Chloe was such a mum. I had no doubt that her strength to keep going was born from a burning desire to see her children again. I had so much more than her, materially speaking, yet I had nothing to live for. So I decided to live for Chloe's kids. They'd lost their dad; they wouldn't lose their mum too.

Standing up was agony. The shooting pains travelling from my bruised shins and thighs combined with the cracked ribs, bruised spine and frozen left shoulder, made my head spin. I felt nauseous and my skull throbbed. My muscles ached so much I had to constantly fight the urge to just lie down and slip away.

But I had seen the light at the end of the tunnel and I hoped to God it wasn't a train.

"I'll be okay," I lied. "Let's go."

I led her back to the ballroom and crossed the stage to the other, locked door. My bruised fingers fumbled with the keys for a bit before I found one I'd not used yet. The door sprung open.

The corridor beyond had another exit to the outside at the far end. On either side was another door. Upon investigation they turned out to be more dressing rooms, his and hers. I wasn't interested in either. I crouched down in the corridor, the lamp on the floor beside me, and I examined the tiles. It was fairly obvious someone had lifted them up and then hastily put them down again. I picked at one and it came loose. It made sense. If there was a body underneath here, and that body had gone walking about the house one night, then its resting place should be somewhat… disturbed.

I pulled away more and more tiles. Chloe helped me, though I'm sure she had no idea why we were doing it. She must have thought I'd lost my mind. It was only when the trap door was revealed that she realized I was onto something.

I opened it up, the hinges creaking with disuse. The stairs were much narrower and steeper than those down into the wine cellar. As we descended into the dark pit, I was aware that the wall that backed onto the wine cellar was not a wall. It was the back of the wine racks. I stumbled over and ran a hand across its surface. Definitely wood, with a multitude of screw holes where the racks were attached on the other side.

And I realized what Percy had done.

This pit was already here, but it was only accessible from the trap door we had just descended through. Heaven knows what its original purpose was, cold storage for game perhaps? It didn't matter. Percy had planned this out in advance. He'd employed workmen to build a proper entrance and staircase from the other corridor. He'd had the wine racks installed but had deliberately blocked off a small part of the underground chamber. Then the workmen finished everything nicely. On the night he killed the priest, he'd brought the body down here, come back up, nailed the trap door shut and asked the workmen who'd constructed the stairs on the other side to tile over this unneeded trap door. If he'd employed different people to do the tiling than those who constructed the wine racks, then nobody would have the full picture of what was going on, and nobody would have been suspicious.

But there it was, in the far corner of the room, wrapped in dust sheets.

Father Jeremy's body.

I approached cautiously. After all, I'd seen this withered corpse moving. It had attacked me for Christ's sake. It was under the control of the entity then, but that didn't reassure me much. The dust sheets covered it roughly—one foot stuck out from the end. It was disturbingly obvious that the corpse had tried to wrap itself after its night of wandering to the library and back.

I uncovered enough of the body to confirm it wore a dog collar. Then I asked Chloe to help.

I didn't tell her who we were carrying. To her infinite credit, she didn't ask. I was using all my concentration to move the damn thing—I had nothing left with which to form words. She wore an expression of determination. She would see this thing through and she wouldn't waste time asking me questions. I admired that. I appreciated her trust. I hoped she wouldn't be too disappointed when she found out I was pretty much making it up as I went along.

As we made it to the top of the awkward stairs and had squeezed the body and ourselves back through the narrow trap door, I became aware that the temperature had dropped dramatically. I collapsed against a dressing room door and tried to recover from the exertion, aware that my breathing was creating steam. Chloe seemed pretty beat too, and I didn't want to send her to check. So I did it myself. I crawled over to the ballroom door and opened it a crack. The entity was in the middle of the huge room, still a swirling mass of energy and confusion. It was moving slowly but there was no doubt as to where it was heading.

The clock.

"Oh Christ," I hissed, closing the door. "It's here already."

"What is?"

"Derek's... ghost."

She fell silent at that, looking like she might burst into tears. I felt the same way. The crushing need to lie here and sob my guts out was overwhelming. But we didn't have time. I knew that if I stayed any longer I might never be able to get up.

"Come on, we have to leave."

Together we dragged the body to the door at the end. I found the right key and we emerged into the fresh air. Still there was no hint of dawn, but we had lamps now and that made a huge difference. We pulled the withered and surprisingly light body around the back of the house to the paved courtyard. Standing waiting for us was the wheelbarrow, with two shovels piled inside.

Thank you, Derek.

With a lot of difficulty we dumped the body in the wheelbarrow on top of the tools. Again I had to stop for a breather. Chloe started pushing but she didn't know where we were going. I forced myself to my feet but stumbled and fell towards her, nearly impaling myself on a wheelbarrow handle. The chill night air kept me conscious as Chloe helped me up again. I took the lead, carrying both lamps, and Chloe pushed the body along behind me. While she'd not been beaten up, she was likely just as tired as I was. But she didn't complain. We moved without a word, too tired to speak. We wore no coats but the cold was the only thing keeping me awake.

Together we bore right, to the side of the lake, towards the Victorian garden.

After a long time and a lot of painful walking, we arrived at the tiny graveyard. This was where they buried Percy, along with his parents and his grandfather, and many other ancestors most likely. This was blessed ground. A Catholic burial site. We took the shovels and we dug a hole. We were both far too exhausted to dig very fast. How I managed to keep hold of that shovel was beyond me, but Chloe moved with steely resolve so I pushed myself to keep up with her.

"So," she said as she scooped another pile of dirt from the small hole we had created near to Percy's grandfather's grave. "We're going to bury this corpse, right?"

"Yes," I said. I had to fight for the breath to talk and dig at the same time, and my head felt lighter the more air I expelled from my lungs. But she'd been patient and now she deserved an explanation.

I leant on my shovel, grateful for the break. "The clock takes five spirits and traps them in the house," I explained. "The fifth ghost gets control of everything: the house, the other spirits, time itself. Percy wanted to silence his grandfather's ghost by becoming spirit number five. Father Jeremy here died to fill a slot. But Percy miscounted. The drummer boy didn't die in the house, so he wasn't trapped by the clock. That meant Percy became number four."

"So Derek is number five?" she asked, plunging her shovel into the soft earth.

"Right. Derek was the next person to die in the house, so he'll be taking the last place. When he takes control he can go anywhere in time, forward or backward, for as long as the clock is attached to the house I guess. I'm not really sure. Percy never mentioned Derek's ghost in his diary, but then I guess Derek doesn't give a shit about Percy and will leave him alone..."

"When did Beth...?" Chloe tailed off. She stopped digging and stared down at her feet. "I'm sorry."

"It's okay," I replied. I started digging again. "Well, it's not okay, but for now it's not happened yet. Beth dies tomorrow night. I'm guessing if she'd died before Derek, we wouldn't be standing in a cemetery burying a three month old corpse right now."

"Is this deep enough now? Does it have to be six feet?"

"Shit no. I'm in no state to dig a proper grave. This will have to do."

We'd only managed to go down about two feet, and the rough rectangle we'd dug wasn't long enough for the priest's body to lie stretched out. Instead we had to curl him in an awkward fetal position.

"So why are we burying this priest?"

I adjusted the body's arm so that it didn't stick up above ground level. "I'm hoping that if we help the priest find some proper eternal rest before the clock closes up, his spirit will be released and can leave the house. Percy will take the third slot and Derek the fourth, and he won't be in control anymore."

"What if it just leaves the third slot open?"

"Then we're screwed. All of this is based on what I read in Percy's diary, and a healthy dose of guesswork. This is the best idea I could come up with. Now, please, read the burial rites while I fill in the grave."

"I'm not a priest," Chloe pointed out, rather redundantly. "And nor are you. You think this will be...?"

RICHARD SALTER

"Legit? No idea. It's better than being dumped in a cellar though. I hope it's enough."

So Chloe read from the burial rites while I filled in the shallow grave. By the time I was done I was utterly spent. I dropped to the ground and lay there, shivering now as the cold bit deep into me. Chloe regarded me like I was dying, but she kept on reading until she was done. Then she made the sign of the cross and sat down beside me.

"Is that it then?" she asked.

"It's all we can do," I said from my prone position.

"Are we going to wait here until dawn?"

"No. We have to go back to the house."

"Back? Why?"

"For one thing, I don't want to die of exposure. I also need to know that it worked. I need to know that Derek's ghost is no longer in control."

"But even if he can't move us around in time or whatever the hell else he could do, his ghost is still in there and he's still pissed. And if Beth doesn't die... sorry... until tomorrow then that leaves the fifth clock still open..."

I hadn't actually considered that. I hadn't thought of anything beyond burying the priest's body. I wanted so desperately to discuss the plan with Derek before he died, but if I'd done that then the entity would have known the plan too.

"Am I right?" Chloe pressed. She was doing pretty well, under the circumstances, but I was bone weary and she was starting to annoy me. I took a deep breath and managed not to yell at her.

"I'm making this up as I go along, Chloe. Honestly, I have no idea if we did the right thing or if we did it in time. The clock could have closed before we buried the priest and he might still be trapped in there. Derek might still be in control."

She could tell I was trying not to lose my temper. It wasn't rational. After the trust she'd placed in me I had no right to be mad at her. But fatigue and pain brings out the worst in people. My tolerance was gone.

"So we have to go back in," she said warily. It wasn't a question.

"Yeah we do. I have to get a look at the clock. I have to know I've got this right. If all I've done is open the third slot for

200

Beth and Derek's still in the fifth… Well I can't leave her like that."

"Okay then, let's go."

I wanted to sit a while longer, maybe for a few hours, but I also wanted this done. The cold was making my teeth chatter and self-preservation forced me to move. Chloe helped me to my feet.

We set off for the house. She supported me as I limped along and for half the walk we didn't speak.

Then suddenly Chloe said, "Hang on, I just thought of something."

We stopped. I collapsed on the grass, happy to take a break and delay our return just a little longer.

"What?"

"Something you said about the clock. You said it was open."

"Yes. It opened when Derek died. When someone dies in the house, the clock opens and sucks in their spirit."

"And when it's open, that's when we had the chance to release the priest."

"Yes."

"But it only opened when Derek died. Yet you'd already got the burial rites book."

I didn't really like where she was going with this. "So?"

"So that means you were already intending to bury the priest when the clock was open. That means you were waiting until Derek died. You were waiting for my husband to die."

"Chloe, it was the only way. Derek was doomed anyway. I knew he had to die before Beth."

"You bastard."

"Chloe, please, it's not like I wanted him dead."

"You had no intention of trying to save him. He had to die for your plan to work."

Chloe was right but it didn't change anything. Not from my perspective. As soon as I worked out who the entity was, I knew Derek had to die. It seemed cold but I knew, if only on a subconscious level, that Derek wasn't leaving the house alive. Although I'd not planned it out in any kind of detail, I intended to have Derek help me bury the body and then return to the house. Then I was just going to wait until he was killed. At that moment, the clock would open and the priest would be free.

Derek died much earlier than I had expected, but that was Chloe's fault for calling to him. Not that I was about to blame her for it.

"Chloe, I'm sorry."

She left me there on the grass with my lamp. She took her own and stalked off towards the house. I tried to follow but my leg hurt too much. It wasn't broken—I couldn't have walked all that way and dug a grave with a broken leg, but it still hurt like a bitch.

I struggled after her. I didn't want her going in the house alone. More for my own sense of security than hers if I'm honest.

"Chloe, please," I called. "I was just going on instinct. I didn't sit down and plan it out. I barely had time to think about it. Please, Chloe. Don't go in there alone."

She ignored me. I crawled after her as fast as I could but she was much closer to the house than I was.

I took a deep breath. This wasn't going to be pleasant and it wasn't fair, but I had to stop her.

"Chloe, the picture on the stairs, of that girl. It wasn't mine. It was Derek's."

She stopped. She turned.

"Derek carried her picture. Her name was Anna. I dated her for a while and then I dumped her. She went to Australia but Derek tried to stop her. He loved her. He never got over her."

Chloe came back towards me then, much to my relief. She was close enough now that I didn't have to shout.

"When the ghost said he didn't love you he was telling the truth. Derek loved Anna. You were a rebound he accidentally got preg—"

Chloe slapped me round the face. There was more shock than pain, but I went down like she'd hit me with a sledgehammer.

"You manipulative little shit," she hissed. "I'm not an idiot. I know he didn't love me. But he was my husband, the father of my children and a good man. He treated me well and he worked damn hard for his family. When was the last time you worked hard for anything?" The steel in her tone was fading, replaced by sobs. Chloe deflated, collapsing to the ground beside me in heaving cries of anguish.

"I know he didn't love me," she said through the tears.

Despite the pain I was in, I reached out to try to comfort her. She slapped my hand away. "Don't you touch me," she shrieked. "Don't you dare! He *hated* you! Anna moved to the other side of the world to get away from you. She wouldn't stay for him. He carried all that hatred and now look what's happened. Look what he's turned into. And it's all your fault. All of it. If you weren't such a selfish, fucking…"

I wanted to protest. I wanted to tell her that Derek was a grown man capable of making his own decisions and seizing his own opportunities. He was never my responsibility. Sure he went ghost hunting with me instead of studying and he failed his exams, but I never held a knife to his throat and forced him to. Sure he loved the girl I was dating, but he had plenty of time before I met her to make a move. I even asked his permission. All this over his jealousy of me? Ridiculous. Without Beth, I had nothing of any worth whatsoever. Derek threw away his family and his life to get revenge on me. And what about the violence, beneath the surface? He was going to beat Chloe. He nearly killed me with his bare hands. That was all him.

But I said nothing. Chloe needed someone to hate, to lash out at, to blame. The least I could do was be that person. Hell I could protest all I liked inside my own head but I deserved it. I'd been a dick. I should have asked Beth to marry me months ago but I was too lazy to get around to it. I liked my easy life. There was no reason to change anything from my perspective. I didn't want to settle down and have a family of my own, at least, not until I realized what I'd lost.

But Chloe, giggly housewife Chloe, turned out to be the strongest of all of us because she had something in her life she could not afford to lose.

"He was a good man," Chloe insisted, as if reading my thoughts. "He could have run when I got pregnant but he didn't. I knew he didn't want to stay but he *did* stay. Putting your family before your own happiness, that's the measure of a good man."

She was quiet for a time. Then she added, "When all this is over, I never want to see you again."

I didn't argue. She helped me up but then let go of me. She made no attempt to help me walk but she didn't rush on ahead either. I struggled to keep up but we arrived at the back door together.

She didn't have to like me to see this through. She did need to work with me.

CHAPTER 19

The house was silent when we entered. I led Chloe through the door into the conservatory, and then into the ballroom.

Nothing leapt out at us. We didn't hear so much as a creaky floorboard. The atmosphere was thick and musty. At least I wasn't shivering now.

We passed through into the corridor to the right of the stage and then through the door to the wine cellar. I almost fell down the stairs but made it to the bottom alive.

The lid of the clock was closed. The first four faces were active, hands telling the same time and moving in unison. The upper clock face had stopped.

Was that a good sign?

"So?" said Chloe. "Did we win?"

"No, you didn't win."

I turned to the corner by the wine racks, raising my lamp. Chloe did the same.

Derek leant against an empty shelf.

"I was supposed to be number five," Derek's ghost lamented. He moved across the cellar, his image literally ghosting as he did so. He left traces of himself in the air as he moved. The door at the top of the stairs slammed shut. Chloe's lamp went out. "What you've taken from me... I was supposed to be in control of everything."

"Derek, we had to do it," I said, trying to guard my lamp, our only source of light, from his approach.

"Of course you did. I wish I'd split your skull open when I had the power to do so. Now, thanks to you, my strength is very limited. But I *can* do this."

My lamp died.

I panicked for a moment. It had been some time since I'd been in total darkness. Having the light denied to me again, it was nearly too much for me to take. But then I remembered I had a backup. I dropped the lamp and reached into my pocket, pulling out my torch. I clicked it on.

Derek's face was an inch away from mine.

I screamed and leapt backwards, nearly dropping the torch.

Chloe had clicked on her light now.

"Look at the clock, Jim."

I pointed my torch at the fifth face of the clock. It was turning backwards rapidly.

"Oh shit."

Derek chuckled. "Yeah, so I feel it's only fair to warn you that while you effectively changed history by releasing the priest and putting me in the fourth slot, there's an entity in the future and the past that still exists. Don't ask me to explain it. I'm just an idiot who failed A-level physics. Either way, when it gets here... When *I* get here, I'm going to be *really* mad at you, Jim. And that skull splitting thing I mentioned." Derek drew close to me again, hissing in my ear. "You're going to beg for that."

I collapsed to the floor. Chloe charged up the stairs and started tugging at the door handle but it wouldn't open.

"Help," she screamed. I had no idea who she was calling to.

While Chloe lost her mind loudly, I lost mine in silence.

The fight went out of me. Every bruise and cracked bone in my body throbbed in pain. My head swam and my vision blurred.

It didn't matter if we changed its past. It was still in control. It could move time around as much as it wanted. It could rewrite history if it chose to. It could force itself to remain in existence. I had no idea how time travel really worked or how history could change, or how the entity could still exist.

It didn't matter.

I'd never felt such utter defeat. I sat there on the floor, my body broken, my mind numb, my spirit shattered.

I had nothing left to fight with. No ideas, no tools, no strength. The entity would be here soon, and when it arrived I was going to die, probably in even more agony than I was already in.

Derek had defeated me.

After all this, after this long, long night, after losing Beth, after all this fucking *effort*, I was going to die in a basement.

The entity formed in the corner of the room. I didn't have the energy to point my torch at it, but from the staircase, Chloe was lighting it up for all to see. Its black malevolence seemed even more intense than before. It whipped up the dust on the floor in a tornado. I could feel the waves of resentment and hatred pouring from it. The noise was unbelievable. The smell of something burning filled my nostrils. It was the only thing keeping me conscious.

Derek, newly dead-Derek, was laughing and laughing. When he spoke I could hear him even though he wasn't raising his voice.

"I don't think I'm supposed to be here at the same time as myself, you know? Hell, the other me probably shouldn't exist at all. But when you can rewrite reality, the rules don't really matter anymore."

The entity advanced on us. Chloe retreated further up the steps.

"Jim," she yelled over the violent cacophony. "Do something!"

But what could I do?

I simply stayed where I was, closed my eyes, tried to shut out the din, and waited for the inevitable.

The noise was incredible, loud enough to rattle every nerve in my body. But there was something else I could hear now. Something familiar. At first I assumed it was the clock ticking, that arrhythmic, jarring, annoying-as-all-fuck tick-tock-tick-tock-tock that seemed designed to keep me on edge. But it wasn't. It was keeping a regular beat. I strained to isolate the sound from the cacophony. There was tune behind it! A familiar melody.

Was that… *Ode to Joy?*

I laughed. I laughed right in Derek's face. Dead or not he seemed taken aback by my outburst. He stopped, confused. He almost looked worried..

It was a message. *Ode to Joy* was a message. Maybe it was calling to me. Maybe I should answer.

So I did. As ridiculous as it sounds, I stood there in front of a dead man and his future malevolent entity-self from beyond the grave and I hummed along. Usually I'd make up some dumb lyrics, but I was too tired, too broken, too terrified to do that. So I just hummed. I hummed as loudly as I could, trying to rise above the noise and the roar, but I couldn't hear myself.

Something new was forming in the room, in the opposite corner to the Derek-entity. I stared at it, my mind too tired to comprehend what it might be. It seemed to be struggling to find form, a much weaker manifestation than the Derek-entity across the room.

On instinct, I switched from humming to singing, "La la la." To my surprise, the new entity seemed to respond to each *la*. I sang louder, my throat aching with the strain. In response, the new cloud of smoke circled like a whirlwind growing more solid by the second. *Ode to Joy* chorused from the cloud as if played by some ethereal orchestra from beyond the grave. I was confused, delighted and scared in equal measure. So clearly was it responding to my caterwauling, it encouraged me to try adding some words.

"La la la, I want to go home,
"Please come save me, la lala."

The whirlwind became a tornado, just like the Derek-entity. But, instead of a dark, swirling storm, this new entity was a brilliant white, like clouds on a summer's day. Something about it seemed familiar. My heart swelled with desperate hope.

The darker entity had now solidified into the recognizable shape of Derek. It was advancing on Chloe, who stood petrified on the stairs. She cried out. I couldn't help her, but maybe I didn't have to.

Recently-dead-Derek was staring at the new tornado with growing panic. He backed towards his future-self, and the two beings merged into one with a weird, reality-bending pop.

By now, the white entity was almost solid. I could see its fingers first, reaching out to me from the tumult, and then a whole arm. The mass of rolling smoke was forming into the figure of a person. I felt such peace as I stared into the maelstrom. My injuries no longer bothered me. The noise no longer hurt my ears, the crippling terror abated, ebbing away from me as I gazed upon that face. I was still humming along, but now I trailed off. It was no longer necessary.

The Derek entity seemed to notice the newcomer for the first time. It turned away from Chloe, rounding on the new arrival, mustering every ounce of malevolence it could find. I could feel the hatred flowing from it in waves.

But the white figure was not serene either. While it provided me with comfort, it was by no means passive. Neither was it silent. It turned from me to face the dark storm on the other side of the room, screaming with fury and anger. It darkened, rolling and spitting with rage.

Suddenly, the two entities hurled themselves together, colliding in the centre of the room. They twisted and turned about one another until they became indistinguishable. The hands on all five clock faces spun in random directions as the titanic battle exploded above the antique timepiece.

I stared in stunned disbelief. The serenity I had felt evaporated as these two entities struggled for dominance. Perhaps this was my opportunity to run, but I could not move. I was transfixed. I had no idea if Chloe was still watching too.

Something was changing. One of the entities seemed to be gaining the upper hand. It was hard to tell, they looked and sounded so similar. I hardly dared hope.

And then, in the blink of an eye, one entity swallowed the other. The noise disappeared in an instant, leaving my ears ringing in the sudden silence. The remaining entity crackled and rolled in darkness for a few heart-stopping moments. And then it calmed and turned white. Moments later, the figure of a woman formed.

Just before I passed out, I realized that she had won.

My Beth was in control, and she had come back from tomorrow to save me.

CHAPTER 20

When I woke up I was still in the wine cellar. The lamps were working again so the room was reasonably well lit. The aches and pains in my body and my hideously swollen left eye told me I was still alive. Chloe was sitting next to me and stood up when she saw me moving.

"We have a visitor," she said.

I raised my heavy head and gazed at the far corner of the room.

There she was, like she had never gone away.

Beth.

I tried to stand but I couldn't. Chloe put a hand on my shoulder to get me to relax. Beth just smiled. She seemed so real, so normal and so alive. There was nothing ethereal or ghostly about her, but to me she looked like an angel.

"What the hell happened?" I croaked.

"I figured you needed some help," Beth said. She sounded just like herself. I wanted to hug her but I couldn't get up. I would not have touched her anyway, for fear that she might vanish.

"Thank you," I said weakly. The platitude didn't even begin to cover it.

"What's it like?" Chloe asked.

"Oh it's weird, very weird. I can feel every part of the house, all its history, all its potential. I know everything that ever happened here and everything that ever will. I can move pieces of this house around like I would play the piano. It's all instinctual. And I can feel the other four spirits. One of them, number four, is really pissed."

"Derek?" I guessed.

"Who else?"

"What time is it?" I asked Chloe.

"It's dawn," she replied. "I looked outside before you woke up. The sun is already nice and warm."

I struggled to sit up. "I have to see," I said.

Somehow I managed to stand, with Chloe's help. I stumbled and tripped and fell a couple of times but I made it up the stairs. We emerged from the side door, opposite the garage. The light was blinding but the feel of the sun on my skin was like the gates of Heaven opening up.

I drank in the light and the warmth. I felt like I'd been in the dark for years. It gave me strength; it helped alleviate some of the pain.

Chloe smiled at me.

"I still never want to see you again," she said.

"You won't, don't worry."

Beth couldn't follow us outside. So we went back in.

***

We sat at the kitchen table, the three of us. Again, Beth didn't look ghostly at all. She was so solid I had to keep fighting the temptation to embrace her and never let go. Chloe and I ate from mini cereal packets. We had no milk but we were so hungry it didn't matter. We drank coffee Chloe brewed on a camping stove and we didn't talk much. We were just enjoying the peace.

An idea was taking shape in my head. I turned to Beth.

"Can you take me back to her—to *you*? When you were alive?"

"I don't think that's a good idea, do you?"

"I think it's an excellent idea," I said. "Why not? You can control time. Take me back so I can get her away from this house before she... before *you* ever set foot through the door."

"I'd love to, but I think the only reason I was able to beat Derek was because he was weakened when the priest escaped. From then on, he was ghost number four and no longer in control. It took time for the change to catch up with him, but eventually I became the last one in. If you stop me from ever coming here in the first place, you'll weaken me too and the whole thing might unravel."

"It will unravel, and then I'll be free."

Chloe and I whirled around to see who had spoken. Derek stood in the doorway. At first I thought we were in serious trouble but Beth didn't seem bothered at all.

"Relax," she said. "I'm in control, remember?"

Derek approached the table. He was ghosting again, not quite all there.

He sat down on a chair, or at least appeared to sit. He watched us, his expression unreadable.

Initially, Chloe reacted with confusion and shock at seeing her dead husband sit down next to her. But she took control of her emotions and stared into her coffee instead. "Here we are then," she said. "We made it through the night."

"Half of us made it," Derek said coldly.

"So what happens next?" I asked.

"I release the other spirits and myself from the clock," Beth said. "I usher us into the next world, wherever that is."

"I don't want to go," said Derek.

"Well you can't stay here," Chloe said, a tear rolling down one cheek. "You need to move on."

We sat silently for a little while.

"I'm sorry about your face," Derek said, indicating my horribly swollen cheek and eye.

"I'll live," I said. In retrospect this was not the most sensitive thing to say...

"So, this has been really awkward," Beth said, rising to her feet. "But if you don't mind, we'll be shuffling off now."

"Wait," I said. "Don't go yet."

"What is it, Jim?"

"I need your help first, before you go."

***

After I had cleared all our equipment from the area, Beth sent Derek's corpse, the stairs, the hall and the drawing room forward in time by two months. Then I asked her to find her eyeless body and move that to the same day as she had placed Derek's corpse. She did this without me having to see her corpse again, for which I was very grateful. I assumed she had stopped moving after last night, but I didn't want to check to find out.

I explained to Chloe my game plan. We would have to clean up the house before we left, and we'd have to make sure our stories were consistent, but if we got it right there was no reason why the police would come after us when inevitably they discovered the bodies. I didn't relish explaining how a violent entity had caused the deaths of Chloe's husband and my girlfriend.

Then Beth and I left Derek and Chloe to spend our last few minutes alone in the drawing room. It was more awkward than I had expected. I wanted to kiss and hug her, but it didn't seem appropriate now she was dead.

"I heard you, by the way," she said. "I heard you singing. I held onto your voice and it guided me. It brought me to you."

"I felt it, I knew it was something I had to do."

Silence. I stared at her face. I already knew it so well, but I realized this would be my last time seeing her.

"I was going to ask you to marry me, you know?"

"Liar," she said with a laugh. "You were never going to ask me."

"Did you want me to ask you?"

"Of course. But don't worry, I would have asked you first."

I chuckled at that. I was lucky in a way. How many people who've lost a loved one get another chance to say goodbye?

"Will you stay in the States?" she asked.

"I don't know. I mean, I have to for a little while but maybe I'll come back here. Maybe I'll find a way to survive over there without you. We'll see."

"I love you, Jim."

"I love you too, Beth."

And then she was gone. One moment she was there and then she was a lingering memory. I didn't want to go on without her, but I had to.

I returned to Chloe. She looked sad but hadn't lost that determined steel in her eyes.

"I don't like lying to the police but I hate lying to my kids more," she said.

"If you want to make sure they're not taken away from you, you'll have to."

She nodded.

We had a lot to do.

We walked down to the cemetery in silence. Chloe obviously didn't want to speak to me but I was too numb and too sore to talk much anyway. The cemetery appeared surprisingly untouched considering we had dug a hole there in the dark. The grave itself did look fresh but we had positioned it in between existing plots, so from the side of the little graveyard the new addition was virtually invisible. Nevertheless, we snapped a couple of older branches off a nearby tree and arranged them with piles of leaves and mud around the site to try to hide our activity. It wouldn't pass a forensic test but then it didn't need to. We just needed to be sure that when Arthur returned on Wednesday he didn't stumble across a freshly dug grave. After that we pushed the wheelbarrow into the lake and threw the shovels in after it. It seemed easier than cleaning them up and putting them away.

Chloe returned to the house while I went to the garage and pulled out the old bicycle. It didn't seem too bad, just rusty and the frame was a bit warped. I rooted around and found a puncture repair kit and an old pump, and in half an hour I'd managed to re-inflate the tires sufficiently to make it roadworthy. I cycled down the path, through the gate and out onto the road. I didn't have to go too far before my phone had enough of a signal to synchronize the date. Sure enough it was Sunday morning, the day after we'd first arrived, which was a relief. We'd not ended up twenty years in the future or in the 1970s, or somewhere equally hard to explain. I couldn't yet make a phone call, so I carried on cycling for about half an hour before I started to see signs of civilization. Here I managed to get a strong enough signal to make a call. I ordered two taxis and then cycled all the way back to the house again.

Chloe met me at the door.

"I'm done cleaning the knives and scrubbing everything else down. There is just one thing."

Chloe indicated the wrecked four-by-four sitting in the driveway, the book case still protruding from the bonnet, windscreen and roof.

"Not much we can do about it," I said. "If anyone asks just tell them Derek and Beth went off with the car and we've not seen it since. Act surprised if they show you a photo."

"And the window?" Chloe looked up towards the library on the upper floor. I followed her gaze and took in the damage.

"We know nothing about it."

Before we left I returned Percy's Catholic Rites to the library and hid his journal again. I went around and locked all the doors. The corridor to the left of the stage still had all the tiles up, but that was okay because there was no longer a body down there. Arthur was unlikely to discover it and so we left it as it was.

Chloe was outside waiting for me. I lingered inside the house just a few minutes more.

It was so calm and peaceful, and so beautiful with the light pouring through the windows, that it was hard to imagine the night of hell we'd been through in this place. I would make my recommendations to my dad and tell him about the room we discovered behind the wine cellar. Then I'd suggest he have the clock removed before reselling the house, just in case.

I walked through the kitchen, conservatory and ballroom, and then down the steps into the wine cellar, clicking on my torch as I did so.

The clock sat silently in the centre of the room as before, only now all five of the faces had stopped and all showed the same time. The maddening tick-tock had ceased completely, which was a merciful relief. Percy and his grandfather, the lavender lady and both Derek and Beth were all at peace now. I snapped a picture of the clock on my phone and left the cellar.

As I passed through the hallway, I thought I caught the notes of the *Pathétique Sonata* hanging in the air. I opened the door to the living room and peered inside. There was nobody in there. The piano was once again hidden by a dust cover and all was quiet. With a heavy heart, I closed the door and crossed the hall to the front entrance.

I joined Chloe outside, waiting patiently with our backpacks and the two bags of equipment. Together we trudged down the road to the lodge, again not talking.

We reached the gate and passed through, then stood by the road, waiting. I had arranged to have the taxis pick us up here, at the bottom of the driveway, so we could avoid the drivers seeing the wrecked car and asking awkward questions.

When the first taxi arrived I let Chloe take it. Despite everything, she gave me a hug and told me to put ice on my face as soon as possible. Then she kissed my cheek, got in the car and was taken away.

My own taxi arrived ten minutes later. The driver helped me load all the stuff into the boot—I planned to leave the equipment in a locker at the airport and post the key to my dad later—and I climbed in. As the car pulled away I didn't look back. I opened the window to let the crisp autumn air in and I fancied that I heard the sound of a distant drum.

The Lies

One month after they first called, the police have brought me down to the station for questioning. I was expecting this, but I am no less nervous. So here I sit in a windowless interview room behind a plain desk on an uncomfortable chair, wondering if I'm going to be able to hold my nerve.

Officer Warrington from Chicago PD is with me. This time however, a middle-aged woman wearing smart business attire accompanies him.

"Mr Randal," says Warrington. "This is Detective Inspector Black of Hereford and Worcester Police in the UK."

I'm surprised to see a British police inspector here. She's come a long way.

They both sit down opposite me. They look sombre. Of course I know what they're going to tell me. My palms are sweating. It was hard enough to lie to them in my apartment the first time. Being here is so much more intimidating. I force myself to remain calm. As long as I don't screw up and say something stupid, I should be home by noon.

Warrington speaks again. "I'm afraid we have some very bad news for you, Mr Randal."

I stare at them in shock. Of course I know why I'm here, but I pretend to have just worked it out. "No," I said. "No no no."

"I'm sorry to say that the body of Miss Bethany Harris was found at Binsham House three days ago."

I gape at them stupidly. Then the tears come. To me this is hardly news, but that doesn't stop the pain from resurfacing. I use the raw emotion to add credibility to my feigned shock. It isn't hard for me to cry on demand these days. All I have to do is think of her.

"I'm very sorry for your loss," Black says.

"We… we weren't together anymore," I say through the sobs. "But I still…" I can't finish the sentence even if I want to. Neither of the officers speaks for a time. Warrington offers a box of tissues and I take one. I try to clean up my face a bit.

"How?" I ask eventually.

"She was murdered in the house."

"*Murdered?*"

"I'm afraid so. We discovered Derek Jackson's body too. We're still trying to determine if his death was an accident."

Warrington says, "I should tell you now, Mr Randal, that your prints are all over the scene."

I glare at them through the tears.

"Is that why I'm here?"

"Yes."

"Am I under arrest?"

"No, Mr Randal. Like I said when we brought you in, we just need to ask you some questions."

"Here's the thing," says Black, her British accent sounding odd to my ears despite my recent trip. "The bodies had only been deceased twenty-four hours when we found them two days ago. We know you've been in Chicago for weeks."

"I went out with friends on the weekend," I say, my voice wavering. "I can give you their numbers. I never left..."

"No need, Mr Randal," said Warrington. There's no trace of you passing through any airports. Plus we've been... keeping tabs on you since Beth went missing. We know you were here when she died."

I act surprised but it's hardly a shock to learn that the police have been watching me. I've been very careful these last few weeks, just in case.

"Then why fly out here?" I ask Black.

She gives me a piercing look. "I'm afraid I need to ask you more details about the nature of Miss Harris's relationship with Derek Jackson. And I need to know what happened that night while you were in the house. The cab driver who took you to London said you were in bad shape and we have security pictures of you at the airport. You were quite a mess."

"Yeah, the bruises, right. Well, I confronted Derek about his... affair with Beth. He got angry. Chloe said he had anger issues. He would hit her regularly is what she told me. The night before I left the house, he beat me up, kicked me down the stairs."

"You didn't check in to a hospital before proceeding to London?"

"No. I wasn't really thinking clearly. I just wanted to get home. I got a lot of funny looks at the airport. They nearly didn't let me on the plane. I told them I got mugged."

"You should have reported Mr Jackson to the police. Leaving Miss Harris with him was putting her in danger."

For a moment my heart freezes. I'd not considered this line of reasoning. Shit, if Derek was capable of beating me to a pulp, why *would* I leave Beth with him?

"As I said, I wasn't thinking clearly. I was in pain and my girlfriend cheated on me. I just wanted to get away. At the time I didn't think about what might happen to her. At that moment I didn't care."

"And now?"

"I miss her every day." I start to cry again. All the nightmares come flooding back. I've been dreading this moment, having to explain myself to the police. I knew it would force me to replay all the horrors in my mind like they happened yesterday.

Black takes a photograph from her pocket and shows it to me. It's a picture of the corpse Chloe and I buried, the priest. "We found this man, Father Jeremy Granger, recently buried in the cemetery on the grounds of the house. He'd been missing for six months. Now, I'm not saying you had anything to do with his death, Mr Randal, because that happened months before you were in England. But perhaps you know how he came to be buried there. Your blood was found near his shallow grave. I'm wondering if you had anything to do with that."

I feel chills again. Is she onto me? Does she know I'm lying?

"That's where Derek and I had a fight. He attacked me in the house, pushed me down the stairs, but I got away. He chased me all the way to the cemetery before he caught me. That's where he beat me up the worst."

"I see," Black says. She doesn't sound convinced but I'm hoping it's enough. "And something else that confuses me, Mr Randal," she continues. She sounds like she's interrogating me now. I can see in her eyes that she knows something doesn't add up. Can she see my guilt? "We discovered the body of Derek and Beth in the hall and the dining room respectively. We swept both rooms for evidence when they originally went missing, and of course your DNA was all over them. So was Chloe Jackson's. You'd all been in the house so nothing unexpected there. But what surprised me was how much of your blood we found *after* the discovery of the bodies. It was everywhere. All over the stairs and the landing, the hallway and the drawing room. Nearly everywhere we looked there were traces of your blood in that area that hadn't been there the first time we looked. And the blood was fresh, Mr Randal. It had only been there a day, not a month. How do you explain that?"

"I… I can't explain it," I say. I am now certain I'm going to jail. I'm going to spend the rest of my life in prison for a crime I didn't commit. Eventually I croak, "Maybe you missed something the first time." It feels like such a weak argument. I hold her gaze, trying hard not to crack. I feel like my world is crashing down. I've worked so hard and built this lie so carefully. I've tried my damnedest to ensure neither Chloe nor me gets the blame for the deaths. And now this wretched inspector is going to find the hole in my story and isn't going to let me go.

She leans in close. "What happened that night, Mr Randal?"

I swallow, trying not to let my guilt glow like a lightning rod in an electrical storm. When Beth had sent the bodies forward in time by a month, so that Chloe and I could prepare alibis in time for their discovery, I hadn't given a thought to the evidence of my involvement that travelled in time alongside the bodies. Derek had nearly killed me on that staircase, of course my blood was all over the scene. And of course it would only have been a day or so old when the bodies were found…

"We heard some weird noises. We saw some strange things. But the four of us were alone in that house. I don't know who buried the priest or who killed Beth. I have no clue how fresh blood got there. I've been here the whole time, in Chicago. I didn't travel back to look for her, though I kept telling myself I should. I don't know what else to tell you. I wish Beth was still alive. I kept hoping she would call me or knock at my door. I can't believe she's gone."

I am sure Black is going to push some more. I expect her to suddenly whip out an incriminating photograph, or some other piece of evidence that proves I am guilty.

"You realize if I can prove you were in England at the time of the murders, Mr Randal, you will be in very serious trouble."

"I wasn't there," I say dumbly, my throat so dry I'm surprised any words come out.

Warrington addresses me now. "About the car, Mr Randal."

"What about it?"

"Tell me again how it got smashed."

He's trying to catch me out. I know now why he didn't show me the photograph back at my apartment on his first visit. He wants me to reveal more now than I knew then.

"I have no idea. Derek and Beth went off in it. They abandoned me and Chloe so we left. After I got back to the States, my dad called me, all pissed off that he had to pay the deductible on the wrecked car. I asked him if anyone was hurt and he said no. But I don't know what happened."

Warrington considers my story for a moment, and this time he decides to show me. It's a picture of the car with the bookcase embedded in it. I've seen it before of course, but I have to act shocked. It *is* pretty shocking.

"Oh my God," I say. The image brings back more unpleasant memories. I'm glad I resisted the temptation to snap some pictures of the wreckage before I left. My phone would be burning a hole in my pocket right now. "How the hell...?"

"We can't explain it either," he says. "Apparently several tons of solid oak bookcase threw itself out of a window and crushed your car. And you know nothing about this?"

"I assumed Derek had just run it into a ditch. I had no idea... I remember the bookcase from the library upstairs. When I left it was still *in* the library..."

We all sit in silence for a moment. Neither of them seems convinced.

"Have you spoken to Chloe?" I ask.

"I spoke to her yesterday," says Warrington. "We've been keeping an eye on her and she wasn't anywhere near Fletchley Park at the time of the murders either."

"How is she doing? Is she okay?"

"As well as can be expected."

More silence. Black seems lost in thought. She's aware that I know more than I'm saying. I know the evidence is not lining up to make a case against me. She's not going to let this go, but unless she can prove that Beth and Derek's corpses travelled in time and make a jury believe it, she has nothing that will stick. All I have to do is keep my cool and wait this out.

"Can I go home?" I ask in a small voice. "I would really like to be alone."

Warrington glances at Black, who nods.

"I'll have Officer Hunt drive you home," he says. "Call us if you think of anything else."

"Do you have any other suspects?" I ask as we stand up. I want to be sure they don't try to pin this on poor Arthur the groundskeeper.

"No," Warrington says. "This wasn't a professional hit, and Miss Harris's death certainly wasn't an accident. Our suspicion is that Mr Jackson killed Beth and then had an accident. But if we do make an arrest we'll let you know."

"Thank you, Inspector Warrington."

Officer Hunt drives me back to my apartment and I ride the elevator in silence. I manage to hold myself together until I get inside my door. Then I collapse against the wall and sob myself into a stupour. I am so relieved to be home, but I know they won't give up that easily, and all of this is stirring up memories I just want to bury for good. They have questions and suspicions but nothing they can prove. The story will never make sense. They will never find Beth's killer. But the relief I feel for surviving today's interview, and the knowledge that I am probably safe from blame doesn't bring my Beth back to me. And it will never erase the memories of that night.

I pull my phone from my pocket and flick back through the photos until I find Beth's picture, the one I took of her playing the piano. I stare at it for a while, and then move forward to the next photo. This one is of the clock in the wine cellar. It's the picture I snapped just before leaving the house for the last time.

I stare at it for a long time.

Something is wrong.

I sweep my fingers apart to zoom in until the five clock faces fill the screen of my phone. I remember very clearly that when I took the picture, none of the clocks were running and they were all set to the same time.

One of them is different now.

I stare at it, unable to comprehend how that is possible. My eyes widen and I feel my hair stand on end like there's an electric current passing through me.

The clock that's different from the others is the fourth clock. Derek's clock.

I can hear the ticking again. I don't know where it's coming from, it's almost beyond my hearing. But it's there. Perhaps it's in my head.

It will be a long time before I sleep again.

ACKNOWLEDGEMENTS

There are, as always with these things, a huge number of people to thank. Undoubtedly I'll leave some folks out, so please don't be mad at me! Firstly thanks to my wife, Jennifer, for being a very honest critic of the early drafts of this novel, and for all your love and support. Thanks to my kids, Aidan and Ethan, for keeping it down long enough for me to get some work done. Thanks to Lupe and Polo, my tireless in-laws, for watching said kids on many Sundays while I got some MORE work done. Mia the dog has no idea how much she helped write this novel, because she's a dog. I tend to come up with my best ideas when I'm walking her, so thanks Mia.

Bob and Jen at Nightscape Press deserve huge plaudits for the work they do every single day for their authors, and they deserve every success (and more awards!). Thanks to Justin for the terrific cover image and for putting up with an annoying author being picky. Additional thanks to Steven Savile, Jordan Ellinger, Richard Wright, Simon Kurt Unsworth, Lou Anders, Trent Zelazny, Mark Scioneaux, James Morrison, Peter Dudar, Peter Giglio, Andrew Lane, Ashley Parkes and Ian Whates. And I'd better leave it there, other than to thank you, the reader, for taking a chance on my first book. I hope you like it. Regardless of what you thought, please consider leaving a review somewhere accessible. That request applies to anything else you read too.

ABOUT THE AUTHOR

Richard Salter has been writing for over 25 years, so you would imagine he'd be a lot better at it by now. He is the editor of a *Doctor Who* anthology and the mosaic novel, *World's Collider*, and co-editor of the charity anthology *Fantasy For Good*, which features some huge names in fantasy fiction and is raising money for The Colon Cancer Alliance. His short fiction appears in various anthologies including *Solaris Rising: The New Solaris Book of Science Fiction, Warhammer: Gotrek & Felix the Anthology, Horror for Good* and *This is How You Die (Machine of Death 2)*. By day he works as a glorified project manager for a telecoms software vendor, and he lives with his wife and two young sons in the suburbs of Toronto, Canada.

Find out more (if you can bear it) at
http://www.richardsalter.com